# SOMETHING IN THE BLOOD

## A HONEY DRIVER MYSTERY

## JEAN G GOODHIND

Published by Accent Press Ltd – 2013

ISBN 9781909520196

Copyright © Jean G Goodhind 2013

First published by Severn House as
Something in the Blood by J.G. Goodhind

Printed and bound in the UK

Cover design by Joelle Brindley

This book is dedicated to

Hazel Godwin, dearly departed, but bubbling with
life during the Bath years

# Chapter One

'Murder, robbery and any other kind of mayhem must be kept at bay in this fair city, my dear girl; hence your appointment as Crime Liaison Officer acting on behalf of Bath Hotels Association.'

Hannah Driver, called Honey by those that knew her best – except her mother who revelled in being different about everything – eyed Casper St John Gervais with incredulity. He was elegant, eccentric and terribly effete, but was he also a little mad?

'Why me?'

'Your experience, my dear girl.'

'I've never been a policeman ... woman,' she corrected.

'We – the association – just want you to act as liaison point between us and the police. You know, my dear girl, how a city's reputation can affect tourism. We have to keep the lid on crime in all its forms. Crime must be swiftly and effectively dealt with. Anyway, besides you having an interest in bed occupancy, I understand you used to work with criminals.'

'I worked for the Probation Service – as a Senior Clerical Officer.'

'Precisely my point.'

'Casper, that means I used to type Social Enquiry Reports, a compilation of circumstances and excuses as to why the client shouldn't be banged up and the key thrown away.'

1

Casper had a very aquiline nose, very thin at the bridge and widely flaring at the nostrils. When he fixed his gaze on her, his eyes seemed to close together, as though a pair of pince nez were perched on his nose. His nostrils flared into black chasms.

'But you're all we have, my dear girl. No member of the association has that kind of experience. And think of the good you could do ... Hmm?'

She only vaguely remembered agreeing to it. Bath Hotels Association had been holding their annual AGM when Casper had made the suggestion. As usual the stuffy bit was followed by a bit of a party – quite a sizeable party in fact.

A well-known wine importer had supplied the drink, and a local caterer the food. Honey regretted arriving early because that meant sitting through the AGM. The bulk of the membership didn't arrive until the meeting was over, heading straight for the bar. Not that the meeting wasn't entirely without refreshments, thanks to a friendly waiter who used to work for her at the Green River Hotel. A few glasses of Australian Shiraz had helped alleviate her boredom. She might have fallen asleep. She hadn't snored – at least she didn't think so.

Casper had taken full advantage of the situation. He'd whispered something in her ear. 'I guarantee that the Green River Hotel will benefit if you agree to this.'

Some semblance of that promise had stayed with her. Upgrading a few bedrooms at the Green River had left her with a chunky overdraft. Running a hotel in a beautiful city was not a bed of roses. Roses had thorns and Casper's promise had poured like honey into her ear. Drat!

Lindsey, her daughter, who was far too mature for her age, offered consolation when she told her.

'Relax. Consider the positive side. It could add a pinch of spice to your life. You need to get out more.'

Honey watched as Lindsey cleared down the bar and

locked up.

'Are you going nightclubbing tomorrow night?' she asked her.

Tomorrow night, Thursday, was Lindsey's night off.

Her daughter shook her tawny head. 'No. I'm going to a concert at the Abbey.'

'Pop?' Honey asked with a hopeful lifting of eyebrows.

'No. Medieval tunes for lute and lyre.'

'My, you are such a wild child. When I was eighteen ...'

'You were irresponsible.'

'Who told you that?'

'Grandma.'

'She's a bright one to talk ...'

Lindsey kissed her forehead. 'I'm off to bed. Now don't worry. Like I said, you could do with a little pinch of spice in your life.'

The little pinch of spice came at the wrong time. Honey loved auctions, especially when there were antique clothes up for grabs. Today there'd been plenty.

Collecting clothes from the past helped her keep sane. Musing over who might have worn those gloves, that button-up boot, that lace trimmed chemise made her forget that the laundry service had mislaid two dozen tablecloths, or that the honeymoon couple in room three had done irreversible damage to the bedsprings.

She had a small but interesting collection of lace mittens, silk stockings and garters plus some very interesting underwear. Today she had hit the jackpot and would have gone one better, then Casper phoned.

'Your first case,' he said. His voice was like tin on the end of the phone. The auction ran full throttle around her.

'OK,' she said, one eye on the auctioneer and the Victorian corset that was up for grabs – all whalebone and laces and made for a waist of less diameter than a modern thigh.

She was almost salivating.

'Where are you? Are you close by?'

Honey looked around her with furtive intent. Should she lie?

'The truth, dear girl,' said Casper as if reading her mind.

'I'm in Bonhams Auction Rooms.'

'Good. Be here by eleven-thirty.'

Here meant his office. The phone pinged like a bouncing bullet. He wasn't taking no for an answer.

And what about the corset?

'Gone!'

She waved at the rostrum.

'Sorry, madam. You're too late.'

Blast! It had been such a pretty little corset, red satin edged with black lace. Definitely French. Definitely provocative.

'But not for you,' she muttered as she pushed her way through the dealers, the curious and the bargain hunters.

She glanced at her watch on the way out.

First she had to settle her bill and collect her purchases. They were large; so was the price.

'Not for you, are they hen?' smirked the cashier.

Alistair was huge, hairy and Scottish.

'Yep! I'm making a tent.'

'Once outside she shoved the Victorian bloomers into her Moroccan leather bag. They'd been listed as having once belonged to Queen Victoria – hence the price. The bag was copious, but the bloomers were more so. A sliver of cotton knicker leg fluttered like bunting between the gaping leather.

The sun came out as she passed the Pump Rooms, turning the elegant façade the colour of honey. Inside a quartet was playing Handel to those taking tea from real crockery with real tea leaves and real cream oozing from

Scottish scones and sugar doughnuts. The music drifted on the air, but did nothing to soothe her slightly savage breast.

Missing the corset rankled. Red satin! And over a hundred years old! Now how rare was that?

Drat Casper St John Gervais! If he hadn't insisted she meet him at eleven-thirty *precisely*, the corset would have been hers.

*It would have fitted me.*

Well, ten years ago it would have. She smiled to herself. Call yourself voluptuous rather than slender, dear. There again, wasn't everybody's waist way beyond the Victorian eighteen inches?

Bath city centre was busy, but it was June and only to be expected. Baskets bursting with geraniums adorned the fronts of offices, banks and shops. Wisps of variegated ivy and purple aubrietia fluttered from lampposts. The stonework of elegant buildings forming Regency crescents and squares turned cowslip yellow when the sun came out.

Month after month the tourists flocked in from all over the world to gape at the Roman Baths, eat the massive buns on offer in Sally Lunn's Teashop and have their pictures taken in front of the Abbey, in the heart of the Royal Crescent or at the end of Pulteney Bridge.

The tourists were the city's lifeblood, the fertiliser that had caused a flowering of aged and listed buildings to convert to hotels, restaurants and guesthouses.

By the time she got to Hotel La Reine Rouge, an elegant edifice overlooking Pulteney Bridge, and within walking distance of the Roman Baths, it felt as though she'd weaved her way through every nation in the world.

The La Reine Rouge was even more elegant inside than out, thanks mainly to its owner/manager's exquisite choice and eclectic mix of antiques, colour and sophisticated lighting.

She patted the arm of a turbaned statuette, one of a gloriously crimson, black and gold pair standing at the bottom of a sweeping staircase that led up to the exquisitely presented accommodation.

'Hi chaps. Is the boss in?'

Neville, a real, life chap with bleached blond hair and wearing a burgundy waistcoat with a gold watch chain answered her question.

'He's waiting for you, sweetie. He's got his manicurist with him. He's terribly tense you know, what with everything that's been happening.'

'Happening? You mean he's broken a nail?'

He threw her a sideways sneer. 'You're a very naughty girl, Honey.'

His attention returned to the trio of white lilies he was placing in a tall green vase. Clucking at them when they failed to fall the way he wanted, he picked them out one by one and started all over again.

'Neville, I hear you can be naughty when tempted.'

Neville blushed. 'Stop teasing me, Honey. You do it on purpose.'

The long case clock standing on a thick Turkish rug chose that moment to chime the half hour.

The flowers continued to behave badly. 'Oh bother!'

Neville's vocabulary was as delicate as his appearance.

Honey considered how much it might cost to have a manicurist call then looked down at her fingernails. The varnish was chipped. What else could she expect? Being a hotel owner meant filling in when the dishwasher broke down or chambermaids didn't turn up.

Tucking her arm through the handles of her bag, she hid her fingers in her pockets and made her way along the thickly carpeted corridor and down the stairs to Casper's office.

At one time the wine cellars beneath La Reine Rouge had stretched the whole length of the basement. After the builders had finished the basics, Casper had turned the area into offices for him and his staff, papering the newly plastered walls with expensive hessian in a rich sienna colour. The furniture was a mix of minimalist settees, Georgian break-fronted bookcases and ethnic artwork. Oh, and clocks. Casper loved clocks. They were everywhere; wall clocks, grandfather clocks, grandmother clocks, skeleton clocks, carriage clocks, all ticking away together. They even chimed together. Casper insisted they all chimed together in unison. He hated untidiness.

'Come in, my dear girl.' His voice rang like the sharp chime of one of his clocks.

The manicurist was buffing the smallest finger of Casper St John Gervais's right hand when she entered. He waved the woman away once that was done.

'Another day, another finger job,' he said with a demure smile.

The manicurist hurried out; no doubt on her way to Neville who would settle the bill. Casper's patrician sensibilities prevented him from anything as plebeian as physically dealing with money.

He was sitting in a honey-coloured leather chair behind a mahogany desk that might once have belonged to Tennyson or Wordsworth. Casper loved items with provenance, a proven history and famous connections. He loved auctions as much as she did, though his preference was for mahogany chests of drawers rather than the cotton type with two legs and a crotch that she favoured.

She smiled at him and brought on the flattery. 'You're looking as lovely as ever, Casper.'

'Thank you, my dear.'

Casper was the prima donna of the catering industry and adored flattery. He sounded like Noel Coward at the height of his success but looked like a rather muscular version of Randolph Scott.

While she stood there, he brought out a feather duster from a drawer and proceeded to flick it at the imagined dust the manicurist had left behind. Casper hated dust and dirt. His hotel, his office and his person were immaculate.

'I trust you have heard the news, so I will not go into detail except to say that your services are required much earlier than one could possibly have anticipated.'

'Well, actually, I've been so busy …'

She didn't get chance to explain that the dishwasher had thrown another tantrum or that a couple from Leicester had climbed out of the window of their ground-floor bedroom that morning without paying their bill. Drat, if only she'd put them on the third floor. That would have foxed them.

Casper was holding forth about the meeting of Bath Hotels Association the week before.

'As you may recall, the meeting took a unanimous decision to appoint a Crime Liaison Officer, someone who could deal with the police on their level and keep the rest of us informed. In view of your credentials, it was agreed that you were the right person for the job.'

'Yes, a little paperwork, a few meetings with the police, and some room occupancy,' she added brightly.

'I think the problem brought to my attention this morning needs a hands-on approach.'

She felt her face tightening as her eyebrows rose up into her hairline.

'Hands on? What exactly do you mean by that?'

Having secreted the feather duster in his top right-hand drawer, Casper used his elegant fingers to flick at an imaginary dust spot on his shoulder – too small a spot for Honey to see even though she narrowed her eyes.

'I mean, my dear, that a little detective work would not come amiss. I think you'd be quite good at it – better than the police in fact. You know how slow they can be, shackled as they are to European guidelines and the Court of Human Rights.' His face stiffened with seriousness. 'I … we want results, Honey. Fast results.'

In her mind she saw herself knocking on doors just like

the police did in their hunt for witnesses, hunting down muggers in their lairs – probably in neighbouring Bristol.

The tingle of excitement melted at the thought of confronting big bruisers with muscles the size of beer barrels.

Her protests were sudden, strident and heart-felt.

'But Casper, I have a job … I've got a hotel to run and I don't really think …'

'As you may recall,' Casper was saying, 'we agreed that crime was the greatest threat to visitor numbers. This honey-coloured city, this haunt of Jane Austin, Beau Brummell and … and …'

He looked up at the ceiling in his search for another famous name.

'Jane Seymour?' said Honey in an effort to help him out.

He frowned. 'Did she live here? I never knew the Tudors graced us with their presence.'

'Not Henry the Eighth's wife. I meant the actress – you know – Doctor Quinn, Medicine Woman?'

He gave her a Paddington Bear-type of stare, hard and vacant. He hadn't a clue who she was talking about. He resumed his diatribe on why she had been lumbered with the job.

'As I was saying, someone with your background …'

'I was nothing very …'

'There are perks of course. You do recall me telling you that?'

Her jaw stopped where it was, her mouth half-formed around a word.

'Yes. You did say so.'

'As I outlined to you, it's only fair that the time you put into this should be recompensed in some way.'

He opened a leather-bound folder lying on his desk. 'I most definitely recall you saying that a block booking had been cancelled and you had rooms to let. Could you find eight rooms for more or less immediate occupation?'

Her voice resumed normal service. 'When?'

'The tenth?'

'Just a minute.'

It was hard to keep breathing. Her fingers were all thumbs. This was a result, the type that put money in the bank.

Without thinking of the consequences, she heaved her extra large shoulder bag onto the leather-topped desk. She should have known better.

'Off!'

Casper's face was a picture of wounded dignity.

'Do you realise this desk was once owned by Lord Berkeley?' Out came the feather duster again.

The feather duster had a strong enough head to sweep her bag onto the floor, but not before the nebulous knickers had spread over the desk.

Casper's raised eyebrows looked in danger of sliding upwards over his shiny forehead. He pointed a trembling finger. There were broad gaps between each word.

'*What ... .are ... .those*?'

Honey muttered vaguely about them having belonged to Queen Victoria and being a collector's item, 'And where the bloody hell is my diary?'

While she rummaged, he picked them up. Eyes poker-wide, he held the waist strings between finger and thumb, peering through the centre of what must have been a singularly draughty garment. No crotch.

'Sorry, Casper. I can't seem to find ... Ah! Here it is.'

Her mind was on business, and this was serious business – especially as far as room bookings were concerned. Once she was all set, she faced him.

It was hard not to laugh.

With a look somewhere between distaste and true blue respect, Casper let the bloomers fall onto the desk, his delicate, white hands remaining at shoulder level.

'What utterly dreadful items! They're big enough to form the mainsail of a decent yacht!'

Honey stuck to the subject in hand. 'So what were those dates?'

Sighing as though life had become terribly difficult, he repeated them.

Honey checked her diary. The tenth had a thick, ugly line crossed through it. Someone had cancelled, and at this time of year she could have sold that room over and over again.

'No worries!' Her face was flushed. Her pulse raced. 'How many did you say?'

'Eight rooms. All singles mark you.'

Singles! Only two thirds of the normal price, but hey, beggars couldn't be choosers; and she was certainly a beggar, thanks to the upgrading of the attic rooms and a deaf bank manager.

He passed her the letter and booking form. 'Here you are. As I said, I think it only fair that you should gain something from these extra duties. We must not allow crime to rise in this city as elsewhere in the western world. We have an image to maintain.'

'Not to mention a bank balance and a lifestyle,' Honey muttered, still scribbling in her diary.

'Exactly. People expect certain standards. Ambience, good service and the standard of personal safety one would associate with ...'

He studied the ceiling as he searched for the right word.

'Disneyworld?'

'Exactly! Therefore, a Crime Liaison Officer can only be a good thing.'

'Oh, I agree.'

Of course she did.

She wasn't quite thinking on the same lines as him. Filling up eight rooms in one fell swoop was fantastic. The alternative would have been to accept lower priced guests

11

from the Tourist Information Office, and even then they would only come in dribs and drabs.

After folding the forms inside her diary, Honey grabbed the escaped undergarment and stuffed it back into her bag.

'So who's been mugged, diddled or been sold a duff budgie?' she said lightly.

A puzzled stiffness came to the face of the chairman of Bath Hotels Association. Street cred and slang were low on Casper's need to know list. If anyone could truly look down their nose at you and make you feel you'd been peddling your body on the street all night, Casper could.

'I'm not sure you're entirely aware of the seriousness of the situation.' His tone of voice was as sonorous as the clock in reception.

Honey felt warm. Things looked on the up and up. She'd made a good bid at auction, the dishwasher man should have finished repairing the blasted machine by the time she got back, and the rooms she envisaged staying empty or selling cheap were full again. It was just a case now of doing this job Casper had landed her with. Surely her first assignment wouldn't be too difficult?

'So what's the problem?'

The way Casper lowered his eyelids, so that she couldn't read his thoughts, sowed the first seeds of worry in what had initially seemed a very fruitful morning.

'I'm afraid an American tourist has disappeared. Not from one of our more refined establishments, mark you. For some odd reason he chose to stay in a bed and breakfast on the Lower Bristol Road.'

Casper said the words 'bed' and 'breakfast' as though he were spitting out broken teeth. It was nothing compared to how he pronounced the word 'Lower' in Lower Bristol Road.

No matter. Honey didn't care. She held on to that warm feeling and set about looking seriously engaged with the situation. 'Are we sure of that? Couldn't he just have gone home early or done something unusual, like visiting Wales?'

'He left his luggage behind.'

'Oh.'

'And his passport.'

Steepling his fingers, he leaned forward. His tone was low, almost secretive. 'Let's look into this ourselves shall we – before we go to the police?'

'I don't think that's a good idea.'

When he threw her a warning look, the eight people in eight rooms melted away to nothing.

It hurt to smile, but needs must. 'On reflection, I think you're quite right. I'll see what I can do.'

# Chapter Two

Casper was OK about her checking things back at the Green River Hotel before pursuing the case of the missing tourist.

Anna, a very willing Polish girl, was running reception. She was sleek, blonde and had a shiny smiling face that nobody could help but warm to.

'Everything OK?' asked Honey.

'Very good, Mrs Driver. Are you OK?'

'Yes, though I have acquired an extra string to my professional bow. I've become an amateur sleuth.'

Still smiling though looking slightly puzzled, Anna remarked, 'That is very nice for you. Does this mean the hotel gets an extra star?'

No, it was not some kind of quality rating, but Honey couldn't be bothered to explain.

'Let's put it this way. It can't do the Green River any harm. And I've bought Queen Victoria's bloomers.'

Anna's big brown eyes were totally *non comprende*. Honey sensed she would have preferred the hotel to have acquired another star. It would probably look better on her cv.

'Never mind.'

Feeling just slightly apprehensive at what she was likely to find, Honey marched to the kitchen and was welcomed by the sound of the dishwasher gyrating with water. Great, that meant she could get on with a few things before paying a visit to Ferny Down Guest House, the bed and breakfast where the American tourist had chosen to stay.

She glanced furtively at the dishwasher which spent more time broken down than actually doing the job it should be doing. She lowered her voice in case the blasted machine heard her and chose to be contrary.

'Fixed?' she asked Smudger Smith, the chef.

'Fixed,' he said without looking up.

Honey sighed. 'Thank God for that.'

He was poking around in the tray of fresh meat just delivered by the butcher. In Smudger's estimation steaks without the right amount of fat threading through them were only fit for the pet food trade.

The dishwasher continued to burble like a bonny brook.

Smudger glanced over his shoulder. 'Your Mother's here.'

Her mother had her own flat at number two, Squires Mews just behind the Theatre Royal. That didn't stop her turning up unannounced and mucking in. Sometimes she was a help, but most of the time a hindrance. Basically it all boiled down to clothes. Her mother was always superbly dressed, not a crease, not a mark defiling her catwalk image.

'Hannah!'

The voice of doom! Her mother was one of the few people who still called her Hannah, but only when she had something serious to say – or at least something she considered serious.

Honey made a beeline for the bar, the only place her mother refused to enter unless it was a life-or-death situation.

Honey made the bar area just in time. The tap tap of kitten heeled shoes moved unrelentingly in her direction.

'Hannah, come out of that den of iniquity. I want to talk to you …'

'Sorry, Mother, but I've got some important business to

15

do on behalf of the Hotels Association.'

The door at the back of the bar was a quick escape route. Although a Catholic, her mother had a Methodist aversion to alcohol – probably because her husband, Honey's father, had had such a liking for it. She never entered the bar. However, she was getting better. Time, as they say, is a great healer.

Lindsey, Honey's daughter, was behind the bar replenishing bottles of mixers. She didn't stop what she was doing when Honey entered, but did throw her a quick grin.

'Grandma's heard about you becoming a private detective. She thinks you might get involved with a policeman and end up drinking in bars all night.'

Honey grimaced as she stated the perfectly obvious. 'I already drink in bars *most* of the night. I run a hotel!'

'Grandma says she reckons you're no good at finding suitable men. She reckons she's going to find one for you.'

Honey lowered her voice. 'Your grandmother's idea of suitable is someone with broad business interests and the personality of a hamster.'

Lindsey smirked. 'And yours is?'

Honey gave a 'don't know' kind of wave of her hand. 'I can go with broad shoulders?'

'As good a starting point as any.'

Honey fidgeted. Lindsey saw her. 'Go on,' she whispered. 'Make your escape. I'll make the excuses.'

Honey kissed her daughter's cheek. 'Did I ever tell you that you're the best daughter in the world?'

Lindsey pretended to think about it. 'Only when I don't ask you for a pay rise.'

'That's my girl.'

'But you never call me that at three in the morning when I *have* been out clubbing.'

Honey threw Lindsey a long-suffering look.

'Mmmm!' She ruffled her daughter's tawny crop. 'It's

just that you don't do it often enough.'

The door slid silently shut behind her, the car started first time, and although it was parked in a tight space, necessity boosted her driving skills. She pulled out and headed for the other side of town. Things were looking good.

It was midway through the afternoon, so the traffic wasn't too bad. She kept to the inner circuit road, skirting the city and sweeping towards the Wellsway then bearing right and immediately left on to the Bristol Road.

Heavy engineering works, scrap yards and devastation had once lined the road on the side fronting the river. They'd since been replaced by swank apartments in former warehouses, smart offices and landscaped car parks.

The other side of the road was unchanged; lined with Victorian villas, some advertising bed and breakfast.

Ferny Down Guest House was one of these. Someone had followed the kerbside attraction rule. Hanging baskets full of purple, mauve and pink flowers hung from ground floor to guttering, obscuring the dirt-streaked façade. A low wall divided a tiny front garden laid with red glazed tiles from the busy road.

She found a parking space wedged between a van advertising carpet cleaning and a truck belonging to the City Council.

There was no garden as such at the front of the guest house. The distance to the front door was no more than two yards and the front door was plastic, totally out of sync with the Victorian brickwork.

Honey took a deep breath then rang the doorbell. Heard it echo inside.

There were other noises, but not the sort associated with someone coming to answer the front door.

Stepping back, she looked up at the windows. Like the door they had plastic frames and were double-glazed to keep out traffic noise. The door remained steadfastly closed.

Honey stepped back from the door and strained to hear something – anything – above the noise of passing traffic.

Grunting sounds accompanied by a few shouts of encouragement came from the alleyway between Ferny Down and the house next door.

Well she didn't have all afternoon. Back she went turning right then right again into the alley.

Three men were manhandling an old chest freezer out of the back gate.

'Careful with my fence,' one of them said. This had to be the proprietor. She'd memorised the details. His name was Mervyn Herbert. Good looks and dress sense were not on his list of priorities.

Overweight, but not obese, he had the worn-out look of someone trapped in a routine he didn't want to be in – like life.

'Mr Herbert?'

She ducked to one side as the men carrying the freezer squeezed out through the gate.

His eyebrows beetled when he looked her up and down. 'You from the council?'

'No. Hotels Association. I came to see you about your little problem.'

For a moment he looked as though she was talking about something personal, i.e. a bad dose of piles or a highly infectious disease, both of which might be of interest to that TV show, *Embarrassing Bodies*.

Sensing he wasn't keen to air his carelessness in public, i.e. losing a paying customer, she mouthed the words, 'your missing guest'.

There was a wary look to his eyes closely followed by relief when he nodded. 'You'd best see the wife. Come this way if you like.'

Once the freezer was on its way to the council truck and the local landfill site, she edged her way around the path carefully avoiding a pyramid of stones that appeared to form a rockery.

Mr Herbert pointed to a plastic-framed conservatory. Through the misted glass she detected a blob of colour moving in a chair.

'She's in there. I'll leave you to it. I've got to make sure this lot from the council don't do any damage.'

He was gone in a jiffy, more concerned with the freezer than he was with her.

'Ere!' she heard him shout. 'Go easy with that!'

She wondered why the men who collected disused domestic items needed to go careful with something obviously discarded. Perhaps because it still belonged to the owner until it was out of sight?

The blob of colour she'd seen in the conservatory, Mrs Cora Herbert saw her, got up from her chair and with a jerk of her head and a hissed command, beckoned her over. 'You from the Association?'

Her perceptiveness took Honey by surprise. She managed a smile. At the same time she took in the too-tight T-shirt, too-tight skirt, black shiny tights and killer-heeled shoes. Mrs Herbert was mutton trying to be lamb.

They shook hands. 'Yes. I'm Hannah Driver. Everyone calls me Honey.'

'Oh! That's a nice name. Yes. I like that.'

Cora Herbert looked impressed, almost as though she wished she'd thought of the name herself.

'Are you American?'

'My father was.'

'I thought you was,' she said, beaming from ear to ear. 'I bet you look like him.'

'I can't remember. He died when I was young.'

Cora's face crumpled with sympathy. 'Accident was it?'

'You could say that.'

Meeting a twenty-two-year-old model at a business do

was accidental. It was hardly an accident that he'd lusted after her, divorced her mother then dropped dead on honeymoon.

Honey took in her surroundings. She'd seen better.

A half-drunk cup of coffee sat on the table. So did an ashtray containing cigarette stubs stained with pink lipstick. The room reeked of tobacco and cheap perfume.

Holding her breath was out of the question. She'd keel over.

'My den where I can do what I bloody well like,' said Cora Herbert as if guessing what Honey was thinking, shooting her down before she raised an objection. 'Are you dry?'

'Sorry?'

'Do ya wanna cup of coffee?'

'No thanks.' Café Latte was one thing. Café Nicotine was another. When she left here she'd stink of stale tobacco. Her hair and her clothes would need instant washing. Dry cleaning bills and suede skirts came to mind. Today she wore linen, thank God.

She got out her notebook and a pen – first requisite of a decent detective. 'So this American …' she began.

'Mr Weinstock. At least that's what he said his name was. But that isn't the name on his passport, nor the address he gave us.'

'Didn't you check his passport details against the address given when he checked in?'

Without so much as a bashful blink, Cora took a cigarette from a packet and lit up. Thankfully, she turned away when she exhaled.

'What for? He paid me cash up front.'

'Ah!' Honey nodded. No point the taxman checking Cora Herbert's records. The passport details had not been entered and neither had the money.

'How long did he stay?'

'A whole week!'

Cora Herbert's tone was the oral equivalent of rubbing her hands together. Her face glowed with satisfaction.

'Unusual for somebody staying in a bed and breakfast.'

'A guest house! We are a guest house,' Cora Herbert snapped, sending whorls of smoke escaping from her mouth.

'Sorry.' Such were the sensitivities of guesthouse landladies, Honey reminded herself.

'Still – a good booking. Few Americans take that long to look round.'

The golden triangle, London, Stratford-upon-Avon down to Bath and back to London; that was the norm, and all done in two weeks with Oxford thrown in.

Cora shrugged her naked shoulders against the gleam of see-through plastic bra straps. 'Whatever. He paid and that was it.'

'So his things are still in his room?'

Cora made a hissing sound through her teeth. 'Ooow, no. I had to clear the room because I had bookings, you see. It's in storage. I'll have to charge him of course.'

'Of course. If he's still alive that is.'

'Well I can hardly charge him if he's dead.'

'Of course not.'

Honey rebuked herself for having misjudged the woman, but on hearing what she said next changed her mind back again.

'If he is dead, then I'll have to send the bill to his family.'

Now burning only an inch or so from Cora's yellow-stained fingertips, the cigarette was stubbed out. A second or two, a little nail biting, and another one glowed red between sequined fingernails.

Honey's eyes flitted to the garden. The rockery was incongruous, but all the same, she longed to sit on its pinnacle while drinking in the air.

She pulled herself back to the job in hand. 'Did he do

much sightseeing? I mean, is there somewhere he might have gone and stayed there longer than planned?'

Cora narrowed her eyes against the rising smoke until they were just slits shaded by thick mascara. 'I don't know about planning to stay anywhere. But he did visit places, though I didn't like to pry. I asked in a general kind of way, and he answered in a general kind of way.'

'Any particular places?'

'Well, the Royal Crescent of course, and the Baths, but I think he went a bit further afield too. Came home by taxi three days following. Handed the driver over roughly thirty quid each time. I saw it.'

Honey agreed that he must have been visiting somewhere outside the city to attract that size of taxi fare. The American Museum at Claverton Down, or even pretty little Bradford-on-Avon? 'Its Saxon church is especially fine,' a Berkeley professor had told her. He'd also related a potted history of the Berkeley family and the castle situated halfway between Bath and Gloucester. He'd looked supremely satisfied on seeing her turn green at some of the gorier details.

'Was it the same taxi cab company each time?'

Cora nodded. 'Busy Bee. The car was black.'

'What about your husband?'

'What about him?'

The tone was soured, the eyes hard as pebbles. No love lost there then.

'Did he speak to Mr Weinstock?'

'Might have done. He was always asking for crushed ice.' She laughed. 'The look on Mervyn's face when he was bashing them ice cubes with a rolling pin – enough to commit murder they were. Why can't he have bloody cubes like everybody bloody else, he used to say.'

Crushed ice. Honey knew from experience that Americans loved crushed ice. It could be annoying when nothing else would do and other guests were making demands. Still, we aim to please, she thought.

'I know your husband's busy at the moment, but I would like a word with him.'

'Of course you would.' Cora got up and poked her head out of the conservatory. 'MERV–YN!'

Her voice clanged around the conservatory like an iron bell.

'No chance,' she said coming back in. 'He's been helping the council blokes to take that freezer. Must have got up a sweat and decided a few pints were needed.'

'He's gone to the pub?'

'Yeah.' Cora screwed up her nose and took another puff of her cigarette. 'It's a home from bloody home as far as he's concerned.'

Honey narrowed her eyes, partly against the damned smoke, and partly because she was making a mental list of all the questions she should ask. She wrote down his name along with a note to locate and question the taxi driver should Mr Weinstock not turn up. She smoothed the page flat with her hand. This was all very satisfying. Wasn't sleuthing à la Agatha Christie based on a process of elimination? Now what else did those detectives on TV do?

It came to her in an instant. 'Can I take a look at his things?'

Cora got up from her chair. 'I don't see why not.'

She led her to a cupboard beneath the stairs. 'There it is.'

Two holdalls, one smaller than the other but neither of them very big.

'Great!' She leaned forward meaning to drag the bags outside.

An indignant Cora stopped her. 'No need to do that and mess up my hallway. I've got guests coming.'

She said it as though she were the Royal Crescent Hotel and expecting a presidential cavalcade not a gang of spotty backpackers.

Before Honey had chance to ask where she could take them, Cora pushed her in with the baggage. 'There. I can't shut the door without locking it, but you'll be all right. You've got a light. Give me a knock when you've finished and I'll let you out.'

Honey swallowed the urge to panic and head for the open air. Stephen King horror stories came to mind. She couldn't quite recall one about a mad landlady locking an unsuspecting amateur sleuth under the stairs, but that didn't mean it wasn't a possibility.

After settling her nerves and giving her thudding heart a severe talking to, she hunkered down and got on with it.

Nothing unusual about the clothes – typically non-iron stuff that anyone with any sense would take on a long-term vacation.

The flight documents and passport were in a see-through plastic zip up. That alone was worrying, though not unusual. Most people carried their passports around unless they had access to a safe. Only up-market hotels had safes.

'So I would take my passport with me if I was staying in a place like this,' Honey muttered to herself. 'But you didn't ...' Her voice trailed away. So why leave it? Unless he hadn't had time or unless something bad, very bad had happened ... The picture in the passport showed a strong-faced man with fair hair. His name was given as Elmer John Maxted, age 43, eyes blue, height 6ft 1 inch, weight 210 pounds.

'You're a big man, Elmer John Maxted,' she muttered and frowned. 'Now why call yourself Weinstock?'

Her eyes flitted over the address – somewhere in California – and dropped on the space reserved for occupation fully expecting something mundane like 'insurance salesman' or 'realtor'. Far from it!

Holding it up to the bare light bulb, she reread the

details on a receipt for travel insurance. Her heart skipped a beat.

'Let me out,' she shouted, hammering on the door. 'Let me out!'

No sound from the other side of the door. Wherever Cora Herbert was, she wasn't close at hand.

Honey dug her mobile out of her pocket and tapped Casper's number.

'Casper. I know you won't want to do this, but you have to call the police.'

He tried a few excuses as to why he shouldn't and asked why she thought he should.

'Look, this missing American; I'm at Ferny Down bed and breakfast, the place where he stayed and he's left his passport here …'

Casper questioned why that had filled her with such alarm.

'Casper, no one leaves their passport behind in a bed and breakfast. But there's something else. His name's not Weinstock, it's Maxted and he's a private detective.'

# Chapter Three

'The police are making enquiries.'

'Is that all?'

Casper's sigh blasted down the phone like the air from a punctured balloon.

'My dear girl, the man has only gone missing. And that, my dear, is more or less what was said to me. They said give it one more day. If he doesn't turn up then they'll put out a nationwide alert.'

The case of the missing tourist had run up against the buffers. Initially she'd been unwilling to take on this appointment. Now she found herself feeling disappointed. This had seemed like a *real* crime case and in retrospect she'd been quite keen to give it a go, but not now. The police had tagged it routine.

On top of that the weather forecast took a nosedive. Storm clouds gathered. The weather god took no notice of her outburst. The rain started at five that afternoon.

'It's June, for goodness sake!'

Thursday. Lindsey's night off and she was hogging the bathroom. The fallout from all manner of scented soap, shower gel, and shampoo was drifting with the steam out of the bathroom window.

Honey was sitting outside beneath a two hundred-year-old canopy. Its metal roof, the original colour turned to the mottled green of aged copper, ran the length of the private patio. Clematis and other plants climbed the fretwork supports. The patio area it covered was further divided from hotel guests by bushes and more plants climbing over a sturdy mesh of wire and stone pillars.

Honey settled herself on a wooden bench. Like the roof, its framework was also of iron and painted white. As she fondled the lion heads forming the arms, she wondered how long before her career in amateur detection restarted.

The sound of the running water coming from the bathroom ceased. Accompanied by a cloud of steam, Lindsey came out wearing a bathrobe and a towel around her wet hair.

Honey looked at her. 'I suppose you'll be late tonight.'

'Tonight? Certainly not. Expect me at around three. You want me to enjoy myself, don't you?'

'You said you were going to a concert.'

Lindsey's voice was muffled by towel and wet hair. 'Mother, I'm trying to appear wild, just as you want me to.'

'You're going nightclubbing?'

Lindsey smiled through fronds of wet hair. 'After the concert.'

The young social scene in the city of Bath was second to none. Trendy wine bars rubbed shoulders with the Theatre Royal, pubs, restaurants and clubs that partied till dawn. Lindsey was part of that scene, but with reservations. Goodness knows where the culture vulture genes had come from.

'Anywhere nice?' Honey asked, trying to sound laid back and modern – even unconcerned. It was far from easy.

Lindsey rubbed vigorously at her hair. 'It depends on my friends.'

*Who was she going out with?* Honey sipped at her drink.

'Three men friends,' said Lindsey before she had chance to ask.

Three men and going to a night club. Buzz words,

every last one of them. But what did they mean? Trying to sound laid back and modern flew out of the window. Mother Hen took over.

'Now look, if you must go clubbing, keep in a crowd and don't let these guys take advantage, and make sure you get a taxi home.'

'Taxis are expensive.'

There was a sense of déjà vu at that statement. Now where had she heard it before? Her response was also familiar. 'I'll reimburse you.'

'Mum! Stop fussing. The guys are great pals and are not going to rape me. Stop treating me like a child. I'm eighteen, for God's sake!'

Honey's mouth dropped as the truth dawned. 'Gosh. You sound just like me. You've inherited my genes.'

Lindsey's eyes echoed the smile playing around her mouth. 'And you sound just like …'

'Hold it right there!' Honey held up her hand, palm facing her daughter. 'I apologise for sounding like my mother. Go out, get drunk, get laid, but don't bring any trouble home.' She kissed her daughter's cheek. 'Just take care of yourself.'

'I will.'

The old coach house they lived in was situated at the end of the long, paved courtyard to the rear of the hotel. There were two bedrooms downstairs plus a bathroom. The upper floor that had once held hay and barley for the horses, now boasted a fitted kitchen and a spacious living room. A stone fireplace graced one wall of the living room and two huge A-shaped trusses supported an exposed apex ceiling panelled in Canadian maple. The panelled ceiling was the reason Honey had created bedrooms on the ground floor and living space upstairs. The view was good. So was the ceiling when you were lying flat on your back, staring into space.

Kicking off her shoes, Honey lay back on the yellow

leather settee and eyed with – affection? Yes, affection, her collection of corsets, silk stockings, and beautiful garters festooned with ribbons, flowers and even tiny birds made of real feathers. Pride of place went to the copious bloomers said to have belonged to Queen Victoria. Like her other favourite items, the bloomers were safely framed behind glass and hanging above the fireplace.

Framing them had been done swiftly before an uninformed member of staff assumed the voluminous expanse of cotton was a tablecloth.

Poor old Queen Victoria. She'd turn in her grave if she knew that someone could actually contemplate setting a plateful of English breakfast on her drawers!

End of the day. The best time. She poured herself a glass of wine. There was something about a good wine that made one see clearer, when in fact by reputation it should make one's thoughts fuzzy.

First, the question of Elmer Weinstock; was he merely missing? Was he here on a secret mission? Or was it that Mervyn Herbert had smashed his last load of ice for the visiting American and decided to smash Elmer's head in along with it? On the other hand, perhaps there was some other reason that wasn't yet quite clear.

Never mind. At least her rooms were full. Dear old Casper had sent more business her way.

She toasted herself.

'Honey Driver. Five-star hotelier, world-famous beauty and famous detective.'

A little over the top, but there …

'Give it time,' she said with a sigh and closed her eyes. She dozed. In her dreams she was wearing a deerstalker hat, toting a magnifying glass and smoking a pipe.

# Chapter Four

It was Saturday night, pouring down and gone one o'clock when Loretta Davies, Mervyn Herbert's stepdaughter, left the Underground Club, which was subterranean, and close to the river.

'Getting a taxi?' shouted one of her friends, tottering on the edge of the pavement and hanging on grimly to her boyfriend who was impatient to be away and screwing her in the privacy of some shop doorway.

'You must be jokin'. I'm skint now ain't I!' The shouted reply was drowned in the drumming of the downpour.

Whatever else her friend shouted back was drowned too. Both the girl and the young man faded into the darkness between the high buildings.

Loretta pulled the collar of her jacket up around her face as best she could. It was plastic, black and shiny. The rain hammered on it before running off in sheets like it would off a tin roof. The Mac was also short, her skirt shorter and her black tights sodden from the thighs downwards. Wisps of hair clung wetly to her face and water dripped from her eyebrows.

Passing cars muted the sound of her DM's splashing on the glossy pavements. Headlights glanced like the beams of a lighthouse through the teeming rain.

Streetlights and headlights lessened once she left North Parade. She kept the gardens on her right aiming to make her way across the road near Bog Island, an old Victorian lavatory that some quirky soul had changed into a nightclub at one time.

As she bent her head against the driving rain, she cursed the night. Her footsteps bounced off the walls in narrow alleys. At times it seemed like an army was following her – or at least one person, possibly more. She shivered inside her raincoat and dug her hands more deeply into her pockets, glad when she finally emerged into a rank of Regency houses.

Square panes in Georgian windows were shut tight around her and curtains drawn. Fewer cars flashed by, most sensible people already home in a warm bed with a warm body. Even the shop doorways were empty, fumbling couples defeated by the wind driven rain, their novice explorations saved for another time when the weather was better.

Empty echoes, lonely streetlights, and heavy rain. Wetness and darkness took the night as their own. The rain hammered so hard and loud that she could no longer hear her own footsteps. She didn't hear his.

A shadow came alive.

She was startled when he stepped out in front of her until she saw who it was.

'You!'

Mervyn Herbert had deep-set eyes. His teeth were yellow. 'Nasty night.'

Loretta was far from pleased to see him. 'Mervyn, stop following me!'

He slipped a hand into his trouser pocket and brought out a twenty-pound note. 'Here you are. I expect you could do with it.'

She hesitated, her gaze bouncing between his face and the money.

She snatched it and stuffed it into her pocket.

'Thought you'd need it. You always did like a pound note, didn't you, girl?'

She didn't correct him and say that there was no such

thing as a pound note, only a coin. The money always came in useful.

'I've got the car.'

His smile was wide. 'Come on sweetheart. I'm only doing my duty as a loving daddy.'

'You're not my daddy!'

Her exclamation bounced between the buildings.

The light from a streetlamp picked out Mervyn's yellow teeth as he smiled.

'We're still family and it's a lousy night.'

The rain trickled into Loretta's eyes and down the nape of her neck. She asked herself whether she could cope with him. The rain increased and lightning lit up the sky.

'All right.'

She was still shivering when she slid into the front passenger seat of the five-year old Ford 'family' car. Family! That was a laugh. Her mother told people she'd been a child bride. She could hear her mother now:

'My Loretta's seventeen. I know I don't look old enough, but I was very young when I had her. Only eighteen myself.'

Hogwash! Her mother had been well into her twenties, but denied herself those extra years, just as she denied the extra inches around her hips and thighs.

She turned as she fastened her safety belt. The rain was unceasing. The streets empty.

The headlights of a passing car picked out a figure amongst the shadows. She sucked in her breath, saw him craning his neck, looking in her direction.

She jumped when Mervyn patted her knee. 'Everything all right, sweetheart?'

She smacked his hand away. 'Keep your dirty paw to yourself!'

Whoever had been watching in the shadows was gone. There was just Mervyn, sitting beside her looking his usual greasy, unkempt self. His complexion was ashen and the sad sod had taken the effort to comb a few strands of hair across a hairless skull. The result was comical rather than complimentary. A sliver of hair slewed over his face and dripped water down his face leaving a portion of his head bald and shiny.

Pointing at it with a painted finger, she giggled.

He pushed it back, a red blush of embarrassment creeping up his grizzled throat.

Loretta laughed out loud.

'Crikey,' she said, firmly asserting the old saucy self. 'You're getting to be a right slap-head aren't ya! Hardly a hair left on yer head.'

His knuckles whitened as his hands gripped the steering wheel more tightly. 'Saucy cow! One of these days …'

'One of these days what?' She laughed openly and loudly. 'You'll do what, Mervyn? Nothing! I'm not a little girl any more. I can stick up for myself, and just you remember that!'

She gasped as his hand grabbed her knee more fiercely and painfully than before.

'You'd be surprised at what I'm capable of, sweetheart. There's more to yer old step-daddy than meets the eye. And you want more money, don't you? You're always wanting my money.'

Loretta suddenly felt scared. 'Let me out of the car!'

He opened his mouth and a cackle came out, like the sound dead men are supposed to make before they die. She wished that Mervyn Herbert were already dead. Better men than him were dead. But that was it. Mervyn was too mean to die, too nasty to end up in consecrated ground.

His hands were back on the wheel. She thought of opening the door and jumping out, but they were travelling too fast. Her tights were new. Her knees would be scratched.

Perhaps out of habit, or some vestige of memory, the old fear returned.

'Please, Mervyn. I'll do anything, anything …'

He grinned, his creased face a yellow gargoyle in the flashing glow of the streetlights.

'Yes,' he said, pausing to slick his tongue over his lips. 'Of course you will.'


The man who'd been hiding in the shadows for the right moment cursed the weather, the car and that bloody little tart. The stupid cow had got into a car, and not just any car, HIS bloody car! Bloody Mervyn Herbert.

The night was black and empty. Everyone was disappearing fast.

Fortunately he managed to flag down what must have been the only available taxi left in Bath.

'Follow that car!'

The driver, a young Asian with white teeth and wearing a white shirt and tie with a black leather jacket, beamed with disbelief. 'You're joking!'

Fingers thick as sausages grabbed his collar. 'No! I ain't!'

The driver stabbed on the gas too fiercely; the car skidded on the water-covered tarmac, careering from side to side as the driver fought to regain control.

Sweat broke out on the glossy forehead. He'd seen this kind of thing happen in the movies. Exciting to watch; in reality too bloody scary for his taste.

The light-coloured Ford was now three cars ahead.

His passenger was impatient, leaning through the partition. He could feel his fingers digging through the sleeve of his leather jacket.

'Overtake! Overtake!' His tone was vicious.

Scared out of his wits, the taxi driver shook his head emphatically. 'I cannot! I cannot! It is far too narrow here! There are many parked cars!'

His passenger leaned further forward and tried to grab the wheel. A car travelling in the other direction blew its horn as they swerved into the centre of the road.

'Please,' the driver shouted; his hands clammy though he gripped the wheel tightly. 'We cannot overtake. It is dangerous!'

Muttering an oath under his breath, the passenger slumped back in his seat. Ahead of them two cars went through a green traffic light. The next went through amber. The traffic light turned red. The brakes squealed as the taxi came to a juddering halt.

The driver eyed his passenger from the comparative safety of the rear-view mirror.

'Where to now?' he asked, unable to control the trembling in his voice.

'Ferny Down Guest House. That's where they *should* be heading. It's on the Lower Bristol Road. Do you know it?'

'Yes. Yes. I do.'

The driver's eyes flickered nervously between the traffic light and the rear-view mirror. Late night passengers troubled him, this one more than most.

The lights changed. The taxi moved forwards across the river and right towards the Lower Bristol Road.

Robert Howard Davies, lately of Horfield Prison, Bristol, made himself comfortable. He knew the taxi driver's eyes were studying him, no doubt wondering whether he'd get his fare or not.

That depends, thought Robert, disgruntled because he'd got so close to reacquainting himself with his daughter. Still, no harm in going to see the wife; and God help Mervyn Herbert if he wasn't there when he arrived. There'd be some explaining to do, and he wasn't in the market for accepting excuses. Never had been. Never would be.

# Chapter Five

One day, one whole twenty-four hours had passed and Elmer Maxted was still missing.

Honey received a phone call. It was Neville, Casper's friend, hotel manager and bedtime companion.

'Casper says you need to go down there and liaise,' said Neville.

'I was thinking the same thing. Whether I want to or not, I have to tell the police all I know.'

There was silence. Neville had placed his hand over the phone. She knew from experience that Casper was in the background giving orders.

'Casper says you are to try and keep the lid on things.'

'At the same time as assisting them with their enquiries?'

Again, silence.

'That's right,' said Neville on behalf of Casper. 'You have to be extremely diplomatic. And quick. He wants you go to the police asap.'

'I can't make it for an hour or so. My receptionist is out sick.'

Again the delayed response.

'We'll send help.'

'Thanks. I appreciate it. How come Casper's indisposed?'

'Casper *never* answers the phone while soaking in the bath.'

Although it was Sunday morning, sauntering along to

Manvers Street Police Station wasn't a problem as long as the promised help turned up. On the contrary, it was a welcome break.

One hour later she was brushing her hair, straightening her white cotton shirt and checking the seams in her stockings. She always wore a skirt on Sunday. The stockings added to feelings of almost lost femininity.

Today had turned out exciting again. Nothing and no one could upset her mood – with the exception of her mother who'd decided to choose this morning to pop in and tell her all about her latest lover.

'I'm going on a cruise this summer. I'm going with a man friend. His name's Christopher Jordan, and he's a really charming man.'

Her mother scurried along behind her like an especially tenacious Jack Russell, all clattering heels and an aura of French perfume. 'Men are such good company. You should get yourself one.'

Honey swung left behind the reception desk. Undeterred, her mother leaned on the counter top. 'I've got just the man to suit you. Have I told you about my dentist's friend? He's got a very nice little business ...'

Honey stabbed at the 'escape' key on the computer. That's what she wanted to do. Escape the reception desk and escape her mother. But Susan, their regular receptionist, had phoned in sick. Honey had been expecting it. Lovesick! That's what she was. A handsome young man from Hungary, working at another hotel close by had moved into the bed-sit below Susan. International participation was bound to happen. And did. This meant that if their days off didn't coincide, they fell sick. Today was the young man's day off – but not Susan's.

Blonde coiffeur, bedecked with expensive jewellery and wearing a silk trouser suit, her mother leaned on the reception desk. Her apricot lipstick matched her outfit.

Honey took shallow breaths in an effort to cope with

the cloud of expensive perfume that fell over her.

'I've arranged for you to meet him in the Roman Bar of the Francis this evening at seven.'

'I can't go.'

'Why not?'

'I'm working.'

'Lunchtime then. I'll rearrange it for twelve noon.'

'Mother!'

'Don't shout.'

'I didn't shout, I merely protested.'

A couple from Sydney, Australia chose that moment to check in complete with three suitcases.

Honey took her time checking them in and giving them their keys, fliers and special offers on local attractions. The plan was that her mother would grow impatient and disappear. She didn't.

'Look, Mother ...'

Jeremiah Poughty, Casper's very close friend, chose that moment to come breezing through the double doors. His fingers brushed over the brass handles as though he were checking for smudges.

'Casper sent me. I understand you're a trifle short-staffed, my darling. So here I am. Lately of the hotel trade, but I do remember which buttons to press.'

'So what are you doing nowadays?' said Honey, purposely turning her back on her mother.

'I've got a stall in the Guildhall Market. It's called, Rice, Spice and All Things Nice.'

Honey looked suitably impressed.

Unfortunately, so did her mother.

Her mother clapped her hands. 'There! You can go on your date and enjoy yourself.'

'No, Mother. I cannot. Jeremiah is taking over reception for this morning only. I have an appointment with the police and tonight I have to work. I haven't got time for dates with your dentist's friend.'

Honey slid herself out of the ergonomically designed swivel chair. Jeremiah eased himself into it.

'He's phoned the police prior to you going there,' Jeremiah went on, swinging his long limbs into the chair and sliding it back into place.

'If that's the case, I can't understand why he hasn't gone along himself, 'said Honey while carefully avoiding her mother's enquiring expression.

'He's not one for men in uniforms,' Jeremiah said. 'Reminds him of the bad old days. Now,' he said, leaning threateningly at the computer screen. 'No need to explain the system to me. Once you've used one, you've used them all.'

Honey grabbed her overlarge bag and slung it over her shoulder.

Her mother followed her to the door and looked worried. 'Why are you going to the police station?'

Determined that everything should run smoothly in her absence, Honey ignored the question and addressed Jeremiah. 'There's a party for lunch coming in at twelve.'

Receiving no reply from her daughter, Gloria aimed her question at Jeremiah. 'Why is she going to the police station?'

Jeremiah was still taking in the orders Honey was throwing at him.

Exasperated, Gloria Cross slammed her hand down on the desk.

'Why is my daughter going to the police station? What has she done?'

Those guests sitting in the comfortable settees around the reception area, waiting for taxis, teas or their check out bill, fell to silence. Curious eyes turned in her direction.

Honey played to the crowd.

'They're accusing me of planning to bury my mother under the patio. I told them it wasn't true and that I'd much prefer to drown you in malmsey, but they didn't believe me. Said they didn't think anyone would ruin good alcohol unless they were batty – or desperate!'

'You're batty!' said her mother, looking thoroughly annoyed.

The guests grinned, chuckled and exchanged knowing looks. Obviously, they too had mothers prone to cause mad moments of sheer exasperation.

Honey threw a swift thank you to Jeremiah who merely nodded and proceeded to tidy up the whole online booking system and the paperwork around him.

Getting to the door had been easy enough compared to getting out of it. Her mother wasn't giving up *that* easily.

'Right. So you're off to the police station on official hotel business. That shouldn't take long. From there you can make your way to church.'

'Mother! I don't do church.'

Too late. A set of impeccably manicured nails were already tapping out a number on her mobile, a determined jut to her chin and a 'no nonsense' look in her eyes. 'Right. Father Trevor's expecting you.'

'I'm not a Catholic.'

'Well I think you should be.'

'My father wasn't.'

Her mother crossed herself. Becoming a Catholic had come late in life – once all the divorces were behind her.

'The service finishes at twelve. No need to hurry back. That nice poof in reception will take care of things until you get back.'

What was the point? Honey shook her head. Her mother didn't know how to spell politically correct let alone apply it. She was one of the old school and not up to speed on courteous terminology.

As she approached North Parade heading for Manvers Street, Honey began questioning Casper's generosity in sending someone over to help out. Casper could be very nice when he wanted to be. At other times he could be downright ruthless.

On her way there she plucked out her phone and tapped into the address book. Casper answered almost immediately.

'Thanks for sending Jeremiah over.'

'Oh! Is that where he is?'

Honey frowned. 'You didn't send him?'

'I asked him to pop over and assist you. He wasn't keen and murmured something about me using him as a stop gap. I told him to go to hell. His interpretation is a little surprising I must say. After all, I hadn't exactly promised him eternal love – just an intimate friendship.'

'Whatever. His presence was appreciated.'

'No doubt.'


Despite the fact that it was Sunday morning, the cop shop was busy. The chalky smell of dried-out paint and well-worn carpet came out to meet her. So too did a tinge of Jeyes fluid each time the cloakroom doors opened in the foyer.

Once the desk sergeant had booked her in, she was told to sit down and wait.

Stressing that she was here by request and on behalf of the hoteliers of the city, and had little time to spare, failed to impress him.

So she sat and studied the people waiting for attention.

They were a mixed bag and therefore interesting.

Irate ex-motorists relieved of their vehicle by some mindless drogue who had fancied his chances at Grand Prix wheelies down over Brassknocker Hill. Grand Pricks were more like it, the cars mangled by now and dumped in some roadside ditch.

A crusty, complete with tangled dreadlocks, foetid smell and a scrawny dog, was demanding the return of his untaxed, uninsured and un-roadworthy vehicle.

An American tourist wearing a tartan cap and matching

Bermudas waited while the desk sergeant took down his particulars.

'What I can't understand is how they knew we were tourists,' he drawled.

Judging by their age, marriage had still been in fashion when they were young. The woman Honey took to be his wife slumped in the chair next to Honey.

Rolling her eyes, she whispered. 'I told him not to make himself conspicuous. But would he listen? I'm not changing my style for anybody, he tells me.' The woman shook her head dolefully. 'Style it ain't.'

Honey smiled. 'Beauty is in the reflection in the mirror. We see gravity taking its toll, and they see Steve McQueen. It's a man thing.'

'You got it!'

A door marked private opened. A man wearing a black T-shirt and stone-washed jeans appeared.

His eyes swept over the waiting room.

Her eyes swept over him. Average height, well-built. The casual clothes and the stubble on his chin, hinted at the rough diamond look. Looking hard added gravitas when you were less than six feet in height. The fact that he had hands like shovels worked for her.

A policewoman lurked in the shadows behind him as though she were watching his back. Honey met the enquiring eyes. The woman's gaze hardened to green-glazed jealousy.

Rough-diamond street cred with stubble scythed over the melee and homed in on her. 'Hannah Driver?'

He had a voice like gravel.

'That's me.'

A waiting room full of curious eyes watched her cross the floor.

It was kind of like being on stage. All the senses kicked in. A few hip-wiggling steps and she was close enough to smell what remained of his aftershave. Three days or so since he'd shaved, but the pong was still there.

'I'm Detective Sergeant Steve Doherty.' He looked her up and down. 'So you're Bath's answer to Miss Marple.'

'Not quite. I don't knit or do crosswords, or frequent vicarage tea parties.'

His surliness travelled to his voice.

'Well that's a disappointment. I would have liked a new pullover or tea with the vicar. But there, amateur snoops come in all shapes and sizes.

'So do cops. I thought you'd be taller.'

For a split second his gaze fell to her 36Cs. He smirked. She guessed what was coming.

'Being of average height has its advantages.'

If looks could have killed, she would have sliced his head off, but he didn't give her time.

'Through here.'

He jerked his thumb in the direction of the shadow in uniform and the corridor behind him.

The interview room was exactly as she'd expected; plain walls, desk, requisite number of chairs and, of course, the tape recorder. Someone had lately run riot with a sweet-smelling aerosol; alpine flowers by the whiff of it.

Doherty flicked the on switch on the tape recorder. The usual words were said, the date and location. Next came the personal details. 'This is Detective Sergeant Doherty. Interviewee is one Miss Hannah Driver ...'

'Mrs.'

Doherty flashed her an impatient look. '*Mrs* Hannah Driver. Also present is Detective Constable Sian Williams. The police woman straightened as though just a mention gave her special rights i.e. access to his body.

'Right,' said Mr Street Cred – who she now knew was named Doherty – sitting back in his chair. 'Tell me your involvement.'

'I prefer to be called Honey.'

'As in Honey Bee?'

'Well,' she began, feeling like a suspect in some cheap television detective series, 'I have been appointed by Bath Hotels Association to liaise with the police regarding any crime connected with tourism ...'

'Yeah! I understand that,' said Doherty, the fingers of his right hand fiddling with the pen protruding from his left breast pocket.

'That kind of stuff out there,' he jerked his head indicating the waiting room beyond the wall. 'Muggings, theft and diddling the exchange rate. Anything that upsets the tourist industry. Must keep ourselves a squeaky clean image mustn't we? Or the Yanks won't be visiting these hallowed shores so the business folk decide an amateur detective is the answer. What a laugh!'

The policewoman covered her giggle with one hand.

Honey sprang to her feet. 'Don't be so bloody condescending!'

He sprang to his feet. 'This is a cop shop not a bloody tea shop!'

They were like bookends, glaring at each other across the table.

Honey slammed her hands palms down on the wipe-clean table surface, rattling the cups and sending a pen rolling.

'Pleased to meet you too! You think you're looking at a soft touch, a woman who knows nothing of the hard knocks of life. Well let me put you straight. I've got a chef that's threatening to slice out the butcher's entrails over the standard of the steaks and a mother who's likely to get herself made into pies if she keeps trying to fix me up with dog-eared divorcees and bog-standard bachelors. Now, I came in here to tell you as much as I know. I didn't ask for the job and I can do better things with my Sunday mornings. Can we get this over with so we can *both* get back to our work?'

'Sit down!'

He did the same, sitting sideways on in his chair, eyeing her out of the corner of his eyes.

She copied his stance, sliding one stockinged leg over the other. He tried to keep his gaze fixed on her, but hell, that skirt was short and those stockings ... No man could resist a shifty glance.

'This bloke disappearing. There has to be something in it, I suppose, what with him leaving his kit behind.'

He sounded sincere, no longer giving her the impression she had no business in the amateur sleuthing game.

She leaned forward, her eyes in danger of popping out of her head. This was so exciting!

'You think he's been murdered?'

He leaned forward too, lower arms resting on desk, hands clasped just inches from hers.

'I don't have a clue. Even private dicks go on mystery trips.'

Honey frowned. 'Are you making fun of me?'

Doherty grimaced. 'I've been appointed as your official contact within the police force. Chief Constable's orders. I'll do my duty, but I'm not happy about it. I think you should know that.'

Deflated, Honey sat back in her chair.

The sound of a stifled snigger came from Detective Constable Sian Williams.

Doherty scowled. 'Shut that!'

The policewoman's pink lips wobbled a bit before coming under control.

Something was not quite right. Honey narrowed her eyes and threw Doherty a piercing look.

She pointed at the tape recorder.

'So why the hell have that thing on?'

He shrugged.

'It doesn't work. I just turn it on for the hell of it. Didn't unnerve you, did I?'

One side of his mouth lurched upwards into a lop-sided grin.

Honey sprang to her feet.

'Well stuff you, Doherty! You may have times for fun and games, but I do not! I have a business to run and it depends on tourism, which, I might add, pays your wages!'

The grin turned into an apologetic smile. He held up his hands in surrender. 'Look, I'm sorry.'

'You're not taking this seriously.'

He nodded at the policewoman indicating she make for the door. It closed behind her.

Doherty noted Honey's brown eyes, the dark hair nicely contrasting with a crisp white blouse, a buff-coloured waistcoat and smart skirt. She was wearing stockings. Not tights. Stockings clung more closely to the skin and he considered himself a connoisseur of such things.

Hannah Driver was not at all what he'd expected. She looked posh totty, but underneath that cool exterior he sensed something hotter.

Honey folded her arms in a way that shielded her bosom. 'I should never have taken this job,' she muttered.

'You didn't want to develop a long-lasting relationship with a crime-fighting member of your local constabulary?'

She cocked an eyebrow. 'Don't flatter yourself.'

'I wasn't exactly spoilt for choice either!'

She didn't go into details of why she'd accepted the role. What would the likes of an unshaved, hard-nosed copper know about business?

'Can we start again?' He sounded as though he meant it.

She considered telling him to get lost, but the shrewder side of her nature stopped her. Casper had promised her fiscal rewards for doing this job and finding the American. Filling her rooms to capacity and every table in the restaurant ordering three courses plus the best vintage wine was not beyond the realms of possibility. She could do with it. The Green River was slightly off the beaten track and could do with all the help it could get.

She sat back down. 'So! What shall we do about this Elmer Weinstock/Maxted or whatever?'

Doherty laid his hands flat on the desk and studied his fingernails. 'So! He was a private detective,' he said thoughtfully.

'Was he here on a job? Have you checked?'

He nodded. 'Yes. We have checked, and no, he was not here on a job. He was on vacation according to his office, tracing his family tree so I was told.'

Honey frowned. So why use an alias?

Doherty gave his own answer to the unspoken question in a voice that was a fair impersonation of Humphrey Bogart.

'These private dicks have a sense of the dramatic. They've been watching too many cop shows on TV. He just liked the deal of being somebody else.'

'You're not going to investigate are you?'

'No. Shall I tell you why?'

'You don't have to, but I guess you will anyway.'

'I think he's met up with a dishy broad and he's gone off to taste a last sip of the sweet honey of life. So what if he doesn't make his flight? Yep. That's my theory. A taste of honey. That's what he's found.'

Honey held back her temper.

'Very poetic, but I think you're wrong.'

He spread his hands and winked. 'That's it, sugar.'

Blue eyes and dark hair. It shouldn't be allowed. A sneaking liking for him developed there and then. Her lips were sliding into a smile without a by-your-leave. She managed to wipe it off before it reached full bloom.

'I'm not going to encourage you.'

She got to her feet.

'So what are you going to do, sugar?'

She paused by the door, rested her hand on her hip and winked. 'I think I'll pay another visit to the house of a thousand ashtrays.'

He grinned. 'Cora Herbert.'

'You bet.'

'You're wasting your time.'

Honey rested her hand on one curvaceous hip and held her head to one side. 'You didn't want to work with me and you still don't, do you?'

His expression clouded. 'It's nothing personal.'

'No,' she said, 'and it won't ever get that way.'

Sian came back after Honey had left, her stockings making a rustling sound as she slid one leg over the other.

Steve Doherty found himself comparing them to Honey Driver's pins. They weren't a patch.

Unaware of his judgement, Sian folded her arms across her uniformed chest and grinned at him.

'You enjoyed that more than you thought you would.'

He stretched his arms above his head and flexed his muscles. 'Take that grin off your face.'

'She's an attractive woman. Getting on a bit, though.'

He spun to face her and pointed an accusing finger. 'Not another word, Williams. I still think this hotel liaison nonsense is all a bloody waste of time.'

She cocked one eyebrow. 'But she makes it more palatable?'

Doherty smirked and a lock of dark hair fell onto his forehead.

Sian Williams went weak at the knees.

His smile was enough to leave her panting for more. Last night his voice had poured into her ear like thick, dark treacle. She'd scored, but she knew from Doherty's reputation that she was just another number on his gun.

Steve Doherty was smiling to himself and whatever

thoughts he was thinking were strictly private.

When he spoke she knew he wasn't really speaking to her. He was advising his inner self, telling it just what to expect next.

'Leave it with me. A little of the old Doherty charm and she'll forget all about being Miss bloody Marple. She'll be putty in my hands. I guarantee it.'

# Chapter Six

Cora Herbert insisted that Honey take Elmer Maxted's stuff away.

'I can't have it blocking up my storage facility,' Cora said indignantly, an unlit cigarette jiggling at the corner of her mouth.

Honey grimaced at the memory of the dusty, dirty cupboard beneath the stairs. Describing it as a storage facility was stretching credibility. Dust, cobwebs and a haphazard mix of jumbled luggage and discarded furniture.

It made sense to take it all back to the Green River and do a more thorough check of Elmer's things.

Back in her office without a hairy-legged spider in sight she took her time. First she took out his passport, flight tickets and official documents and took them into her office and her private safe. On studying the flight ticket, the return date was only two days hence.

There was a mystery here. Two days until he flew home? He should be making plans to go right now, checking railway and bus schedules or making arrangements to drop off a hire car – if he'd ever had one.

And there was something else. If Elmer was tracing his forebears, why no birth, marriage or death certificates, or even a half-completed family tree?

She couldn't suppress the tingle of excitement that ran down her back. This was a real conundrum – as the old sleuths of the nineteen twenties would have said. Neither could she throw off her first instinct – that Elmer Maxted was dead. Murdered. But how and by whom? And why?

The hospitality industry consisted of sixteen-hour days, seven days a week. Public holiday times, like Christmas, Easter and the height of summer, were their busiest times of the year.

She reminded herself of where he'd been staying and the nature of the people running the place.

Even during normal times, she rose at dawn and didn't fall into bed until the early hours of the next day. Tiredness led to short tempers. Had Cora or Mervyn snapped and done something stupid? She thought about it. Cora? No. The woman wasn't Mrs Cordiality of the Year, but the only murdering that went on in their guest house was probably burning the sausages at breakfast time.

The door to the office was well oiled, so she didn't hear Lindsey come in.

'Mother! What are you doing?'

'Are you trying to give me a heart attack?'

'Why would I?'

Lindsey was wearing her gym kit, her navy and white bag slung over her shoulder. She grinned. 'Not unless you've left me a fortune in your will. I might chance it then.'

'I suggest you speak to your grandmother on that score.'

Gloria Cross had had three husbands. All of them had been millionaires including her own father. He'd shoved off back to Connecticut with a trophy wife. Undeterred, her mother had sued for settlement, got it, got a new millionaire and drank a toast to her former husband's memory when he'd died in bed on his honeymoon.

'A fitting end to a man who loved women,' said her mother. That night she'd drunk two bottles of Krug and ate a whole lemon meringue pie – her favourite. It still was.

On marrying a Methodist she'd become teetotal. He

51

was dead and gone. It was a matter of time before champagne corks popped again.

Honey smelled her daughter's freshness as though she'd just showered.

'What are you doing?'

Honey began tucking the passports, papers and flight tickets back into the plastic zip-up and then into the safe. Before finally turning the key, she paused, her eyes again falling to the calendar.

'There's a disparity between the booking he made at Ferny Down Guest House and his return flight from London Heathrow. Where did he intend going between those two dates? Had he booked in somewhere? Had he failed to arrive?'

Lindsey shrugged. 'Perhaps he was going to stay on at chez greasy spoon a few more days.'

Honey thought about it, then shook her head. 'To book in for a week at a bed and breakfast is unusual in itself. Most tourists aren't that specific – certainly not in an establishment like Ferny Down. It caters for the lower end of the market.'

'We're not being snobby here, are we?'

'Realistic!'

Lindsey didn't argue. She was as aware as her mother that most tourists staying in certain establishments had definite travel plans. Depending on budget, one or two days sufficed in each place they visited.

'But there are always exceptions.'

Honey waved the airline ticket. 'He was flying home two days from now. That doesn't leave long for travelling anywhere. A day at most. The last day would have been set aside for travelling to the airport.'

Lindsey agreed. 'Most people travel up to London the day before.'

Honey fluttered the tickets against her mouth as she thought things through.

'That means he would have left for the airport tomorrow.'

'And what else?'

Honey slid her eyes sidelong. 'He was researching his family tree, and yet there are no birth, death or marriage certificates in his luggage. I find that strange.'

Lindsey sighed and looked at her watch. 'So you think he's been murdered.'

'Do you think so?' Honey's eyes stretched and a mix of fear and excitement tingled in her ample bosom. The possibility had entered her mind, but surely there was no hard evidence. Had Lindsey spotted something she hadn't?

Her daughter's response swiftly removed any hope of enlightenment.

Lindsey grinned. 'It's my off-the-cuff opinion – purely because I've got no time to consider anything else.' She glanced at her watch again. 'Oops! Must get changed. I've a bar to open.'

'Where do you get your energy?'

Lindsey kissed her mother's cheek. 'I inherited it from my mother along with her good looks.'

'Really?' exclaimed Honey while studying her muted reflection in a glass fronted cabinet.

Lindsey wrapped a loving arm around her shoulder.

'See,' she said, her head resting against that of her mother. 'We're more like sisters than mother and daughter. But it's a safe bet that my love life is more intriguing than yours.'

'You wait. I am an amateur detective you know. Who knows what delicious men I might come across.'

'And today you went to the police station. So tell me. Did you meet any good-looking policemen?'

Honey opened her mouth to deny the fact when Doherty popped into her mind.

Lindsey had insight which, in Honey's opinion, wasn't right in a girl of her age.

'Mother, you're blushing.'

'No, no, no, no, no. It's my age.' She waved her hand in front of her face. 'Hot flushes. See?'

Lindsey stood by the door, a glint in her eye, her brown legs smooth and shiny. 'You may be my mother, but you're also a woman. I think it's time you lived for yourself not for me. Have a slice of romance, mother. You deserve it.'

Honey gaped. When Carl died in a boating accident, Honey had promised herself that she would put Lindsey first in everything. For that reason she'd shied off permanent relationships. She'd seen the problems they could cause. She'd never voiced that promise, so it came as something of a surprise that Lindsey was aware of her sacrifice. And now?

Like a thickly iced cream slice, Doherty came to mind again. Naughty, but nice.

Perceptive as ever, Lindsey winked. 'That good, huh?'

Once she was alone, Honey dragged her thoughts back to the missing tourist. Cupping her chin in her hand she stared out at the blank wall beyond the small window. If he had been murdered, where was the body?

She shook the thoughts from her head, zipped up the bags and shifted them into a far corner.

There were other possibilities of course. He could just have gone walkabouts. Perhaps he'd met some old relative while tracing his family tree and was making up for lost time.

As she shut the door behind her and prepared to check in a nice couple from Ontario, another thought crossed her mind. Would a man seriously searching his family tree leave the paperwork behind? Perhaps that might explain there being none in his luggage. But if that were the case, why leave his passport and airline tickets?

She shook her head, her mind in overdrive.

'We have a room booked in the name of Whittaker,'

said the nice middle-aged man.

Plastering a smile on her face, she entered their names on the system, checked their passports and handed them their room keys, menu cards and a map of the city.

'There's plenty of information in the folder in your room,' she added, 'but don't hesitate to ask if there's anything else you require.'

They thanked her before moving off, Daniel, porter, handyman, native of Croatia, helping them with their luggage.

Her phone rang.

'DS Doherty here.'

Blue eyes, dark stubble. 'I was wondering ...'

'So was I. If Mr or Mrs Herbert had murdered Elmer Weinstock, Maxted or whatever his name is, where would they bury him?'

'That wasn't what I was going to ask you.' He sounded disappointed.

'I suppose if you were looking for a body, you'd dig the garden up first, wouldn't you?'

Steve Doherty prided himself on being a bit of a ladies man. No woman could fail to fall for his suave looks, his rough, masculine charm. So why wasn't she listening to him? He was about to tell her to forget it when an idea occurred to him. Humour her. Make her think this really was going to be a serious case.

'I've had second thoughts about this case and a few possible theories. Can we meet for dinner and talk about it, you know, away from interruptions?'

'You do think he was murdered!'

Doherty felt himself being drawn in by her enthusiasm. It wouldn't be in his interest to contradict her, so he didn't.

He smiled in that secretive way he'd practised in front of the mirror, the sort of smile Bogart used to use. Left-hand corner of mouth lifted, right-hand corner turned downwards. He'd throw it at her in the flesh once they were alone together.

'Let's just say I have a hunch.'

Honey was all ears. This was just what she wanted to hear. Getting involved in murder beat washing dishes hands down.

Slumped back in his green leather office chair, Steve Doherty kicked at his desk which sent him spinning in the chair. She was putty in his hands.

'Great. Where and what time?'

'Sometime after midnight, say about 12.30? The Zodiac?''

Doherty covered the mouthpiece and swore. Wanting to get her alone had backfired. The Zodiac was a restaurant beneath North Parade. A set of narrow steps led down to a barrel-roofed cellar that swept out beneath the road. At the other end to the entrance a glass-covered archway looked out over North Parade Gardens. Laid out in the eighteenth century, the gardens were below the level of the road.

It was a lovely spot, the green lawns plastered with tourists by day sitting on the benches, rubbing their bare feet and swearing not to go on any more ghost walks, Austen Walks, and tours of the Roman Baths.

Trouble was the Zodiac didn't open until nine o'clock at night, and didn't shut until three in the morning. Hence the city's hoteliers and publicans, their only free time being between midnight and dawn, frequented it. Like vampires, thought Steve Doherty, they only come out at night.

Doherty visualised his duty roster. On duty until ten tonight, and on again at six tomorrow …

'OK,' he said, cursing himself for being so easily led. 'I'll be there.' He pulled his face out of shape as a thought occurred to him. Sian Williams would be on duty with him tonight and a bird in the hand …

Honey made things easy for him. 'But not tonight. Not this week in fact. How about Friday week?'

His whole body relaxed. That was when the roster changed. At least he'd get a lie in the following morning. And Sian Williams would be on a different shift. Best to keep women divided. It kept them interested.

'Suits me fine.'

There was no one hanging around in reception except for Mrs Spear pushing the vacuum cleaner. She was singing along to whatever she was listening to on an iPod.

Honey gave her a wave. She didn't notice.

A totally frameless conservatory, an extravagance she'd never regretted, led off the reception area. Through its unsullied glass she could see the abbey, the mansard roofs, the tall chimneys framing the green hills circling the city like giant arms.

This was the view that tourists came to see; so why had Elmer Maxted stayed at a cheap guest house frequented by those on a very tight budget? His luggage was expensive and although private detectives were portrayed as dirt poor in TV programmes, it wasn't necessarily true and certainly not in his case.

Her thoughts were interrupted.

'Honey! Honey, darling!'

She recognised the voice of Mary Jane Jefferies, who'd been a regular visitor to the Green River for years.

Wearing a pink caftan over equally pink trousers, the tall woman floated towards her waving a copy of the Bath City bus timetable.

'I have a problem,' she said. Five amazingly long fingers dug into Honey's shoulder. Firmly gripped, she was steered into the sitting room.

'Or rather, I think you have a problem,' said Mary Jane, her voice dropping to not much more than a whisper. 'Take a seat.'

Mary Jane was a doctor of parapsychology a ghost goddess as she'd explained to Honey when they'd first met.

'Which is why I keep coming back here, Honey. You have a resident ghost.'

That little morsel of wisdom had been exclaimed in one of Mary Jane's earlier visits.

Honey had accepted the fact without argument. Yes, she knew the place was old and it creaked and groaned through the night, but then, didn't all old buildings do that? And yes, it was old, but not old when compared with Stonehenge or the Roman Baths. The outside was imposing but promised comfort; the large, oblong windows glowed amber with inner light at night and by day sparkled in sunlight. The décor was fresh and fitting for the age of the house. Honey had no trouble sleeping between its aching walls. What was two hundred years in the great scheme of things?

As Mary Jane chattered on, talking about her relative that just happened to live in the same room she was currently staying in, a retired university professor from Connecticut strolled past the window, her mother walking beside him.

The sound of her mother's voice drifted through the window. 'Families used to stick together in the past and marriage was for life ...'

And this coming from a thrice-married woman. Honey almost choked.

Her mother loved meeting hotel guests and did her bit to help out. She regarded herself as the official social secretary of the Green River Hotel, a bit like those she'd met on cruise ships.

At least it kept her out of the kitchen. Gloria had learned first-hand that Smudger was likely to reach for the meat cleaver if she interfered in his domain. Honey had backed him up. Good chefs were hard to come by. Interfering mothers were two a penny.

Mary Jane broke into her thoughts.

'I told her she was mistaken. He doesn't come from that side of the house. He always comes out of number five and walks along the landing. Mrs Goulding is trying to say that he's coming out of the closet and that he chases her around the room. Well! It's nonsense. All wishful thinking and a figment of her imagination I think!'

Honey eyed the tall, gaunt woman sitting beside her. Where exactly was this conversation going?

'I'm sorry. I'm not quite getting this. You're saying that Mrs Goulding reported a man chasing her around the room?'

'Sir Cedric! She reckons he's coming out of her closet, when both you and I know very well that he lives – or rather – materialises from the closet in room twelve.'

'You mean our resident ghost!'

It sounded wacky, but Honey had got used to it. Mary Jane was in her seventies and claimed she knew all there was to know about the afterlife and the spirits residing there. That's why she kept coming back to the Green River Hotel, which, according to her, was much favoured by the spirits of the departed. She particularly liked the eighteenth-century gentleman who resided in the closet in room twelve – the room Mary Jane always booked in advance. Sir Cedric was her particular favourite, mainly because she was certain they were related.

Honey listened patiently. 'Have you seen Sir Cedric lately?'

Mary Jane looked hurt. 'Well, no. But that doesn't mean he's deserted me. After all, I am his great, great, great, great, grand niece.'

She patted Mary Jane's liver-spotted hand. 'I'm sure she's just imagining things. And as you point out yourself, Sir Cedric wouldn't desert you in order to take up with a perfect stranger, now, would he.'

Mary Jane's crumpled face unfolded. 'No! Of course not. There's the family honour at stake! I told her that, but she dared question whether Sir Cedric really was one of my ancestors. I told her straight that I'd traced the family tree myself.'

Honey's ears pricked up at the mention of tracing family trees.

'Of course you have. How very interesting. Tell me,' she began. 'Is it true that a person needs birth certificates and all that stuff if they're tracing their family tree?'

'Someone serious about tracing his or her ancestors accumulates as much paperwork as possible. It's imperative. The fact is that if you've got gaps in your knowledge there's always specialists willing to give you a hand.'

'There are? I didn't know that.'

'Of course. A little information – some bits of family gossip and hearsay can go a long way.'

'Where's the best place to start tracing a family tree if you happen to be an American?'

Mary Jane's twinkling blue eyes twinkled a bit more. 'It varies. But I can tell you where I started. Are you going to do yours?'

Honey shook her head, one ear cocked to the sound of her mother's voice and footsteps pattering past in reception. 'I'd rather not know,' she said, pulling a face and shaking her head.

'Parish registers are good. So is the local registrar of births, marriages and deaths. The first thing I would do is speak to the relatives.'

'Could you do that for me? I could give you some basic information. The name's Maxted.' She frowned. 'It doesn't sound very Bathonian or even North Somerset.' She shrugged. 'But it's all I have. What I'd really like to know is if an American named Elmer Maxted has contacted anyone about tracing his family in the last few weeks.'

Face bright with enthusiasm, Mary Jane nodded. 'I'll

get on to it right away. Now,' she said, fumbling for a pen in her purse, 'in your case the best thing I can do is to interview your mother ...'

'No. You misunderstand. I told you. It's not for me.'

Mary Jane looked surprised then disappointed.

Honey dropped her voice to a whisper and leaned close. 'This Mr Elmer Weinstock I mentioned, alias Maxted, has gone missing. He was researching his family tree.'

'You don't say!'

'Do you think you could help?'

Mary Jane's response was diametrically opposed to the Philip Marlowe low-key approach. She looked like a fizzing firecracker about to explode.

'Ye–sss,' she hissed, the word elongated because she was trying so hard to suppress her excitement. 'I know just what he would do. First, he would speak to Bob the Job.'

'Bob the Job?' Odd name, thought Honey, for someone specialising in research of any kind.

Mary Jane explained. 'He's the first port of call in this city if you're looking to trace your pedigree.'

'Well, well.'

It never failed to amaze Honey what went on in Bath. There were worlds within worlds and experts on everything from Jane Austen to sex toys for the over-sixties.

The sound of clattering kitten heels sounded as though they were coming her way. Honey decided it was time to split.

'I have to go now, but I'd appreciate you making enquiries.'

Mary Jane was scribbling Elmer's name on the back of the bus timetable. 'If he's a serious player, Bob will know all about the guy.'

*'I'm sure my daughter would love to hear about your research on the Pilgrims' Trail.'*

As her mother's voice came closer, Honey began her

dash for the French doors.

'*Well, I really don't think I've got the time just now ...*'

A male voice. The professor was stalling – thank God!

'Leave this with me,' Mary Jane was saying as Honey backed out through the doors and through a herbaceous border.

The pages of magazines on a table near the door fluttered on the incoming draught.

Mary got up and shut it. She said something Honey couldn't hear. She guessed from the movement and shape of her mouth that she was telling her to have a nice day.

'I will,' she called back, waved and ran.

It might have been something to do with the fresh air, but suddenly she was hit by an intelligent thought.

Somewhere in the city was a taxicab that had ferried Elmer Maxted around the city before he'd disappeared.

Cora had told of a black Ford with the name, 'Busy Bee Taxi Cab Company', emblazoned in red on its side. That, she decided, was as good a place as any to start.

# Chapter Seven

Devotees of Jane Austen and all things Regency thronged through Bath's elegant crescents and leafy squares. Some narrowed their eyes in an effort to blank out the traffic and pretend that Mr Darcy was striding the pavement, resplendent in tails and tight trousers.

Keener on cameras than books, the Japanese snapped pictures of each other leaning on lampposts or posing outside McDonalds.

The Australians made for a decent brew in a reasonably priced café or a pub. The Americans did the tours at lightning speed, determined to get as much value as possible from their transatlantic flight.

This morning those looking over the parapet towards Pulteney Bridge were very subdued. Something had happened that attracted everyone's curiosity, something that certainly wasn't on the tourist trail.

Uniformed police were filtering people around the blue and white 'incident' tape fluttering around the steps leading from the road and down on to the towpath.

The river thundered over the weir throwing up clouds of foam and filling the air with spray – a sight by itself that was worth a look. But there was more than that going on today. Much more.

Doherty narrowed his eyes at the span of Pulteney Bridge, its stone piecrust gold. The rain had cleared. Licked by the early morning sun, the crescents, parades and avenues of Bath tiered upwards like steaming slabs of honey to the crisp blue of the sky. What a spot! All blue and gold on postcards sent home to Mom in Illinois or Auntie Meg in Alice Springs.

He was down on the towpath examining the body. Above him, the curious watched in hushed silence until an incident tent hid the bloated body.

Flanders the Scene of Crime Officer, a man with pale eyes and even paler skin, gave him the low down.

'Been dead a while. Look at him. Reminds you of a ...'

'Stilton cheese,' Doherty interrupted. 'Blood congealing in the veins.'

Flanders pallid features took on a dejected look. He so loved flaunting his knowledge, especially if it meant he could make someone sick with the details. It was easier to make young constables sick. More difficult with seasoned detectives, especially this one.

Doherty had burst his bubble on the first count, but he wouldn't on the second; Flanders was pretty sure of that.

The man had been found fully clothed with a sack covering his head. Flanders carefully removed the sack. The side of the man's head was caved in.

'Blunt instrument,' he said flatly, as though he'd seen thousands in his life. He had and had long ago giving up counting.

He picked up a transparent evidence bag.

'See this piece of wood?'

Doherty narrowed his eyes. The piece of wood was old and weathered.

'Part of a door,' said Flanders, warming to his subject. 'It had a number on it at one time. One of them little brass ones, or even plastic. See?' He pointed to the faint indentation on the wood. 'A nine or perhaps a six. It was lodged beneath his armpit.'

Doherty's attention strayed to a group of office girls, leggy, lovely things and young enough to be his daughters.

Doherty smiled at the office girls before barking out

orders to the assembled team. 'Come on lads. We've got work to do. Let's be having you. I want it swept with a toothbrush if need be. No skimping and no moans about bad backs and cups of tea.'

One of the forensic boys chose that moment to lean over the wall and spray the towpath with a shower of whatever he'd had for breakfast that morning. The office girls groaned and began to disperse.

Flanders kept on about the piece of wood.

Doherty refused to be impressed. 'So what? The river's high. There's always flotsam and jetsam floating about.'

'Do you want me to throw it back in?'

Flanders was being sarcastic. Doherty had no time for that and it showed in his attitude.

He snatched the wood. 'The second word's off!'

Flanders bowed to his job, his white plastic siren suit crackling as he carried out the last rites as far as a cop is concerned – going through the deceased's pockets.

'No money on him, no watch, just a white mark where it used to be. A dead cert mugging.' His probing fingers hesitated. 'Hello, hello! What have we here.

Flanders held up the Amex credit card so he could more easily read the name. 'Elmer John Maxted.'

Doherty watched with narrowed eyes as it was slid into yet another transparent evidence bag then escorted Flanders back up to the road.

'Give you a full report later!' Flanders puffed once he'd reached the top of the towpath steps and was only a few steps and a few more puffs from his dark green Citroen.

Nearby a traffic warden checked her watch, pursed her lips and clenched her jaw. This morning her routine and her tally were sharply curtailed and she looked pig sick about it.

Once Flanders was swinging the Citroen away from the kerb, Doherty took out his phone and scrolled down the numbers until he got to hers.

She answered after the fourth ring. It sounded as though she were in a hurry.

'Hannah – Mrs Driver? This is Detective Sergeant Doherty.'

'I'll ring you back.'

He frowned at the phone. It wasn't the response he'd been banking on. He'd been about to eat humble pie. Well sod the bloody woman. He'd tell her in his own good time.

# Chapter Eight

A row of taxicabs waited on the rank alongside Bath Abbey. A few of them were of the old-fashioned London black cab variety, like a row of black beetles queuing for a meal. The others were smart and shiny saloons. Only Busy Bee Cabs proclaimed their trade, in red lettering along their sides.

After making enquiries, she was directed to a man named Ivor Webber, a stocky Welshman of West Indian descent.

'He's the one who got the fat fares last week,' someone told her. 'Bloody Welsh Tafia!'

Ivor was sitting in the driving seat of his cab sipping at an elderberry crush and reading what looked like a copy of *Mein Kampf*.

'Sorry to interrupt you,' she said, bending down close enough to see that he really WAS reading Hitler's one and only attempt to woo the world with the written word.

Ivor flipped his sunglasses back on to his forehead. 'Where to, lovely?' he said. He closed his book and placed it on the seat beside him.

Honey jerked her chin in its direction. 'A surprising title.'

His teeth flashed in a healthy white smile. 'Well there you are, lovely. I'm a surprising man. I like to form my own opinions, you see. It attests more reasonably to my intellectual growth. Now where can I take you?'

'Nowhere.' She leaned on the door. 'Just a question.

Do you remember an American you picked up from Ferny Down Guest House?'

His amiability was undiminished. He threw back his head and slapped the steering wheel.

'You mean good old Elmer. Wish I had a few more like him in a week – a most generous tipper. There's not many of them nowadays, what with the exchange rate and all that.'

Honey smiled and nodded, sensing she was off to a good start. 'Must have been some journeys. Where did you take him?'

'Here and there.' Ivor Webber had a happy face.

She fancied the smile was a permanent fixture.

'Pretty far, so I hear.'

He nodded. 'I did.'

Honey brought out her notebook and pen. 'So where exactly?'

His smile melted. 'You the fuzz, lovely?'

'Now what makes you think that?'

The wariness of a man who hasn't always been upright and law abiding came to his eyes. 'Instinct, lovely, just instinct.

She decided to come clean. 'Look. He's gone missing and his relatives are wondering where he's got to.'

OK, so it wasn't one hundred per cent clean, but a little white lie about worried relatives wouldn't hurt surely?

Ivor showed the whites of his eyes. 'Is that right, lovely? Well I never. I took him to a few places – bit of sightseeing – usual stuff like Bradford on Avon, St Catherine's Valley, Lacock – you know – that place they use on a lot of historical dramas on television and film and suchlike.'

Honey nodded appreciatively. This was going SO well! 'You sound as though you like history,' she said.

'I do, but not that fancy pants and heaving bosom stuff. I prefer World War Two myself. See?' He held up the offending tome. 'Not so much the military and political side, though that of course is interesting. I like to investigate how it started you see. Just in case. You know what they say about history, don't you?'

Honey didn't bother to tell him she knew very well; he was going to tell her anyway.

'History repeats itself,' he said with the air of a man who's spent his time analysing world politics while awaiting a fare.

When her phone ran she thanked him before turning away to take the call. This time it was her mother.

Her voice was thin; not exactly wavering and weak; more wavering and worked on.

'I fell down the stairs, dear.'

Honey raised her eyes to heaven – or at least as far as the pigeons squatting around the fancy bits on the abbey roof. It was the way her mother said 'dear' that raised her hackles – and falling down the stairs had nothing to do with it.

'Mother, you've done this before.'

'It's my age, dear. One gets very tottery as one gets older. I need you here.'

Honey gritted her teeth. 'That wasn't what I meant.'

'Oh dear! I feel quite faint.'

Her instinct told her that she'd probably only tripped down one stair and that if she phoned Lindsey she'd get the truth. Her sense of duty made her head for home, but she had an inkling her mother had an ulterior motive for getting her there.

# Chapter Nine

It was gone midday and Lindsey was on reception when she got back. She looked extremely business-like, a pen in one hand and a pile of invoices in the other. Her eyes slid sidelong in the direction of the lounge.

'Grandma's in there. She's got a man with her,' hissed Lindsey.

Honey hunched her shoulders questioningly.

Lindsey mimicked the same action. 'I've no idea who he is.'

Forewarned but wary, she followed the smell of fresh coffee.

Her mother was semi-prone on a settee, bandaged ankle resting on a stool.

Someone was sitting on a chair opposite her. She purposely refrained from looking at him, positive it was bound to be the professor from wherever; the one her mother wanted her to meet. The one she *didn't* want to meet.

If she didn't look, perhaps he would disappear.

Her mother looked up. 'So! You came back to see how I am.'

'You look good.'

'My ankle doesn't.'

'I suppose it could be better.'

'You bet it could!'

Normally she avoided the men her mother chose for her. On this occasion the set of his shoulders and the casual demeanour attracted her attention. She forced herself not to give in and faced directly forward.

Her mother didn't leave things there.

'Hannah? This is John Rees.'

'Mother, I can't stop ...'

Her first inclination had been to throw a killer look at her mother and a contemptuous one at the man she'd found for her. Instead she found her brittleness melting away in the warmth of his smile.

'Hello.'

'Hi.'

American.

'John's just opened a bookshop in Rifleman's Way. He's from Kansas.'

John took her hand and shook it firmly. 'Originally from Kansas. I live in San Diego nowadays. Or rather, I did. Now I live here. In Bath. Best little city in the world.'

His voice was like silk. His hair was light brown shot with just a little white at the temples.

'Well that's ...'

She was about to see how nice that was, but the first notes of Beethoven's Fifth were throbbing against her chest.

'My phone,' she said, inwardly groaning as she plucked it from her bag.

Making sincerely meant excuses she backed towards the door.

She recognised the rough-diamond copper's voice. 'I thought you'd like to know; we've found Elmer Maxted.'

'Great! How is he?'

Her eyes strayed back to John. He was tall and lean and had a merry look in his eyes – not at all the dusty professor or accountant sort her mother kept digging up. For once this could be fun. And she had time now didn't she? The case of the missing tourist was all but over, wasn't it?

The police officer – Doherty – was saying something.

'Sorry. Can you repeat that.'

'He's not OK. He's dead. Murdered. I need to talk to you.'

Honey placed her hand over the phone. Her smile flew like a bird to gorgeous John.

'I'm sorry. I have to take this call, but if you'd like to leave your details, perhaps we can get in touch. Unless you'd like to wait.' She bit her lip. Business and pleasure were colliding here. She was presuming he was here to arrange a conference or something. Anything. He looked interesting.

'Honey? Are you still there?'

The sound of Steve Doherty's voice seeped through her fingers.

Reluctantly, she bent her lips back to the mouthpiece. 'Sorry, I just had something to arrange.'

'Can you meet me at the place where he was staying? What was it again?'

'Ferny Down Guest House on the Lower Bristol Road.'

'That's it. I'll see you there.'

'Sorry,' she mouthed to the delectable John Rees. She wriggled her fingers in a wave at her mother.

'What about my ankle?' her mother called after her.

'Ask Chef for a bag of frozen peas.'

She tried to phone Casper to see if he'd heard the news but he was out of the office and never, ever used a mobile. She asked Neville where she could find him.

'Not a clue.' Neville sounded snappy. They rowed infrequently. It had to be about something important. She made the mistake of asking him what was the matter.

'He wanted harvest beige in reception and I wanted blush pink.'

'Heavens! Who won?'

'He did.'

'So where is he?'

'I don't know.'

72

'Oh come on. Casper tells you everything. You're his bosom buddy.'

She sensed the stiffening on the other end of the phone. 'Not all the time! Sometimes he's in a world of his own. No consideration. None at all!'

Casper was aloof, superior, elegant, efficient and homosexual; she'd never known before that he could be secretive.

'Tell him ...'she began, meaning to convey that Maxted was dead.

Neville interrupted. 'I suggest you tell him yourself!'

The connection was terminated with an angry click.

So Casper has secrets. The fact surprised her. She wondered at his response once he knew that their missing American had turned up dead.

Her mother had got to her feet. 'Are you staying for lunch, dear?'

Honey glanced down at her mother's ankle.

Her mother noticed. 'I have good genes. I heal quickly.'

Honey looked beyond her mother's shoulder into the lounge. John Rees was finishing his coffee. She was sorely tempted, but Doherty and a dead body awaited her. She shook her head.

'I can't.' She threw a smile in John's direction. 'Sorry I can't stay, John. Duty calls. Another time perhaps?'

He got to his feet on incredibly long, strong legs.

His smile was to die for.

'Sure. I'll make a note of your number.'

For the second time that day she was in two minds about a situation. Lunch with a charming guy or suffer the dead ash in Ferny Down Guest House, courtesy of Cora Herbert. Curiosity overwhelmed temptation. She couldn't resist. On passing through reception she remembered Jeremiah Poughty. Lindsey traced his number and asked him if he knew where she could find Casper. He told her.

# Chapter Ten

Casper St John Gervais appreciated balance and having things in perfect order. He also found it mesmerising just how quickly one minute flowed into another. That's why he collected clocks. Clocks were one of the reasons he visited Simon Tye. Simon was as at home with the underworld of a small city as he had been in a large one. In London he'd upset the wrong people – which is why he'd headed west and opened a clock shop.

Tye's Timepieces was tucked away in a bow-fronted shop down a set of damp green steps. Only crumpled pavements and a mass of wandering tourists separated it from the sticky aspect of Sally Lunn's teashop.

Casper paused before pushing the door open. Already his heart was beating faster. What would he find inside – Simon Tye of course. But what gems of mechanical chronology would he have there to tempt him?

'Get a grip,' he muttered into his impeccably knotted tie.

He smoothed his hair back from his forehead in an effort to calm his nerves. Once properly under control, he pushed at the door.

An old-fashioned doorbell clanged overhead. Mechanical whirrs, taps, ticks, scrapings and dull thuds filled the air. So did the pungent, cloying smell of bees' wax and linseed oil. No matter how hard he attempted to maintain his self-control, something akin to passion clutched at his heart.

Brass, mahogany, oak, maple, and marble decorated with French Ormolu, the clocks surrounded him, their ticks and their chimes as sweet as words of love to his keen ear and knowledgeable mind. Instinctively, he knew there was something special for him here.

It was set on a chest of drawers with a serpentine front and hanging brass handles, as fragile as fine string. Simon always did have a way of showing things off to best advantage. 'Presentation is what matters, guv,' he always said. He was right. The honeyed glint of the satinwood emphasised the ice-cold perfection of white porcelain. It was brilliant, four feet wide and three feet high Dresden figures grouped around a china-faced clock figured with brass.

He ran his fingers over the beautifully defined muscles of the crisply carved shepherd. 'Divine,' he breathed.

'You wan it?'

Like a grinning satyr, Simon Tye's face appeared over the top of the clock, one bony elbow close to the porcelain shepherdess who leaned nonchalantly against the round barrel of the clock face.

Casper stepped closer, his eyes taking in every intricate detail; the shepherd, a lamb flung around his shoulders, the shepherdess, a crook in her dainty hand, her skirts piled like a pumpkin between her narrow waist and her graceful little ankles. Sheep and lambs gambolled before the pair and graceful naiads held the clock above them on porcelain ribbons.

It was gorgeous and there were myriad questions he'd like to ask about it, but knowing Simon Tye of old, his mind calculated the price. 'It's very nice, but not the best I've seen.'

He was lying and he could see from the shopkeeper's face that he knew it. Never mind. He would brazen it out.

Simon grinned as though he were looking through him and knew the truth. He looked almost part of the clock itself, yet a lot less beautiful. Wide mouth, almond-shaped eyes with straggly mass of blue-grey hair that hid a hunk of reddened gristle and gaping hole; all that remained of his left ear. That's what came of grassing up blokes in the East End of London. No wonder he'd headed west and opened up a clock shop.

'I knew you'd want it the minute you saw it, Mr St John, sir.'

Casper licked the dryness from his lips. Damn the man! He tried to ignore the smile that was spreading across Simon's face like melting cheese. To hell with it! Unable to resist, he reached out and trailed his fingers over the gleaming glaze. A thrill shot through his body. He breathed deeply before he asked the first question.

'Dresden?'

'Dead right!' Simon's smile was unaltered. Someone else's discomfort, especially someone as wealthy as Casper, was incredibly enjoyable.

'Made for the Paris Exhibition of 1900. Brilliant, ain't it!'

Casper squirmed inside but hell's bells, he certainly wasn't going to take it all without giving some out.

'Did you get it legally, Mr Tye?'

Simon looked hurt. 'Mr Tye is it, not Simon, my dear friend as it usually is? Are you tryin' to throw me off balance, get the better of me an' 'ave it away for nix? It was a legitimate purchase. Cross my 'eart.'

He made the usual sign on his narrow chest in the place where his heart might have been.

Casper took advantage. 'So?' He lifted his eyebrows questioningly.

'To tell you the truth I bought it off a lady who brought it 'ere in her car. Said the 'ouse was cluttered with stuff and she needed the room. Took a song for it she did – though, I shouldn't be telling you that.' His eyes narrowed.

Casper shook his head and tutted reproachfully. 'What

sort of person would want to get rid of a lovely thing like that?'

'A woman who don't like too much dusting, I s'pose, though mind you, she didn't look the type that got her 'ands dirty too often.'

'No taste,' said Casper, his eyes fixed on the clock.

'No shame,' echoed Simon.

'How much?' he asked, the words spitting from his mouth as though he had no control over his tongue at all.

Triumph shone in Simon's watery grey eyes and slinked in shiny wetness along his wide, flaccid lips.

'I could get seven at auction.'

'Hundred?' said Casper hopefully.

'Leave it out! Thousand,' Simon retorted feigning insult.

'Exorbitant!'

Simon's eyes were pinpricks in narrow slits. 'No it ain't, and you know it ain't.'

He was right. Casper laid a well-manicured hand across his chest. His heart was racing like an express train. It was now or never. He braced himself to forego the temptation. He even made a half turn towards the door.

Alluringly, the clock began to chime its siren song, the note lucid – heavily seductive to a clock collector's ear.

He stared at it, aware that Simon was watching him like a hungry hawk, his fingers thoughtfully tapping at his bottom lip, scratching at his chin. But his eyes stayed fixed on Casper's face.

His self-control wobbled like a jelly and finally toppled. 'I'll give you five.'

'Well ...' said Simon thoughtfully. His eyes were hooded. He was looking downwards so Casper couldn't see how delighted he was. 'Let's say five thousand five hundred shall we?'

Not to be outwitted, Casper fixed his gaze on Simon and set his jaw in a firm, determined line. 'Let's say five thousand two hundred.'

Simon chuckled and shook his head. For a moment Casper was almost panicked into raising his offer. He forced himself to hold out though his mouth was as dry as the bottom of a birdcage.

'It's a deal!' Simon spat on his palm and reached out.

'Fine,' said Casper, declining to shake a hand smeared with spittle. 'I'll get it collected,' he said before the brass bell jangled and the door chamfered shut.

Simon Tye's warm smile melted the moment the door was closed. The clock was sold and he was damned glad it was. He hadn't found out the provenance of the timepiece until after he'd paid the asking price. The clock was worth twice what he'd just accepted, but he wanted it gone – before the rightful owner came calling and police got involved; both were things he could well do without.

Casper was dead pleased with his purchase. Wonderful day, he thought to himself, smiling at the world that eddied and flowed around him.

A coachload of German tourists was taking photographs of the flowers, the edifice of the Guildhall, the entrance to the Roman Baths.

He beamed at them as they methodically set up their shots, checked their lighting and posed their portraits.

This year would be a very good year for the city and for La Reine Rouge.

The day was a good one and remained so – until he sauntered into his favourite restaurant.

The Saville Roe, which served all manner of seafood, nestled beside an alley of polished cobbles just behind the Theatre Royal. Panelled walls, alleviated by the use of white damask tablecloths and silver-plated cruets, gave it a rich, Gothic-style ambience. The clientele were well-heeled and on a lunchtime businessmen outnumbered tourists. He was shown to his usual table in the far corner. A menu card and wine list as white as the table linen was brought within a minute of him sitting down.

Just as he was deciding between a goat's cheese and salmon concoction and slices of sea bass flambéed in pear juice, the waiter brought him a cordless telephone.

'For you, sir,' said the handsome Italian as he handed him the phone.

It was quite usual to receive calls at his favourite haunts from those who knew him and also knew of his distaste for mobiles. He only spoke into proper phones. A cordless just about met his approval.

For a brief moment he eyed the proffered receiver with something close to disdain. He was also slightly miffed that his habits had become so – well – habitual that people knew where he could be contacted.

Never mind, he told himself as he accepted the call; you've had a good day. It's June and the sun is shining, business is good and you've had a stroke of good luck. That clock is worth far more than you paid for it. You've done well and all is well with the world.

Then Honey spoke and told him about Elmer Maxted. Suddenly the June sky dulled to November.

# Chapter Eleven

It became obvious to Honey from his attitude that it wasn't Doherty's idea that she should accompany him to Ferny Down Guest House.

'I don't see the point,' he told her bluntly.

He'd adopted a glum look, an unmistakable grimness around his mouth as the disgruntled grumbler took over.

She stated what she thought was the matter. 'You were told I had to come along.'

He shoved his hands in his pockets. 'The Chief Constable thinks he might get more media coverage with you on board. He likes having his picture in the press.'

He said it through gritted teeth.

'Never mind.' Honey patted his hand. 'Oww. Your hand's cold.'

'Cold hand, warm heart.'

'Well there you are then. Warm to me. We're in this together.'

He grunted something unintelligible.

'I'll take that as an affirmative.'

There was nothing for it but to settle comfortably into her seat in Doherty's sports car.

Doherty sat silently beside her.

Honey made a point of eyeing the passing scene.

'The flowers look lovely this year. I like pink and mauve together. Don't you?'

'Mrs Driver, this is hardly the time to be noticing flowers.'

Maintaining her smile and her bright disposition, she tilted her head sideways so that a sweep of hair blanketed her right shoulder.

'It's a question of keeping things in perspective. Flowers are like music; they soothe the nerves. That's what I'm here to do. Think of me as a flower.'

'What?'

The car swerved towards the central reservation earning a blaring horn and a two-fingered salute from white van man.

Showing no sign that she'd noticed, Honey carried on.

'This I think is the way to proceed when we speak to Mrs Herbert. You act like a stone, steadfast as you ask Mrs Herbert a lot of questions. I'm the fragrant flower that calms her nerves.'

Doherty shook his head in disbelief. He also sniffed the air. French perfume. Honey smelled good and looked good. She was wearing a pink checked jacket, cream skirt and candy striped shoes. Good enough to eat.

'So!' Honey went on. 'Are you going to arrest Mrs Herbert?'

'I didn't say that.'

'But you're not discounting it.'

'That depends on the evidence and her answers to my questions.'

Doherty's square chin turned squarer. She sensed his confusion, personal and professional colliding behind the resolute exterior.

'I doubt that she did it, though she is a criminal – of sorts. She should be locked up just for her choice of clothes and make-up. Now that's criminal!'

'Yeah, yeah, yeah,' said Doherty as he turned off the engine. 'Right. Now there's a few questions I've got for you, flower.'

'I'm all ears.'

'You said that her old man was manhandling a chest

81

freezer out of the back gate when you first visited.'

'That's right. The council truck was waiting outside to take it to the recycling plant for degassing before it was crushed.'

There was a rasping sound as he stroked his chin. Three days stubble. 'Are you sure about that?'

'It's an environmental thing they have to do.'

'I wonder whether they've crushed it yet. I'll get it checked.'

He made the call before they got out of the car, telling somebody to check it out.

The flowers in the hanging baskets were wilting slightly. Honey wondered whether Mervyn had been the one who looked after them. Not necessarily of course. It could be Cora but she was down in the dumps and had forgotten. Not surprising.

His expression was deadly serious as he rang the doorbell. Comprehension regarding Honey's innuendos blinked into his eyes when Cora Herbert answered the door.

Her sense of style hadn't altered one iota. She was wearing a cropped black top and chequered skirt with a ragged fringe around the hem. Her eyes were heavily outlined. A gold droplet dangled from her pierced belly button. Her flesh was white like dimpled bread dough. The gold droplet heaved in and out as though it were gasping for air.

Her black-rimmed eyes landed on Honey.

'What? You again!'

'It's me,' Honey said trusting her smile would override the hint of hostility in Cora's voice. She needn't have worried. Cora's attention swerved to Steve Doherty. A deep intake of breath ballooned her bosoms.

If Doherty had been the cream and she'd been the cat, he would have been gobbled up by now.

She was straight to it, her eyes shining and her red lips

smiling. 'And you are?'

Doherty took a side-step. Partially shielded by Honey, he flashed his identity card.

'Detective Sergeant Doherty. I need to speak to everyone who was in this house on the day he left.'

'Me, me husband and me daughter.' Cora gushed the information.

Doherty's chin shot forward when he nodded. The stubble rippled as his mouth moved.

Honey watched it move. Funnily enough, it was exactly the same length as two days previously. It occurred to her that he trimmed it to just the right length in an effort to make exactly the right impression.

'Just the three of you live here?'

'And guests when we've got any. Mind you, I can always find room for a nice-looking bloke like you.'

A nerve ticked a muscle beneath Doherty's right eye, but he kept his nerve.

'I need to speak to you, your daughter and your husband.'

Thick with mascara, Cora's eyelashes flickered like the wings of tiny bats.

'Our Loretta's up in her room. Merv isn't here. In fact, you could say that I'm all by meself.'

Honey recalled Cora telling her where her husband usually enjoyed his quality time.

'Perhaps if you could tell me which pub ...'

The interruption was unwelcome. Cora glared and her tone turned frozen as a fish.

'He's not gone to the pub. He's gone away. He's allowed to go away isn't he? God knows but we work hard enough, put up with enough ...'

Aware that her attempts at flirtation had flopped, the belly she'd attempted to hold in relaxed into its natural pudding shape.

'For goodness' sake,' she muttered, 'it's only a tourist

gone on a mystery tour! That's my opinion anyway.'

Steve Doherty's face set like quick-drying cement.

'Mrs Herbert, today a body was pulled from Pulteney Weir. We believe it to be the body of your former guest, a Mr Elmer Weinstock, also known as Maxted. We would like you – or your husband – to make a formal identification.'

The wind knocked out of her sails, Cora Herbert's botoxed bottom lip hung puffy and quivering. Her eyes stretched prominently in the podgy, pallid face.

'Can we come in and discuss what you know?' asked Honey.

Cora nodded and retreated into the green and white hall.

Honey recalled the fug in the conservatory and prepared to take small shallow breaths. To her relief they were shown into the guests' lounge instead. A 'no smoking' sign was prominently displayed on the mantelpiece. The room had a pleasanter smell than the conservatory by virtue of a can of air freshener. Lilies of the Valley by the whiff of it, Honey guessed.

Cora Herbert didn't invite them to sit down, but they did anyway. Cora perched on the arm of a chair immediately opposite, like a vulture deciding whether to fly off or stay and pluck their eyes out.

Doherty got out his notebook and a smart-looking pen.

Honey eyed him sidelong. He seemed relaxed. He was making a list on the pad and ticking the items off, too slowly for her liking. An overwhelming urge to know *everything* and *at once* took hold of her. She found herself counting the seconds he was taking to ask the first, relevant question.

It was obvious that he was terrified of Cora Herbert. But for goodness sake, he was a policeman. Weren't they brave, fearless and bold?

Apparently not. She jumped in herself.

'Can you tell me who was here the last time you saw the man you knew as Mr Weinstock?'

Policemen were usually forceful – or at least they were on television. Doherty remained relaxed. Silent.

As is the way of some women of a certain age, Cora did not seem to welcome a dominant female. Her reply was aimed directly at Doherty. Her hands smoothed her skirt following the contours of her thighs. 'First there's Mervyn of course, then my daughter, Loretta.'

'How old is she?' Doherty asked.

'Seventeen.' Her smile was weak, but her simpering spilled out, unhindered by recent events. 'I had her very young you see ...'

The door to the lounge creaked open. The truth bounced into the room.

'I'm nearly eighteen and my ma isn't as young as she makes out!'

The correction came from the over-made-up girl poking her head around the door. Her blonde hair was streaked with three shades of copper. Her earrings were big enough to swing on and she wore six rings on her right hand alone and another in her nose.

Doherty nodded a greeting and turned back to Cora.

'The man you knew as Mr Weinstock is dead. Did you have anything to do with him while he was staying here – you know – general stuff like saying hi in the morning and how's the weather?'

Loretta's earrings made a tinkling noise as she folded her arms beneath her pert breasts. Honey took note of those rings. Definitely six rings on three fingers of each hand and one on each thumb. None on her index fingers.

She was wearing a red sweater with a keyhole design over her cleavage that left nothing to the imagination. Like her mother, her belly button was pierced.

Loretta shook her head. 'I didn't have much to do with him meself. He chatted to Mervyn a lot. They used to booze a bit in the den.'

Cora smiled at Doherty. 'I don't think this nice policeman has got any more questions for you, Loretta.' She turned back to the girl, her expression hardening just a teeny, weeny bit. 'I'll be along shortly to make yer lunch, love.'

Honey saw the contempt in Loretta's eyes and knew beyond doubt that her mother's affectionate tone wasn't a regular occurrence.

Honey smiled at her. 'Cool rings.'

'Thanks.'

'Be great if you could remember anything about the bloke. I know it's kind of humdrum, but you know – anything at all?'

Doherty cottoned on to her game.

'You might have spotted something that less observant folk might not. We'd appreciate your help.'

Honey was trying not to stare at Loretta's skirt. If it had been much shorter, she would have seen her dinner.

'Was your father friendly with the American guy?' asked Doherty.

Loretta's expression was petulant.

'He's not my father.'

'My first marriage,' Cora explained with a weak grin to them and a warning look to her daughter.

Loretta shrugged. 'The other night when I heard him talking to Mr Weinstock was the last time I saw him – or more like, heard him. He was talking to Mervyn.'

There was something in the way she said her stepfather's name and the careless way she shrugged that set the alarm bells ringing – at least for Honey. She glanced sidelong at Doherty. Did he have teenage children?

No. He did not. He hadn't seen that telling slide of the eyeballs that was meant to show casual indifference but in fact meant something entirely different.

'You overheard what was said?'

'Yes. They were in the kitchen. Mr Weinstock had asked Mervyn for ice.' A wicked grin crossed her face. 'Mervyn hated having to get crushed ice. Not that it was any big deal, wrapping cubes in a tea towel and bashing them to smithereens. Is it true he's dead? The American?'

Doherty nodded. 'The man you knew as Mr Weinstock is dead, yes.'

Loretta's eyes lit up. 'Bludgeoned to death? Could it have been done with a rolling pin? Old Merv was a dab hand with that rolling pin. That's what he used to crush the ice.'

'You little bitch!' Cora sprang to her feet. Fingers like claws reached for her daughter's throat.

Honey got in between them. 'Now calm down.' She frowned at Doherty. 'So how was he killed?'

'We're not sure yet,' said Doherty. 'Once we have the details of the post mortem, I can ...'

Honey was losing patience. 'Can we get to the point, please?' Both the policeman and the teenager looked surprised. A cloud of perfume emanated from the trendy teenager when Honey addressed Loretta. 'What were they talking about?'

A thunder-faced Cora butted in again, her lips quivering slightly. 'She's just told you. Mervyn was crushing some ice. That's all.'

'You said they were talking,' said Honey, fixing her gaze on Loretta and refusing to take notice of the sour looks Doherty was throwing her way. 'Now to my mind that means after the ice was crushed. Is it possible that the man you knew as Mr Weinstock had his own bottle of whisky? Quite a few Americans buy their own to save on bar prices. Could he have asked Mervyn to sit down and have a drink with him?'

Loretta began fiddling with a wispy strand of hair caught around her earring. 'Yes. They were. I could tell they'd had a drop by their voices. It echoes a bit in the den anyway.'

Doherty jumped in. 'The den? What den? I thought they were in the kitchen.'

Loretta studied her fingernails in a nonchalant, cocky kind of way. The polish looked black or at least dark purple. 'They were in the kitchen first getting the ice, and then they went into the den. Mervyn was showing him his watch collection.'

'He collects watches? Old pocket watches – things like that?'

Loretta nodded. 'Yeah.'

'Interesting.'

Honey could feel Doherty's eyes on her.

She didn't tell him that Casper, who had enrolled her for this job, collected clocks. Mervyn collected watches. Now what sort of coincidence was that?

# Chapter Twelve

Mervyn opened his eyes but saw nothing. Everything was dark and his head ached. The dryness on his tongue was like iron filings and, for some daft reason, he could smell something that reminded him of Christmas.

With each breath the sack covering his head was sucked up into his nostrils, the sweet-smelling dust drawn up into his nasal passages. What with that and the gag in his mouth, it was difficult to breathe.

A sense of panic overwhelmed him. He was going to die. Not comfortably, perhaps not even quickly, but slowly suffocating, struggling for even the slightest morsel of air.

He tried to remember exactly what had happened, but all he could think of was Loretta. Everything began and finished with her. Even in this his worst nightmare, the thought of her nubile body assuaged his fear. Eventually his fear won the battle.

What was he doing here!

Mentally, he retraced his movements. Somehow he couldn't move forward from Cora's first husband giving him a beating. All he'd done was to give Loretta a lift home. He'd tried to explain that it was raining, but to no avail. The blows still fell hard and fast.

That was when he'd made the decision to leave. If that moron was walking free, then he was off. For good! First get some money together ...

Something about that gelled in his brain. Money! Sometime after that he'd arranged to meet someone, but for the life of him he couldn't remember the guy's name or why he'd arranged to meet him.

He shivered. His clothes were chill and damp against his skin. He knew he'd sweated a lot. Now he was cold, terribly cold. One shiver came fast upon another. If he hadn't been gagged his teeth would have chattered.

He tried moving his arms, flexing his fingers, squirming against the ropes that bound his wrists.

Suddenly he became aware that someone was there. The footsteps were muffled because of the sack over his head. He tried to lift his head, to roll away.

He never saw the hand that killed him. He saw only the wasted years of his life flashing before his eyes before even the memories drained away along with the blood and bits of brain.

The cellars were deep, one tier upon another. A thin scum of orange silt covered the cracked concrete and dented cobbles, a result of the times when the river was swollen, the lower levels flooded.

It was like that now, slippery and smelling of river mud and untreated effluent. Coke cans and plastic shopping bags bobbed around just below the ledge that dipped into the river. This was the very lowest cellar and slowly, with the passing of the years, the river was claiming it as its own.

The body had softened and was faintly marbled by virtue of resident bacteria. He'd covered the head with a small sack so he didn't have to look at the staring eyes. The sacks were readily available. He used them frequently for other things, less gruesome things.

The rest of the body was wrapped in a length of polythene that crackled when he lifted it up. The man wasn't light, but not too heavy either. Carefully so as not to slip, he carried Mervyn Herbert down the last flight of steps. There was a good flow on the river, a welcome result from the earlier rains. On the opposite bank he could see ranks of sodium streetlights winding through the darkness. Spots of reflected amber light danced on the racing river.

On his side there were no lights only the black square shadows thrown by the circling colonnade above. The night was his, as dark as his mind.

Gently, still holding on to his precious piece of polythene, which had once covered a mattress, he let the body slide into the water. It bobbed about a bit, clung to the bank as if unwilling to leave him.

Beneath his breath he cursed the strong flow and with the help of a torch searched behind him for something to poke the body away from the bank and into the main stream.

What had once been a door lay cobwebbed and rotting against the wall. Just as he'd done before, he tore a piece of rotten plank from it, green paint clinging in odd patches over its rough surface.

With the fingers of one hand, he gripped the crumbling door lintel overhead. In the other he held the wood. Still holding on to the flaking masonry, he reached out and poked at the body until it was safely carried into the current. Then, carelessly, no longer interested in the bloated flotsam he had consigned to the water, he flung the piece of wood after it.

Unafraid and uncaring, he watched it ebb into the black night and black water. What was it to him? What was anyone to him? Except with one notable exception, one person who he loved more than himself.

The rush of water and a slight bumping sound made him look back again.

The body had returned, the river current pinning it against the bank.

There was no option but to drag it back on to the slime-covered flagstones. It had to be got rid of, but where?

He sat down and thought about blame and throwing the police off the scent. Blame and guilt. He knew a lot about them and about loss and restitution, making things up to those you loved.

An idea came to him. Suspicion fell initially on close acquaintances in a murder case. So, if the body was found in the right place ...?

## Chapter Thirteen

One-thirty. Smudger the chef was complaining about the butcher again.

'I swear to you, it's rubbish. Trust me. Let me tell him that if he don't up his standards, I'm for chopping out his liver!'

Honey rolled her eyes. How was a woman to cope? A batty chef *and* a mad mother.

Her mother was rabbiting on about a very upright and uptight type she wanted her to meet. 'You must meet him, Hannah, darling. I'm sure you'll get on like a house on fire.'

'Mother, I can arrange my own dates.'

Her mother shrugged. 'Well it doesn't seem that way to me.' Digging her painted nails into Honey's shoulders, she flipped her round to face her.

'Tell me the truth, the whole truth and nothing but the truth. Do you have a man friend?'

'Yes.'

'Yes?' Her mother sounded incredulous. She clapped her hands and looked extraordinarily happy. 'You do? Who is he?'

'Just a guy.'

'What's his name?'

'Jeremy.'

Her mother frowned. 'I don't know him. Do I?'

'Right. You don't know him.'

First, deal with the chef.

'Smudger? You will not threaten the man. If he fails to deliver decent meat, then he doesn't get his bread. Savvy?'

Smudger's sandy-coloured hair curled out from beneath his tall, chef's hat. His eyes glittered. 'Great! I can't wait to see his face when I tell him to stick it.'

'No!' Honey wagged a finger at him. 'That isn't what I said. Just insist that he keeps his standards up, or else ...'

'Or else I chop him!'

A gleaming meat cleaver was waved with gleeful anticipation.

'Smudger, hurting comes in many forms. A light bank account hurts more than a wound!'

Smudger looked disappointed, but accepted her judgement.

'And for my next trick,' she muttered to herself.

She wheeled her mother away from Smudger's realm and into the conservatory.

'Doesn't the garden look lovely?' she said, a calming measure in anyone's book.

Her mother glared up at her as they marched the width of the conservatory until their noses were almost flat against the glass.

Her mother eyed her accusingly. 'You haven't got a boyfriend, have you? You were lying.'

'Yes.'

'Well I've got one for you.'

'I don't want one.'

The conservatory looked out over an enclosed garden. The trees had grown high and wide obliterating the view of other buildings. If you lay flat in the grass and stared directly upwards, you could almost forget you were in the heart of the city. But there was no grass. Just paving slabs.

Her mother looked puzzled, her lips parted as though there was something she wanted to say, but she wasn't quite sure how to phrase it.

'So you've met someone you think suits me. Where did

you meet him?'

'At the dentist. He's a widower.'

The vision of the gorgeous guy she'd seen standing beside her mother at the beginning of the week flashed into her mind. Somehow she hadn't envisaged him as being a widower.

Giving herself time to digest this, Honey banged on the window at Mary Jane and waved. Mary was practising her tai chi out on the flagstones and managed to include a slow wave amongst her movements.

Accompanied by her mother's list of reasons why she should meet this man, Honey continued to watch Mary Jane's sinuous arms rolling and wafting outwards, one leg slowly raised, one little twist of her spine.

'OK, he's a bit of a steady Eddie, but I'm sure he's the right man for you.

This last sentence sunk in. 'I'm really surprised. He didn't strike me that way,' said Honey.

'But you haven't met him yet.'

The vision of the cool dude in casuals was shattered.

Her mother smoothed her corn-coloured tunic as she settled gracefully into a chair.

'You haven't met him, dear.'

'But he was here the other day. You said he was a bookseller. His name was John Rees.'

'Not him. I meant Edgar Paget. He's my dentist. And a very good one,' she added, as though that in some way recommended him as a potential suitor.

'Mother, I don't think I can take to a guy who makes a living from peering into people's mouths.'

'He's not just *any* dentist! Private patients only.'

Honey turned her back on Mary Jane who had just entered into the final movements of her daily routine.

Folding her arms across her chest, she eyed her mother with a mix of disbelief and total confusion. Was this woman really her mother? And what was she trying to do?

Get her to notch up the same number of marriages she'd gone through herself?

But first things first:

'So this bookseller. What was he here for?'

'To organise a book fair. He wanted to make a booking. I just got talking to him. He seemed very pleasant.'

Honey's jaw dropped. 'A booking.'

Her mother nodded. 'Yes, dear.'

'So why didn't you pass him to reception?'

'Because he asked to see you.'

Honey sighed. 'I'll have to phone him.'

'So what about my dentist – Mr Paget?'

'No!'

Her mother rarely frowned. *It causes wrinkles, dear.* Her indignation showed in the way her heart-shaped face became elongated as her chin dropped. The wrinkles came anyway and would have looked good on a bloodhound.

'Well, that's a change of attitude, I must say.'

Honey's thoughts were on the gorgeous guy who'd called in earlier in the week.

Mary Jane caught her just as she was rushing from the conservatory and into reception.

'I'll speak to you later,' Honey called over her shoulder.

'There's no need to panic. He said he'd call back,' said her mother, yet again scurrying along beside her.

Honey refused to listen, rummaging among the bits of paper in a basket marked 'file'. Everything that didn't have a home – which included the calling cards of salesmen selling disposables – went into the 'file'.

'Have we had a booking for a book fair?' she asked Deehta, who came in to cover on Tuesdays and Thursdays.

Deehta shook her dark head vehemently. When it came to efficiency, Deehta was top of the pops. Honey had no choice but to believe her.

There was no sign of a business card marked

'*bookshop*'.

'Never mind,' Honey said once she was satisfied that her filing tray was its usual, uninteresting, self.

Mary Jane, who let nothing interrupt her *tai chi* session, called out to her.

'We need to talk,' she said quickly in a hushed voice, as though secrecy and speed were paramount.

'I know where he went,' hissed Mary Jane. 'That guy who went missing; I know who he was asking about and where he went.'

Honey took hold of Mary Jane's bony elbow, hauled her into her private office and shut the door. 'Tell me!'

'He enquired about a family called Charlborough.'

'Do you mean *the* Charlborough family? Landowners, plantation owners, and allegedly members of the Hellfire Club?'

Mary Jane's face shaped itself into a question mark. 'You mean they were members back in the eighteenth century?'

'Allegedly. They live at Charlborough Grange out at Limpley Stoke.'

Mary Jane's face brightened. 'That's the place. That's where he went.'

It added up. Ivor the taxi driver had taken Elmer to the church at Limpley Stoke, though he hadn't mentioned Charlborough Grange.

'And Elmer was related to Charlborough?'

Mary Jane shook her head. 'Oh, he couldn't say. He wasn't specific according to Bob.'

Honey entertained some pretty fast-moving thoughts.

'Am I right in thinking our missing tourist would have learned a lot from a parish register?'

'He sure would,' said Mary Jane. 'That's one thing you can say about the church, they certainly kept tight tabs on everybody.'

# Chapter Fourteen

The hotel had been busy, she'd gone for a mid-evening doze and the alarm woke her just after eleven p.m. A quick shower, fresh make-up and hair dried; a search through her clothes; jeans, a black T-shirt and pearl earrings. Casual but classy, she thought, after a brief glance in the mirror.

On the way to meet Detective Sergeant Doherty, she looked for Ivor's taxi but couldn't see him. If she had she would have asked more about Elmer's visit to Limpley Stoke. Mary Jane's report was clear enough, but it wouldn't have hurt to confirm it.

The night air was still and cool. The lights of the city obliterated the blackness of the river. The river was running high and fast and didn't look its normal friendly self. Possibly there'd been heavy rain upstream.

Doherty awaited her.

As she descended the steps down to the solid oak door of the Zodiac Club, she considered whether she should tell him what Mary Jane had told her about Elmer having been in touch with a man named Bob the Job. Crazy name, but there, people hoping to find fame or notoriety in their background were a bit crazy; devastated when they realised their ancestry contained nothing more than generation after generation of farm labourers, housemaids and itinerant drunkards.

Should she tell him where she'd *thought* Elmer had gone, or should she check out this oddly named guy, Bob the Job?

The Zodiac was a private club. On ringing the bell, a small slot opened. A pair of eyes looked out and a muffled voice asked for her name and whether she was a member.

'It's me.'

The eyes opened wide in recognition and the door opened.

'Good evening, madam!'

'Good evening, Clint. I think that's the first time you've ever called me madam.' She looked him up and down. 'Nice suit.'

Clint, her part-time washer-up, grinned from ear to ear. Despite the spider's web etched into his skull and the gold earring, Clint looked both presentable and slightly menacing, in fact ideal for the job.

'I got it at Oxfam,' he said, running sausage thick fingers over the silky lapels. 'Not bad is it.'

'No. Not bad at all. Should last you a while as long as you don't go washing up in it.'

'I won't be doing that. Serving in me mate's shop is my daytime job, washing up is early evening, and this is my night-time job.'

'So when do you sleep?'

There was a whole load of innuendo in the wink he gave her.

'When I can. Got to have a social life, ain't I?'

'You certainly do.'

And all for cash, thought a bemused Honey. It occurred to her that he could be making more money than she was, and enjoying a better social life.

'Look,' she said. 'I'm expecting a guest. His name's Steve ...'

'Doherty. Yeah.' His grin collapsed into a stiff grimace. 'The dude's already here.'

There was no point asking him how come he knew a member of the local constabulary. She could guess, but Clint (Rodney Eastwood to give him his full name) was

Clint and his business was his own.

Threading her way through the room brought to mind old black-and-white movies; night clubs where shady characters clustered in dingy alcoves. The ceiling was barrel-vaulted and the walls bare stone. Down-lighters picked out swirls of blue smoke drifting from the sizzling steaks being grilled al fresco in the restaurant. Apart from them the lighting was minimal.

Steve was propped up in the corner of the bar. A space had opened up around him; news of his profession had no doubt travelled.

Isolation didn't seem to worry him. His eyes were everywhere but stalled once they landed on her.

'Drink?' Shifting his stance he dug into the pocket of his black leather jacket.

'Vodka and tonic. With ice and lemon.'

He took the money from his pocket. No wallet, she noticed. A cautious man. She wondered where he kept his credit cards.

'Are you hungry?' he asked her suddenly.

She shook her head. 'I've eaten.'

She eyed the clientele, noting who was playing after hours. Hotel and pub managers mostly, plus those who owned, ran and worked bloody hard in their own hotels.

'Cheers.'

He clinked glasses with her while they studied each other, a meeting of eyes, a furtive appraisal of each others attributes.

For his part Steve admired her clear skin, a handsome rather than pretty face. Her hair was dark, her eyes brown and her legs went up to her shoulders – or at least, that was the way it seemed.

Honey glimpsed the glint of a gold bracelet on his right wrist. His hair was cut short. It suited him.

'So,' she said after taking a generous sip of vodka and tonic. 'Have you informed the relatives?'

'It seems our American friend doesn't have any. Apparently there was a sister, but she died a few months ago.'

'So he went travelling to get away?'

Doherty shrugged. 'I suppose so. Who knows? They reckoned he was well into doing research. Tracing ancestors was the latest thing. Before that it was haemophilia.'

'The bleeding disease.'

'That's the one. Someone in the family died of it.'

She finished her drink. He insisted on buying her another.

Do I deserve another?

She answered her own question. You bet!

Weekends were hard in the hospitality trade. The world and his wife came away on weekend breaks, and from Friday night to Sunday lunchtime the locals were out wining and dining. Add that to the huge influx of tourists at this time of year, and you've got a punishing schedule.

It came to her suddenly that they were in competition with each other. He wanted all the glory in cracking this, and so did she. She hadn't thought she had before, not when the job had first been foisted on her. But now? Something was stirring.

Unfortunately for '*good ole*' Steve, it wasn't passion that had coloured her decision to meet him, but curiosity, a driving need to find out exactly what was going on. That was the reason, she told herself, but still her eyes kept sliding sidelong.

She shook the thoughts from her head.

'Bubbles,' she explained on seeing Doherty's quizzical expression. She cleared her throat. 'Are there any clues?'

'Minor things. A piece of wood jammed into the side of the deceased. The river's full of debris following heavy rain. But it was interesting. There was an indentation on it where a number used to be. Could have been a nine. Could have been a six.'

'Depending on whether you're Australian.'

She smiled as she said it. The vodka had gone to her head.

Doherty had a blond moment. He didn't have a clue – or perhaps just no sense of humour.

She took it slowly. 'Upside down. A six if you're upright and living in the northern hemisphere, and a nine if you're upside down, i.e. Australian.'

'Very funny.'

He gave a weak laugh, though his expression remained serious.

No sense of humour, she decided, but then it wasn't a very good joke.

Doherty went straight into the facts. 'He had a sack over his head. Not a big sack. A small one. It had a smell. Not a nasty smell. A nice smell.' He said it as though only he knew its significance.

Honey nodded appreciatively as though she somehow knew the significance of such a thing. But why should she? A sack, was a sack, was a sack. And the smell? Hemp surely?

She noticed how quickly he had spoken, giving away information that perhaps he shouldn't. Anything to maintain her interest.

He fell to silence. She sensed him looking at her. Decided it was her turn to speak.

'And he never was in the freezer?'

He shook his head. 'No. We checked. It was still there waiting to be de-gassed and whatever. It was empty and there were no signs of him ever being in there.'

'Do you prefer to be called Steve or Stephen?'

She didn't know why she asked, it just felt as though something was needed to fill the sudden silence.

'Doherty.'

'I prefer to be called Honey. Only my mother calls me

Hannah.'

He regarded her for a moment and nodded slowly.

'So! I take it you're divorced.'

Was that a hopeful look in his eyes?

'No. He died in a sailing accident.'

'I'm sorry.'

'That's what everyone said. But I wasn't. Not really. Racing and delivering sailing yachts had taken precedence over his married life. The more impassioned he'd got with his sport, the less we'd seen of him. It didn't help that most of the crew he hired had been female. He reckoned they bonded well and did everything that he asked of them.'

'Any children?'

'One. Lindsey. She's eighteen.'

'Get on! You don't look old enough.'

'Very kind, but I've heard it before.'

'I meant it. Does she look like you?'

She wasn't sure that he did, but at least he was treating her as a woman. Besides, it was the best chat up line she'd heard in a long while.

'She looks like her father and like me.'

He nodded sagely, as though she had said something very profound.

She asked him about himself. He told her he was divorced – something she'd already guessed – and that he'd moved to Bath from London.

'To make a new start,' he added. 'Got fed up with the pressure of work in the Met.'

He told her he rented a flat in Lansdown Crescent, but was looking to buy. 'When I can find something affordable.'

She knew where he was coming from. Bath was expensive. Georgian houses of elegant proportions, horrendously expensive to maintain, had long ago been divided into flats. Their elegance undiminished, their interiors furnished in a suitable style with expensive antiques, nothing in a really good location came cheap.

She let him make the headway until judging the time was right to make her excuses.

'Sorry, but I have to split. I'm cooking breakfast in the morning.'

It wasn't strictly true. Smudger never did breakfast if he could possibly avoid it. Dumpy Doris, a woman of dumpling roundness with arms a Sumo wrestler would be proud of, cooked up a cardiologist's nightmare; fried sausages, fried eggs and fried bacon. It was sometimes joked about that even the cornflakes would be fried if Dumpy Doris had her way. But she filled the gaps and good help on a weekend was hard to come by.

'I'll walk you home.'

'No need.'

Clint opened the outer door for them, his eyeballs bouncing between her and Doherty.

'It's no trouble.'

'It's no distance.'

Doherty threw a backward glance at Clint before the door slammed shut.

'I know him.'

'Everyone knows Clint.'

She didn't want to know what Clint did when he wasn't washing dishes; she didn't want to know what offences Doherty might have charged him with in case it put her off of ever employing him again. When they got to a certain age, automatic dishwashers were notoriously unreliable. Clint was not.

'Are you sure you'll be all right?' he said once they were up on pavement level.

'Fine.' She nodded vehemently. 'It's not far.'

'I insist.'

'Will you frogmarch me if I refuse?'

'Possibly. You know us cops; brutal, insistent – but

cute.'

She tried to pretend that he didn't appeal to her. Not easy.

'Shouldn't you add conceited?'

'I can't see why.'

Bath didn't have the night smell of the big city – the stewed traffic fumes, the dank river and the heat rising like dust from concrete buildings. Set like Rome in a sweeping valley surrounded by tree-topped hills, its lawns and well-kept flowerbeds lent a spring-like freshness in the air. The mellow walls of ancient buildings glowed in the borrowed gleam of well-placed lighting. Even at this hour the streets had a safe feeling about them, as though the ghosts of the past stood sentinel over those treading its cosy alleys and broad thoroughfares. Late night revellers wending their merry way home raised a hand, called and waved goodnight.

Pulteney Street flew straight as a dart from the centre of the city to the Warminster Road. The Green River Hotel was close to the very end, tucked away down a cul-de-sac.

Doherty sniffed the air. 'I love this place. There's something immortal about it. It looks beautiful, even at this hour. It's sacrilege that we're talking murder.'

She agreed with him though it occurred to her that he hadn't mentioned much about the murder tonight, though, goodness, she was grateful for the details he had given.

'Almost there,' she added, her footsteps slowing. She stopped and faced him. 'Look. You don't need to come any further.'

She smiled as she said it. No, she did not want him to see her to the door. The windows would be black, the minimum of light falling from the reception area; everyone would be – or should be in bed. Not necessarily so. Like a lot of seniors, her mother, who'd decided to stay overnight, was a light sleeper. Questions would be asked. She'd prefer them not to be.

She turned swiftly away before he had a chance to kiss her. She wasn't ready for it. Not just yet.

'Goodnight.'

'Goodnight.'

He sounded disappointed, perhaps even hurt. She glanced back to ensure he had indeed strolled off towards Lansdown Crescent and his bachelor pad. His form, his shadow and the sound of his footsteps faded into the night.

Walking on tiptoe was never going to be easy. The flagstones skirting the cul-de-sac were uneven and badly worn from centuries of use. Her steps slowed the closer she got to the hotel. At last, once she was sure he was gone, she stopped and turned round.

The night breeze was cool as water against her face when she looked for him. The coast was clear.

Counting to ten she waited, then slowly, still with her heels held barely off the ground, she retraced her steps. She heard a car and presumed he'd got a taxi. Certain she was right, she increased her speed, then paused as her fingers felt something in her pocket. Why was she bothering to walk to the taxi rank? Ivor Williams had given her his number.

Taking out the business card, she held it to catch the gleam of a streetlight, took her phone from her pocket, and dialled the number. Ivor answered.

'How's the book going?' she asked.

'Too busy for reading at present, lovely. What can I do to help you?'

It was obvious by his response that he didn't recognise her voice.

'It's the hotel lady that was asking questions about Elmer Maxted. I suppose you've heard the news.'

'Yeah.' He sounded horrified. 'Poor bloke. Who would have thought it, eh?'

She counted off all the bits of information she'd come across. Was Bob the Job for real or was he as spectral as the ghost Mary Jane insisted came out of the closet? Was her information likely to be pure fabrication?

'When you drove him around, did you ever take him to Limpley Stoke?'

'Sure. I told you. He wanted to visit the church. Took his time of course. Wanted to meet the vicar you see. Had things he wanted to ask so he said.'

She breathed a sign of relief. Her confidence returned.

'What sort of things?'

Ivor paused before his words began again in that very Welsh, singsong way. 'Well, I can't say for sure, mind you, but it was something to do with family.'

'His family?'

'Yes.'

'And he stayed there quite a while?'

'Three days in a row.'

'Three days!'

She couldn't help sounding surprised. Why would anyone – even the most ardent sightseer or family historian, want to spend three days peering into old and very dusty archives? Surely he couldn't have spent all that time in the company of the vicar? Just in case she was wrong, she asked Ivor.

'He saw the vicar on the first day. I saw them talking. But not after that. He just went into the church and walked around the gravestones and all that. Took some time that did. I waited until he came out and we went sightseeing. Not that he seemed that interested in the sightseeing. He was quiet when he came back. Doing a lot of thinking you see. Finding out about your ancestors can be a bit daunting you know.'

After thanking Ivor for his help she put her phone away and headed home. So Mary Jane's friend was right. There was no mention that he'd actually visited Charlborough Grange and introduced himself to the family. According to Ivor he'd gone no further than the church and its grounds.

Would searching through the archives take three consecutive days?

That, she decided, was a question that had to be answered. The hotel was in darkness. Loud snoring drifted out from the settee in the room just behind reception. The night porter was (almost) on duty. She took off her shoes.

'No point trying to creep in, mother.' Lindsey's head bobbed up from where she was lying full stretch on a brown leather chesterfield.

Honey jumped. 'I wish you'd stop doing that.'

'Scaring you or waiting up for you?'

'Both.' Honey eased herself onto the settee beside her daughter. 'Are you spying on me?'

'Yes. You're such a virgin when it comes to men.'

'Excuse me?'

'Don't remind me that I'm your daughter etc., etc., I mean you haven't indulged for a while. That's why I've got to look out for you.'

'Lindsey, I've only been out for a drink.'

Lindsey reached over and made a lengthening motion from the tip of her mother's nose.

'OK, my nose is growing like Pinocchio's.'

Lindsey huddled forward, her face, even in the gloom, glowing with interest.

'So! Tell me what he's like.'

'Who?'

'The policeman. And don't try and look so innocent. Grandma told me you had a date with him.'

'There's nothing to it.'

Lindsey gave her that '*who do you think you're kidding*' kind of look.

Honey held her head to one side and looked at her daughter. 'Are you always going to be looking out for me?'

Lindsey nodded.

'I thought so.'

# Chapter Fifteen

Honey was taking a shortcut through the Guildhall and feeling as fizzy as an uncorked bottle of champagne.

For the first time since becoming an amateur sleuth, she was approaching her mission in a relaxed manner. Her mind was open to possibilities. In fact it was like a great white board on which the problem is detailed in green felt tip and all the connecting factors are entered around it.

The Guildhall market was a magical place, where stalls dealing in antiques jostled with those selling a wide variety of cheese, garlic sausage and dried flower arrangements.

She sniffed the air, enjoying the way the mix of fragrances cleared her head and her mind.

Suddenly she had a eureka moment. it was there – the unmistakable tang of oriental spices. The sack covering Elmer's head had reeked of spices.

She looked round in the hope that she might find the source of the smell, perhaps a suspect. Stupid really. Was there likely to be a sign saying 'Get your small sacks here – ideal for placing over the head of your victims?'

When she saw where the smell was coming from and the stallholder, she smiled; Jeremiah Poughty, the very same who had taken over her reception area on orders from Casper.

She could tell by the look on his face that he wasn't missing the hospitality trade one little bit.

Cloves, cinnamon, bay leaves, turmeric and a host of other scents filled her head and cleared the excesses of the night before. There was a clichéd exoticism about them. A hint of the east, Persian markets, the Alhambra and over-indulgence of the senses.

It was all for sale under the sign printed in garish red letters on an apple green background, which screamed HERBS AND SPICE AND ALL THINGS NICE.

Jeremiah's stall. He waved before turning a beaming smile on a woman customer who, even at this distance, Honey could tell was giving him aggro.

'What's that one?' The woman's voice had all the enchantment of iron filings.

'Turmeric, honey.' Jeremiah settled one hand on his slim hips which were tightly clad in tan suede trousers. He wore a matching waistcoat festooned with embroidered flowers. The waistcoat was worn over a peasant-style shirt. His lipstick was purple and his complexion was as shiny and brown as a conker.

'And that?' The woman poked her finger at another small sack and sniffed.

'Paprika, dahling.' He nodded a greeting to Honey. 'Looking for something exotic to spice up our life are we?'

The woman did not appear to notice that he was talking to someone else. She pointed a podgy finger.

'Pretty colour. Got much taste?'

'Lots of honey, honey.'

The woman frowned and shook her head.

'I'm not sure. I normally only buy such things when uncontaminated by human hand. Preferably in plastic bags and on a supermarket shelf. Are your hands very clean?' said the woman, her small eyes narrowing in her pudding face.

Jeremiah threw her an indignant look. 'If you want something in plastic, go trot along to the supermarket.

Jeremiah was committed to all things green and free trade and free love and everything else that didn't come pre-packaged and with a hefty price. His tone was dead end and don't pass go.

The woman took on a shocked expression, wrapped her sheepskin coat more tightly around her body, then shuffled off to the next stall.

Jeremiah recovered quickly. 'Win some, you lose some. Oh well. There's great demand for what I sell.'

As stalls went Jeremiah Poughty didn't have a bad one. It was a well-stuffed pitch – wooden shelves at the back filled with sacks of vibrant-coloured powders, beans, nuts and other items she didn't recognise. Bunches of herbs, thyme, parsley, fennel and sage hung in bunches overhead. Some substances stuffed in between looked questionable.

'Jeremy, can I ask you something?'

His eyelids fluttered nervously. 'Sure. But if it's a date, I'm not your type.'

She smiled. 'No, and I'm not yours.'

She looked over his stall and upwards at the sign.

'Nice little spot, Jeremiah. Herbs, Spice and All Things Nice.'

Suddenly Jeremiah was all teeth, wide mouth and floating hands. 'Spice adds a little colour to your cooking – you should try some.'

The words came rat-a-tat-tat out of his mouth.

'It's mine and Ade's.' He nodded towards his partner who was wearing a green T-shirt, matching silk scarf and trousers too tight for decency. Like an unripe banana, thought Honey.

He smiled briefly by as he was bagging up half a pound of dried beans for a crusty with three rings in his nose, in the usual uniform of ragged parka jacket and half-shaved head, with a half-starved dog.

'I will. But not today.' Honey dug her thumbs into the waistband of her jeans. Designer of course. Bums and thighs were a nightmare without a good cut.

'On the house,' he said, offering her a small bag of dried herbs.

Honey grinned. 'Can I put this in my mother's curry?'

'What you do to your mother is your affair. It's a free sample – we give it to other customers too.'

She eyed him quizzically. 'Just how highly spiced is it?'

Jeremiah pursed his beautifully sculptured lips. 'I told you. Purely legit, dahling thing.'

Honey took the brown paper bag and slid it into her leather one.

'Go on,' he said. 'What do you want to ask me?'

'About these sacks …'

The necks of the sacks containing the spices were rolled over revealing the brightly coloured contents. Honey fingered them thoughtfully.

'They're just sacks,' said Jeremiah with a nonchalant shrug. She noticed his eyes slide sidelong to his partner.

'A sack like these was found covering the head of the man they dragged from the weir the other day.'

'Oh my!' Jeremiah jumped and grew taller. Although his teeth showed he wasn't smiling. 'He was murdered?'

'He was that.'

'How terrible! Poor man! Suffocated with spices and hit over the head with a blunt instrument.'

She wasn't sure either from his expression or tone of voice whether he was being facetious or strangely enraptured. She didn't know him well enough to judge but felt obliged to burst his bubble.

'You know I'm Crime Liaison Officer for the Hotels Association, don't you?'

She hadn't been given a formal title or had it described in writing, but the handle seemed close enough.

He looked askance at her.

She took advantage of his off-guard moment.

'He was killed three days ago. Saturday night sometime.'

'Dreadful.'

112

'Where were you last Saturday?'

His features froze before he burst out laughing. 'You're just joking. You can't really ask me questions. You're not a policeman, dahling.'

She raised one questioning eyebrow. 'A sack smelling of spices? You've got loads of them here.' She spread her hands, indicating tier upon tier of small, filled bags. 'A friend of mine who *is* a police detective would be interested in hearing that.'

'You wouldn't!' Jeremiah's hand splayed across his mouth. He looked horrified.

She nodded.

'I would.'

He glanced nervously towards his partner, then back at Honey. His eyelashes fluttered darkly over his cheeks. Honey was sure they were made of nylon.

As he leaned closer, the smell of his perfume obliterated that of the spices. 'I was out two-timing my boyfriend,' he said softly. 'You won't say anything, will you?'

Honey fixed her eyes on Jeremiah's partner who was still serving. 'Who were you with?'

His tongue swept along his bottom lip. 'I really couldn't …'

'Perhaps I should ask your friend.' She made a sideways move. Jeremiah followed her like a mirror image. 'No! There's no need to.' He glanced over his shoulder. Ade was now talking with the young man from the coffee stall. 'Andrew Charlborough. I was with him.' The name came out in a rush of breath.

Honey asked him to repeat what he'd just said, and he did. She wasn't often amazed at what people with status and money got up to in their spare time. She'd seen Sir Andrew Charlborough at a number of auctions. They were hardly on nodding acquaintance, but she'd judged him as an upright, respectable citizen, the sort that's in bed by eleven with a good book and a long-term wife.

'You mean the antiques dealer?'

Jeremiah nodded. 'And before you jump to the wrong conclusion about the man, I was invited to give a quote for some plants he wanted. A bloke who works for him and sometimes delivers for us asked if I'd be interested. He introduced us, said he was interested in very big tropical plants.'

'So why wouldn't you want your partner to know?'

Jeremiah chewed at his lip. 'I kept the deal to myself. And the money.'

Honey's mind was already darting elsewhere. It kept coming back to her that Elmer's head had been covered with a small sack smelling of spices. 'So what happens to the sacks once they're empty?'

Jeremiah shrugged. 'Mostly I give them away. Or chuck them. Some people buy by the sack – the big customers that is.'

She eyed him speculatively.

He wasn't long interpreting her look.

'I have not a killing bone in my body!'

She shook her head. You couldn't detect a murderer just by the looks of him. Just because he denied the fact didn't mean anything either. She'd hedge her bets.

'Can you provide me with a list of regular customers? The bigger buyers?'

Jeremiah shrugged his narrow shoulders. 'There's only a few. Shipping orders ain't our style. Half a pound here, a pound there. That's what I call big, honey.'

Honey kept her gaze fixed on Jeremiah's face. 'Please. It would be a great help.'

Recognising he had to put himself out, Jeremiah sighed and nodded. 'I'll do what I can.'

Her jovial mood had turned greyer, just like the weather. Elmer had found his way to Charlborough Grange. So had Jeremiah.

# Chapter Sixteen

The next morning, before doing anything else, she phoned Doherty and asked if there had been any developments.

'No.'

Not very forthcoming. Well two could play at that game.

'OK. So I won't tell you what I know. See you.'

'Hang on there!'

Schooldays came to mind. *I won't show you mine unless you show me yours.*

'We're tracing his movements. We've spoken to the taxi driver who ferried him around.'

'I guessed you would. I hear Elmer was interested in the Charlborough family. Do you know them?'

'I'm only a common copper, but I have heard of them. What's the connection?'

'I think they figure somewhere in Elmer's family tree. It's possible that's why Elmer went to the church. He was checking out the parish register.'

'Whoa right there. That line of enquiry is a dead end. Elmer was taken there and back by the taxi driver. It's not a case that he went missing in the grounds or thereabouts. We found him in the river, which means he must have been killed somewhere in the city. Mrs Herbert did say he went sightseeing there and on the night he disappeared, he went out quite late.'

She had to concede that he had a point.

'So there you are,' he crowed. 'That's the way it was.

We have a witness who overheard Elmer arguing with Mervyn Herbert. She also gave us a very good description of his car.'

'So Mervyn Herbert is the chief suspect. You're still looking for him?'

'Yes.'

He asked her out. She said she'd take a rain check. It wasn't that she wasn't attracted to him; she was. It was nerves. Plain and simple.

As if there wasn't enough to do in running the hotel, her mother had stopped over and was hounding her about having carpet laid over a truly lovely stone floor. 'Look, Allied Carpets are doing a great deal ...'

She was in the middle of checking the new menus – Smudger liked to change them every three months – and having her mother breathing fire over her shoulder did nothing to help her concentration.

Lindsey saved her bacon.

'That nice bookseller is here to see you again,' she said as she flounced past, a litre of Gordon's gin in one hand and a bottle of Glenfiddich in the other.

Honey stopped what she was doing.

Lindsey's footsteps went into reverse. 'I know you're fancying this policeman, but so what? Two guys are better than one.'

'Lindsey! That's two-timing – even though neither have quite started yet.' She tried to look shocked.

Her daughter shook her head.

'Even if you dump both of them in the end, play around a bit first. It'll make you feel good about yourself.'

Honey's jaw dropped.

Lindsey made a clicking sound, gave her customary wink and resumed her trek to replenish the bar.

Honey shoved the menus into a folder until later.

'Lead me to him. Mother, this is the sort of man you should have found for me in the first place.'

Her mother frowned. 'A bookseller? Do you think I would introduce you to a bookseller? You know there's no money in selling books. It's a mug's game. Besides, he's American.'

Honey's mouth dropped. 'Dad was an American.'

Her mother made one of those sounds a senior citizen makes when she's been caught out and is reluctant to face the consequences.

Mary Jane waylaid her on her way to greet John Rees.

'I need to make arrangements to hold a séance,' she said. 'Do you know of anyone whose loved ones have passed over who might be interested in attending? Older people in particular take great comfort from it.'

Honey turned round just in time to see her mother beating a fast pace across reception.

'Mother! Mary Jane would like a word with you.'

Her mother came to a giddy halt. It wasn't often she got trapped into doing something she didn't want to do. She was usually the trapper.

Mary Jane's lucid voice rang across reception. 'Gloria, my dear …'

Honey exchanged a secretive smile with her daughter who had just emerged from the bar.

Lindsey shook her head. 'Granny won't be pleased.'

'Never mind. It'll keep her occupied for an hour. Now, where have you put my visitor?'

'Prince Charming awaits you in the lounge with a cup of coffee,' said Lindsey then smiled as Honey unconsciously tidied her hair as she passed an ornate French mirror.

'I wonder, is he really Prince Charming or a frog in disguise?'

'You won't find out until you kiss him.'

Nothing was going to stand in the way of her plan to drive out to the church at Limpley Stoke. She'd phone the vicar first to make an appointment. John Rees had delayed her plans, but even a girl pushing forty has to have fun.

His hair was sandy, his face slim and warm hazel eyes danced with humour behind frameless spectacles. He removed them when she entered and stood to greet her. It was old-fashioned and oddly touching. She half expected to look down and see that her sensible skirt had turned into a crinoline.

'Mr Rees. I'm so sorry I missed speaking to you when you last called. There was a misunderstanding. I thought your being here was my mother's doing.'

One side of his face seemed to rise in amusement, his eyes twinkling as though he'd read her mother just like – well – a book.

Standing in front of him like this made her nervous. She rubbed her hands down over her hips and offered to pour another coffee.

'No. Thank you,' he said.

Making the effort to sound the professional hotelier, she tucked her skirt beneath her as they both sat back down.

'So! What can I do for you?'

'I want to hold a book fair.'

Green River had a very handsome conference room overlooking the park at the rear. Conferences and wedding fairs brought in good revenue. Why not a book fair?

'I think we have exactly what you are looking for. Our conference room holds sixty people ...'

'No,' he said. He raised his hand, his palm facing her like a halt sign. 'You misunderstand. I'm holding a book fair at the shop. I run themed evenings complete with wine and cheese and whatever – and sometimes the books are about wine and cheese. I pick a theme you see, select the books covering that particular subject, and objects featured in those books. For instance, I've done a modern art theme. The books were on modern art – the wine and cheese were the same – but I asked local artists to lend me their paintings for the evening – price tags included.'

Honey wasn't quite sure where this was going, but hazarded a guess.

'You're going to use hotels as a theme? Haute cuisine perhaps?'

The thought of the inclusion of the latter sent a shiver down her spine. What if the Epicureans attending were niggardly with praise and slated whatever dishes the Green River produced? Smudger didn't take criticism. He got huffy very easily and it was her that had to contend with his moods.

'I favour a Victorian theme for my next event and that, of course, will include the clothes of the era. Not the big crinolines and stuff like that. I don't have the room, but smaller things; gloves, mittens, hats ...'

'Underwear?' said Honey as the Queen's voluminous undergarments, already displayed behind glass, came to mind.

'Exactly,' he said. 'Just enough to set the scene. I understand from Alistair at the auction rooms that you own a very famous pair. I'd like you to display them if you don't mind. And then I'll select the books to go with it.'

Honey nodded. 'Victoria's pantaloons are yours for the asking.'

The fact that she wasn't going to earn anything out of his fair wasn't important. But something else was.

'Am I invited?' she added.

He smiled. 'Would you come?'

She smiled back. 'Of course I will.'

# Chapter Seventeen

Casper St John Gervais enjoyed the good things in life. He took pride in running a superbly furnished and well-run hotel. He adored cashmere sweaters, tailor made jackets and trousers, and felt nothing could compete with a pure cotton shirt made by a skilled Indian gentleman in Saville Row, London.

His exquisite taste extended to his surroundings. His hotel had graced in-flight brochures and *Hidden Hotels of the World* magazine, and was frequented by the rich and famous, confident they would receive excellent service and absolute discretion.

He didn't live there himself. He lived in a beautiful house, one of the impressive twenty-four that made up The Circus, that ring of mathematically produced elegance from the fevered brain of John Wood.

As with many Georgian houses, the ceilings were high and the windows large. The Georgians had excelled in letting in as much light as possible in the days before Edison lit up and invented the electricity bill.

The paintwork was finished in traditional colours; the furniture was even more elegant than in his hotel. Gilded mirrors reflected the star bright quality of the chandeliers, prisms of light flashing outwards.

Thick Turkish rugs hushed his footsteps. The only other sound, besides the beating of Casper's heart, was the incessant ticking of his clocks. He had more in his home than at his hotel.

He was sitting admiring his latest purchase when the front door bell rang. Sighing, he put his single malt onto a silver coaster to avoid marking the small piecrust table near his chair, then walked along the passage to the front door. He opened it to find Simon Tye standing there.

'Did you smell the cork out of the whisky bottle?' he said casually.

'If you're offering, I'm accepting,' said Simon and, without being asked swept past him, striding through the hallway purposefully as though bad news had come with him.

Simon was oddly quiet as Casper poured.

'Enough?' he asked raising the glass so Simon could inspect its contents.

Simon's eyes were fixed on the porcelain clock, his brows furrowed as if he could see some flaw in it that he had not seen before.

'Don't say the woman who sold you it wants it back,' said Casper as he handed him the drink.

'No,' said Simon. 'But her husband does.'

Casper raised his eyebrows quizzically.

'It appears she never had permission to sell it.' Simon clutched his glass with both hands and looked totally embarrassed. 'I'm sorry mate, but Charlborough wants it back.'

Casper was all attention. 'Charlborough? Do you mean who I think you mean?'

Simon nodded. 'Yes, the same bloke who bid against you for the Chepstow long case up at Marlborough in the summer.'

Casper took a slug of whisky. So did Simon.

'He reckons he's goin' to sue if he don't get it back.'

Casper caught the caginess in the sidelong expression Simon threw him.

'I told him I sold it to you.'

Casper groaned as he slouched back in his chair.

Simon shook his head mournfully. 'Sorry, mate.' He began to dig in his pocket. 'Here's your money.'

Casper eyed the bundle of fifties Simon placed on the table. They looked grubby, beneath his fastidious cleanliness. He would get Neville to gather them up, or otherwise use the pink washing-up gloves kept in the kitchen drawer.

'I'll take it now if you like, though you'll have to help me.'

'I don't do lifting,' said Casper with a shrewish pout. He gazed blankly into space. The thought of letting the clock go too quickly gave him great pain. Perhaps he could persuade Charlborough to let him keep it, offer him more, double what he'd paid Simon Tye. It was certainly worth a try.

He put it to him.

Simon shook his head. 'No,' he said resolutely. 'It has to go back.'

Casper sighed and although there was still plenty in his glass, he set it dumbly down on the table. He nodded in tacit agreement. 'You can count on me to make arrangements.'


His second visitor that night helped the situation along.

'I've come to make my report,' she said, breezing in more joyfully than Simon Tye had done.

She told him what the taxi driver had told her.

'Couldn't you get in trouble for withholding information from the police?'

Honey shrugged. 'Doherty, the cop they've assigned to me, has his own theories. He's adamant that the victim was murdered close to the river because that's where they found him. I must admit, he does have a point. And he's quite amiable about it.'

'He's trying to hit on you?'

'Something like that. Anyway I thought I'd go along

and ask the vicar what our American friend had found out about his family tree.'

She looked surprised when Casper stated he would go with her, though he didn't look too pleased about it.

'Two birds with one stone, my dear girl. We both have quests to perform at Charlborough Grange.'

# Chapter Eighteen

The Warminster Road winds up a hill out of Bath passing substantial Victorian villas with far reaching views over the meadows dipping down into the Avon Valley. Like a blueprint from history, a canal and a railway line run alongside the river. Together they span the centuries.

Further out, the villas are replaced by modern detached houses, and further out still the sunlight twinkles through battalions of tall dark trees standing sentinel at the roadside.

The road to Trowbridge branches off to the left, under a railway arch and into the village of Limpley Stoke. Some way up the hill, in the older part of the village, the church nestles amongst houses of its own age, built in the years of the Stewart kings.

Casper insisted they first return the clock before she made her enquiries of the vicar. He'd explained the situation to her and how he'd phoned Charlborough and offered more money, but had been refused. His mood was sullen and it was a fairly silent drive.

It was no trouble for Honey to alter her appointment. As she drove she rehearsed mentally the questions she thought relevant.

Casper was a picture of sullen resentment. He was brooding on the fact that he had to travel at all. That woman! That bloody Charlborough woman had upset his equanimity. He wished her ill. No, he thought, changing his mind. He wished her dead.

Pamela Charlborough had come back from Spain under duress and she was dead pissy about it.

If her husband Sir Andrew hadn't discovered she'd sold the clock she would still be out there lunching in one of the smaller but more select quayside restaurants in Puerto Buenos, rubbing shoulders with the owners of luxury yachts. As it was, her personal bank account was sadly lacking so she was here in England and bored stiff.

'I needed that money. You're such a skinflint.' Her comment and request for more money had been ignored. 'You care more for that clock than you do for me.'

Annoyingly he'd agreed with her.

She paced the conservatory, which was an old and elegant structure erected by some Victorian antecedent of her husband's. The man should have been named Midas but was more formally named Reginald. He'd spared no expense on this particular monstrosity. The place was filled with tropical plants from all over the world. It was lush, almost beautiful, but there was a wild carelessness about it. The plants were huge, thick-leaved affairs. Rather than the place being somewhere pleasant to sit among palms dotted around, it was the chairs that were dotted, the foliage that was over-abundant.

There were two views from the conservatory. To the rear were massive greenhouses full of even larger tropical plants. Huge leaves pressed against the glass as if trying to escape from the dank humidity that prevailed inside. She'd gone in there once. Once was enough.

From the other end of the conservatory she could look over the drive and the wide steps that led up on to the parapet to the front door. She sighed. The drive was empty and she was lonely. Oh for a bit of red-blooded company.

She took a red leather address book from her handbag, opened it and ran her finger down the letters of the alphabet stopping at the letter 'P'. With one well-manicured fingertip, she flicked the book open at that page and smiled at the entry. She kept the book open, picked up her phone and dialled. It rang for a while then was answered. The sound of his voice made her go weak at the knees.

'Well hello,' she purred. 'And how is my favourite little pussycat? Due for some well-earned leave yet? Spain is still very warm you know.'

The response on the other end of the line was negative. Her smile stiffened. Expensive heels of exquisite shoes dug into the tiled floor and her smile faded.

'You haven't got time? For me you should make time.' She gritted her teeth and her lips felt stretched and dry.

He said something about their time together being long past. She scowled at that and regretted phoning.

Her tone turned sour.

'Don't worry about it darling. After all, you're just a number on my list – just as I am on yours. One of my older numbers of course. Adios, amigo!'

She snapped the phone shut then flung it as far as she could.

'Damn you!'

It bounced off the back wall and disappeared into the greenery. The sound of car tyres crunching on gravel made her look towards the drive.

# Chapter Nineteen

'I smell money,' said Honey.

Her eyes took in the fudge-coloured stone, the lead-paned windows set into stalwart mullions of stone. Elizabethan?

'Old money,' corrected Casper suddenly breaking his silence. 'Enough of it to allow Sir Andrew to do more or less what he wanted in life. Started off conservatively enough – Eton, Cambridge, followed by the army, followed by some acting and then the writing of his memoirs.'

'About his time wearing tights?' asked Honey, determined to raise Casper's spirits.

'Don't be facetious!' He sighed. He ducked slightly so that his gaze could sweep unimpeded over the elegant façade. 'Apparently the place was in danger of falling down back in the nineteen fifties. Annoyingly gorgeous now!'

Honey noticed that Casper kept his eyes averted from the clock draped like a beautiful woman on the back seat. Her car of course. He'd made perfectly relevant excuses as to why they couldn't use his.

'Darling, mine's a two-seater. Isn't yours one of those people-carrier contraptions?'

She'd told him that no, it was not, but owning up to a two-seater was no contest. Of course they'd have to use her car.

Casper slammed the car door as if banning the

timepiece from his mind. She knew he would do his utmost not to look at it again.

Looking distinctly unhappy, Casper clumped up the mossy steps to the next level of gravel.

Italian terracotta pots lined each tread and terrace, containing a froth of straggling lobelia, nasturtiums and variegated ivy.

The front door opened as if by magic. Andrew Charlborough had white hair and strong features. The ruddiness of his complexion was indicative of a man who'd served in the army, climbed mountains, and tramped through the jungles of Borneo. Not too good on an actor perhaps, but his bone structure was good.

He wore a powder blue sweater and matching trousers. A crisp white shirt collar emphasised the colour of his complexion.

He glanced swiftly at his wrist. The gold strap of a very expensive wristwatch glistened.

'You're late.'

He addressed Casper, turning away once the words had been snapped.

Unfazed and mildly respectful of gentry, Casper replied. 'Do accept my apologies, old boy, but due to circumstances beyond our control.'

'The traffic was heavy,' added Honey, suddenly irritated by Casper's flowery words.

Charlborough barely glanced at her. Again he addressed Casper. 'Have you brought it with you?'

'Yes indeed, though the thought of returning such a wondrous object weighs heavy in my heart.'

It sounded like Shakespeare, but Casper had made it up himself. Honey raised her eyes heavenwards. Casper was doing everything to impress.

Charlborough was unmoved. 'Bring it in here.' He turned away. Casper looked as though he was about to blow a gasket.

'I do not hump!' he said, both hands resting on his silver-topped walking stick.

Honey looked down at her shoes in an effort to hide her grin. Did Casper realise what he'd just said?

'My butler is not here today,' said Charlborough, his expression unaltered. 'I'll see if someone else can give a hand. Perhaps you'd like some coffee while I arrange things?'

Casper grabbed the chance to have a nose round – just as Honey knew he would.

They stepped into a hall where the walls were lined with heavy oak panelling and the floor was thick with the rich colours of ancient Oriental rugs. There was a dark green tapestry along one wall where a hunter sat on a pale horse, his dogs and retainers around him. A falcon perched on his wrist. Against the tapestry and set on a long Jacobean table with barley twist legs was a display of eighteenth-century silver. It was an incredible collection, handed down rather than purchased.

Above a stone mantelpiece sat a skeleton clock, its workings suitably protected beneath a dome of Victorian glass.

'Such exquisite items,' breathed Casper, his eyes shining with delight. 'Absolutely exquisite.'

All the clocks stated it was two thirty-five.

Honey checked her watch. They were quite correct.

Casper gave it one last try. 'I came here to see if we could not come to some understanding. I'm willing to offer more than your wife was paid for the clock.'

Charlborough paused and eyed him as though he were considering the depth of Casper's pockets. His eyes narrowed, their greyness only a shade darker than his hair. His jaw was strong, his features chiselled – like a Roman general or emperor.

'Haven't I seen you at Sotheby's?' Andrew Charlborough directed his question at Casper. So far he'd hardly glanced at Honey.

Casper visibly grimaced. 'We've bid against each other on a number of occasions.'

'Really?'

'Really.'

'In that case I'll ring for refreshments,' said Charlborough.

Honey asked if she could use the bathroom.

Charlborough hardly looked up as he indicated a corridor of panelled wood and more tapestries running off the main hall.

'Take that passage, turn right then left at the end. It's on the right.'

She cursed the elderflower concoction her mother had foisted on her at lunchtime.

'The ginseng will put a spring in your step,' her mother had told her.

It didn't, unless you count having to move smartly in the direction of the nearest loo!

She heard Charlborough tell Casper that they would talk in the study.

After ogling and using the Delft-tiled bathroom, it was time to play hunt the study. It has to be off the reception hall, she told herself and began trying a few doorknobs. Some were locked.

'Can I help you?'

She started. The thick carpets had smothered the sound of his footfall. He looked pleasant enough, around thirty. He was carrying a tea-tray.

She smiled. 'I'm looking for the study.'

He smiled back. 'Follow me. Andrew asked me to bring you tea.'

She wondered at his familiarity, calling Sir Andrew by his first name.

'Are you a member of the family?'

'I've been here for some time,' he said, which didn't

really answer anything. 'I suppose you could say I was. But I get paid for being here.'

His smile was disarming.

'In here.' He indicated a door. She opened it.

The study was as impressive as the rest of the house. Rich spines of old books lined packed shelves; there was a white marble fireplace of a later age than the house and an over mantel above it of later age still. The clock was of black marble, round and nestled on a mock carriage of gold ormolu and decorated each side with fat bottomed puttees.

Bunches of carved grapes wound in fertile splendour up and around the huge mirror hanging above the mantelpiece. Honey mentally assessed its height at around eight feet and it was about the same across.

There were a few pictures on the wall; black and white snaps and one or two coloured; family shots, a wife, a child. And later, just a young man, the child grown up perhaps? But no wife. No woman at all.

Sir Andrew did not acknowledge the young man who'd brought the tea. He left with as much deference as he'd entered.

'Would you like to pour?'

Honey realised Sir Andrew was directing the question at her.

Her first inclination was to say no, but she changed her mind, aware that Sir Andrew was eyeing her.

There were only two cups on the tray.

'No tea for me,' said Charlborough, and got to his feet. Three decanters sat on a silver tray on the sideboard. He pulled out the stopper and began to pour himself a drink.

Casper and Honey exchanged contemptuous looks. Tea for them, brandy for him.

'I admit to being disappointed,' said Casper as Sir Andrew seated himself behind a desk that was almost big enough to be a dinner table. 'I bought the clock in good faith.'

'I apologise,' said Charlborough. 'My wife had no business selling the clock.'

'But would you reconsider …?'

Honey was surprised. She'd never known Casper wheedle to anyone. He was certainly wheedling now.

There was an awkward silence during which she allowed her gaze to drift. Even once conversation resumed, she was not included.

Out of boredom as much as anything else, she got up and paced the perimeter of the room.

Charlborough was spouting his personal history.

Latching on to the subject, Honey interrupted.

'Had quite a career in the army, sir?' She nodded at a line of photographs that covered a good footage of panelling. They were black and white, unmistakably in foreign parts and full of smiling soldierly faces. Most of those pictured looked boyish. Charlborough, who she just about recognised, looked more head boyish and a touch superior.

He seemed pleased that she'd noticed, his voice booming.

'Indeed yes. Great days. Great boys.' Charlborough's jowls drooped with nostalgic sadness.

He was on his second glass from the decanter.

'Do you know Jeremiah Poughty?' She adopted her sweetest voice. 'West Indian parents, born in Gloucester, now runs a spice stall in the Guildhall Market.'

If Charlborough was taken by surprise, he didn't show it. 'I've never heard of the man.' His voice was even.

'He deals in spices and plants. You invited him here to talk about plants, I think.'

He shrugged. 'Perhaps I did. I don't recall the name.'

'You might recall what he looked like. He's very …' she paused for the right word. There was only one. 'Colourful! Both in skin tone and clothes. A bit of a peacock you could say.'

Charlborough remained as cool as his powder blue sweater. 'Oh yes. The plants. I don't handle the domestic side of running this place. Anyway, what's that got to do with my clock?'

'Nothing really, except that the sacks ...'

Uneasy with the line of questioning, Casper got to his feet. 'Look I'm sorry about this, we really have taken up too much of your time, but if you should ever reconsider ...'

'The clock is not for sale – at any price! And now ...' The glass was slapped down.

Honey recognised the sign for goodbye. Sir Andrew had had enough.

He pressed a buzzer fixed to his desk. 'Mark will show you out.'

The young man who'd brought the tea quickly appeared looking as though he'd swapped the kitchen for the garage.

Honey eyed the black T-shirt, the tight-fitting jeans. He smelled slightly of oil.

'Ah! The butler.'

'Hardly,' he said with a smile as he accompanied them to the door. 'It's Trevor's day off, although he's probably around somewhere. I'm the back-room boy. I take care of anything mechanical.'

Casper pouted all the way down the steps to the car. As he walked he swung his silver-topped walking cane.

'Careful,' cried Honey, ducking to one side. 'You look as though you're going to bash someone with it.'

'That man! Why couldn't he indulge his wife a little, let her sell the clock and spend the money at will? I could swear, I really could!'

He slumped in the front seat and slammed the door.

Honey got behind the driving wheel and turned the key. 'Don't do that, Casper. We're off to see the vicar next.'

133

## Chapter Twenty

A downcast Casper opted to stay in the car.

'Walk it off,' Honey said to him.

He glowered.

She persisted. 'A bit of fresh air will do you good.'

'I don't want to be done good! I want that clock!'

'Children,' she breathed quietly and headed for the arched and ancient entrance to the parish church.

The interior was very dim by virtue of its narrow Saxon windows. The walls were whitewashed but looked ice blue as the light diffused through the stained glass.

A woman arranging flowers told her where she could find the vicar.

'Through the chancel and down the steps to the crypt.' She pointed a skeletal finger tipped with bright pink nail varnish. 'He's got an archive down there.'

Apart from her painted fingernails, the woman seemed a sensible sort. She wore a flowered dress and lace-up shoes. Her eyes darted over Honey as swiftly as her fingers did over the flowers.

'You could do with wearing something warmer. Cold as death it is down them steps – though only to be expected I suppose. It's only a skip and a spit from the crypt where they're all cold and bones.'

'Charming. What better way to spend a warm spring day?'

Stone steps led down into the chancel. Cold air met her at the bottom and she shivered.

The Reverend Reece Mellors was bending over what could only be a parish register. It was huge, big enough to make a tabletop – a coffee table at least.

'Reverend Mellors?'

He looked up.

She beamed warmly. 'I'm Hannah Driver. I rang you.'

'Well good afternoon!'

His deep baritone ricocheted off the cold walls and coffins. His hand swallowed hers.

The Reverend Mellors was something of a surprise. She'd expected a pasty-faced vicar with horn-rimmed spectacles and a vague look in his eyes. Instead she was confronted with a tall man who had to stoop beneath the vaulted roof. Black was the best way to describe him; black hair, black eyes, black bushy eyebrows, and dressed in black. The blackness contrasted eerily with his pale complexion. Like Count Dracula, she thought, and found her gaze fixing on his mouth when he spoke. No sign of fangs though – and that name was vaguely familiar.

'I spoke to you about an American tourist, a Mr Elmer Weinstock, though he may have used the name Maxted.'

The vicar's smile lifted his saturnine features. 'Ah yes. Interesting chap. Couldn't quite get out of the habit of using a pseudonym I think. He told me both names and that he had his reasons. He also swore me to secrecy as to his real name. I had no problem with that. In my opinion I think he liked the excitement of having two names. I can't think of any other reason for him doing so unless he didn't like the one he was given. Still, we can't help the names we're given, can we?'

Honey conceded that vicar could be right. It was just the habit of a detective's profession.

'Were you of any help in his quest?'

'Oh, I think so, although he had done quite a bit of groundwork himself.'

'I wouldn't have thought either of those names would

be very common around Bath.'

'They're not. He wasn't tracing his own kin. He was tracing his wife's, and even then only by marriage. His wife's cousin married Sir Andrew Charlborough in this very church.'

'Is that so?'

Now this was interesting.

'That is so.' His finger traced a relatively late entry in the parish register.

'She died about twenty years ago.'

Honey recalled the photographs: black and white of Charlborough and his lady and a child, then a later one of a young man, presumably the child grown into manhood.

'And the son? Is his name and birth date listed?'

The Reverend Mellors slammed the book shut. 'Not in this one.' He reached for another hard-covered book. 'His baptism would be in here.'

She watched as he rustled through the pages.

'Ah! Here it is. Lance Charlborough was baptised eighteen years ago.'

Honey's thoughts returned to the photographs of the handsome young man. Some had been fairly recent. And his mother had died twenty years ago. She was just about to point this out, but Mellors beat her to it.

'Not his birth date, you understand,' said the vicar having noted the expression on her face. 'That would be in that book,' he said, patting the former epic tome he'd been perusing.

'Aren't baptisms or christenings usually done within a few weeks or months of birth?' she asked him.

He pursed his wide sensuous mouth when he nodded. 'They always were. There must have been some reason, perhaps that they were abroad at the time. Sir Andrew did serve in the army I believe.'

'Did Elmer have children?'

'No. I did ask him, you know, out of interest as one

does in the course of a conversation. He said something about his wife having had an inherited disease, so they'd chosen not to. Apparently she died some time ago. He's alone now. Or was. I did hear of his demise.'

It was on her tongue to ask him to look up Lance Charlborough's birth date, when the woman who'd been arranging the flowers called down the stairs.

'There's a phone call for you vicar. I took it in the study.'

'I'll be right there,' he called back.

He grinned ruefully. 'Sorry about this. I quite often put my phone on divert so I can take it on my mobile, but Mrs Quentin puts her trust in God not modern technology. She picks up the receiver within the first three rings.' He sighed. 'Oh well. Sorry about this.'

'Never mind.'

'I'll look it up for you and give you a call. Shouldn't take too long. Is that all right with you?'

'Of course.'

Mrs Quentin, the swift-moving flower arranger, escorted her down the aisle to the church door – a bit like a wedding in reverse.

'The vicar's a bit lax when it comes to security,' she said quickly as though impatient to get back to her flowers. 'But I like to make sure that anyone who comes visiting is properly interrogated before seeing the vicar and shown off the premises if they've no business being here.'

'You're a gem, Mrs Quentin.'

She meant it. Women like Mrs Quentin didn't need a computer-based diary when it came to recalling who had visited, where they'd come from and what were their intentions. The naturally nosey had a ten megabyte memory installed at birth.

Honey asked the obvious question.

'Do you recall an American who came checking out his family tree?'

'Ooow, yes. Mr Maxted. He came here three days on the trot poring over the old registers and asking questions. He snooped around a lot. I caught him behind the church. That was when I realised he wasn't just interested in his family tree,' she said, her voice falling into a disdainful hush. '*She* was there. I saw her out back on t'other side of the fence. Hussy, she is. Lady Charlborough indeed. No lady her! The first Lady Charlborough, now she was a lady. But that one!'

A woman! Was Elmer having an affair?

'Did you happen to overhear what they were talking about?'

The baby pink lips pouted with disdain. 'Certainly not! I am not in the habit of listening in on private conversations!'

Honey mumbled an apology.

'Besides, they were talking normally, not like that man who came along after him that day. Scruffy-looking individual he was. Perhaps that's unfair. Not so much scruffy as pallid and bland. And loud. 'Twas a wonder they didn't come to blows. The American was none too happy with him I can tell you.'

The sun warmed the coldness of the crypt from her back, but a fresh chill ran down her spine. The description was familiar. Dare she ask?

Mrs Quentin shook her head. 'No. But I saw his car.'

It was hard not to cross her fingers and wish or shout Hallelujah, but Honey contained herself. 'You don't happen to remember what make or colour of car.'

The powdered cheeks puckered into a knowing smile. 'I do indeed! One of them cars that keeps the lights on all day. And it was dark blue. And an estate. Let's see, it begins with a 'V' … '

'A Volvo?'

'V for Volvo. That's the one!'

Honey resisted the urge to skip all the way back down

the churchyard to her waiting car.

'Home,' muttered Casper, who was laid back in his seat, his hat pulled down over closed eyes.

'Not yet,' said Honey, hardly able to control her excitement. 'I think our American might have been having an affair with Charlborough's wife.'

Casper peered out from beneath the brim as she swung the car away from the kerb.

'Steady on old girl. Still, could be to our mutual advantage. If old Charlborough finds out and shows her the door, he might need some money for the impending divorce and sell me the clock.'

Honey made no comment. Accelerator stabbed to the floor, they were off down the road heading back to Charlborough Grange.

'I declare I am totally wearied by all this detective work,' muttered Casper. 'I only asked you to liaise with the police, not run the case.'

'I never do things by halves, Casper.'

He waved a hand in surrender. 'Please yourself. But don't expect me to go back into his superior presence. He is not the type I would wish to include among even on my "b" list of acquaintances.'

Now that was a turn up for the books! Casper was a born snob.

'Never mind him. Now listen to this Casper. According to the vicar Elmer was Sir Andrew's brother-in-law by marriage, but not the present marriage. The first marriage.'

'You're suspecting familial skulduggery,' he said profoundly. 'Or might I suggest, that you hope it is.'

'Do I sound as though I do?'

'Yes. Like a bulldog. You have sunk your teeth into this bone and you're not letting it go.'

'There's more. One of the women who does the flowers in the church heard Elmer having an argument. Guess who with?'

'Go on. Tell me,' Casper said wearily, the brim of his hat bouncing on his nose.

'Mervyn Herbert!'

'Ah! We have our murderer.'

'We would if we knew where he was.'

Swinging the car down the drive, she targeted the gap between the stone pillars on either side of the entrance.

'Elmer also met Pamela Charlborough.'

'At the Grange?'

'No. At the church.

'Just the church?' asked Casper in that sharp, sudden way of his.

'Just the church,' she replied grimly. 'Ivor said he was there for hours, three days on the trot.'

'Pretty church,' said Casper. 'I took a walk all around its perimeter.'

Honey remembered thinking the interior was a bit gloomy.

'It was dingy inside.'

'As I said, my dear, I walked around the perimeter. There's a very neat graveyard surrounded by ivy-covered walls and laurel hedges.'

'How very Gothic.'

'There's also a stile and no more than two fields between it and Charlborough Grange.'

Honey's hands tightened over the wheel.

'So Ivor, the taxi driver, wouldn't have known if he'd visited Charlborough Grange or that he met Pamela Charlborough. He couldn't have seen from where he was parked.'

'Should you not be calling her *Lady* Charlborough?' said Casper in a passable resemblance to Noel Coward.

'From what I've heard, she's far from that!'

'You're prejudiced. And don't think I am not aware of where your thought process travels. You are assuming she was having an affair with our American friend.'

'Right. If he wasn't having an affair, then why did he make her acquaintance?'

'The meeting could have been prearranged or it could have been by chance. Either way, there's still our missing Mr Herbert to consider. Mr Maxted is found murdered and Mr Herbert has disappeared. To use detective parlance, I think it's an open and shut case, guv.'

Honey shook her head. 'I can't see that it's that simple. If his wife's cousin was dead, what was the point?' A spine-chilling answer sprang into her mind. 'Unless he hadn't known she was dead. Unless he suspected …'

'Now you're talking pure fiction. You're making up the plot as you go along.'

She wasn't listening. Absorbed in 'what ifs' and 'whys', she shot past the main gate of Charlborough Grange. Casper cried out in alarm as she spun the car round on the spot.

'Sorry. I was miles away.'

Casper righted himself and readjusted his hat.

'So was I. If it wasn't for my seatbelt I would have flown through the windscreen.'

This time no one answered the front door of Charlborough Grange.

Honey looked down towards where she'd left the car parked on the gravel drive at the bottom of the steps. Casper looked comfortable enough, his arms folded over his chest. His hat was pulled down over his eyes, but she knew he was brooding. He'd lost the clock and he was pig sick about it.

The door stayed shut. The windows looked out sightless over the warm stone terraces simmering in the afternoon sun. The shadows of trees were growing longer across the lawns and the heads of flowers quivered with honey-seeking bees. The air was ripe with floral perfume and ripe green leaves, the smell of grass gently baking in the summer sun.

She made a snap decision and followed the path along the front of the house, through an arch and into a rose bower. A tunnel of blooms heavy with scent, yellow roses vying with white ran the full length.

Through a gate and she found herself in a walled garden where fruit trees clambered over warm, red brick. Such gardens had existed in medieval times; perhaps this one predated the present house, the house itself standing on the ruins of an older dwelling.

The workmanlike surroundings, the rubbish bins, a small cement mixer, a ride on lawnmower waiting to be put away, led her to the tradesmen's entrance. The rear of the house was as silent and bereft of human contact as the front.

'Hello?' she called out.

The sound was lost in the warmth beating against the red brick walls, the sturdy metal objects standing sentinel at the side of the path.

She stood absolutely still drinking in her surroundings. If you listened hard enough and were very observant, you could almost smell danger. She did just that, bringing all of her senses into play.

Nothing!

No surprised countenances appeared at the windows; no curious eyes watched as she found a back door, opened it and went in.

She found herself in a conservatory where the greenery was as vigorous as in the Amazon rain forest.

'Who the hell are you?' A female voice.

Even before she turned round, Honey guessed she was in the presence of Lady Charlborough.

She was sitting in a wrought iron chair, her finger poised over what appeared to be a diary or address book. A gold sovereign hung from a chain around her neck. She wore a gold belt, gold high-heeled sandals and earrings to match. Despite the contempt in Mrs Quentin's voice,

Honey had expected a mature Chelsea rather than Essex girl. It was hard to keep the surprise from her voice.

'Are you Lady Charlborough?'

The woman, whose hair was Scandinavian blonde, had a tan only obtainable from somewhere like southern Spain. She was holding a glass in her free hand. The liquid in it was clear and sported a slice of lemon. Gin rather than water.

Plucked eyebrows rose, and dusky rimmed eyes opened wide with a mix of street acquired caution and upper crust disdain.

'Yes. I'm Lady Pamela Charlborough. Who the hell are you?'

'Honey Driver.' Her hand shot forward. It wasn't taken.

Pamela Charlborough threw the book she'd been reading to one side. 'Is that supposed to mean something?'

'I suppose not. I really wanted to ask you about your brother. You know he's dead, don't you?'

'My brother? What brother?'

'You don't have a brother?'

'That's right. I don't.'

'Ah! And I suppose you're not the first Lady Charlborough?'

It was something else Honey already knew, but it seemed best not to let on that she'd been prying.

The expertly made-up face stiffened. 'No! I am not. I'm the second wife,' Lady Charlborough said. 'The trophy wife you might say.'

The words chipped and tarnished trophy came immediately to mind.

Lady Pamela slugged back the remains of the cut-glass tumbler, took out the lemon and ate that as well.

'So what the hell do you want?'

'An American tourist was fished out of the river the other day. I was under the impression he visited you here. His name was Elmer Maxted, though he did sometimes

143

call himself Weinstock. You might have him written down in your address book.'

Lady Charlborough tapped her pen on the chair arm, her glazed expression as brittle as old glass.

'I've never had the pleasure.'

'No?' Honey sounded surprised. 'So do you often go hob-nobbing over the church wall at the bottom of your land? Or were you just passing by? You were seen talking to him.'

The pink lips twisted into a snarl.

'Old Mother Quentin. Nosey cow! Time she was pushing up the daisies in that bloody churchyard instead of putting them in pots!'

'Were you having an affair with Elmer?'

Lady Pamela's jaw dropped. 'How dare you! Who the hell do you think you are!'

'I'm working hand in glove with the police. I can't help the questions being asked. The police will ask the same once it's confirmed by Mrs Quentin that she saw you with him. Still. Your choice. Maybe it's better if you told me the truth rather than them.'

'You're not the police?'

Honey didn't flinch. OK, it was all bluff, but bluff might baffle brains, that's if Pamela Charlborough had any.

For a brief moment the flesh beneath the made-up face squirmed as though Lady Pamela's skin had got too tight to cope with. Telling the truth and saving face were fighting it out.

Honey hadn't been too sure how long she'd take to snap, she just knew she bloody well would.

'OK. I saw this bloke on the other side of the wall and we passed the time of day. There's no law against that, is there?'

Honey shook her head. 'There's no such thing as coincidence. I would have believed your story except that

144

Elmer Maxted married a cousin of Sir Andrew's first wife. Now that's what I call too strong a coincidence!'

Lady Pamela raised herself from the chair. Her botoxed lips curled back displaying perfect teeth.

'That's the way out,' she snarled, wobbling slightly as her legs took her weight. 'Now get out before I call the police!'

'You can if you like, bearing in mind that I've already told you that I happen to be working with the police.'

'Don't care! Clear off! Go on! Clear bloody off!'

Honey paused. 'OK, Mrs Charlborough. I'm off.'

'*Lady* Charlborough, if you don't mind!'

'Are you kidding? As long as you've got two nostrils in your nose, you'll never make a lady!'

Her ladyship clutched an empty wine glass. Honey shut the door just before the glass hit.

'Temper, temper,' she muttered to herself.

While retracing her steps through the warren of passages, she tapped in Steve Doherty's number on her phone, determined to tell him all she knew. There was no signal. She needed to get outside. Surely in these spacious gardens there should be somewhere she could pick up a decent signal.

There was a kitchen to one side, an empty place with deep white sinks and the sort of atmosphere left over from the Victorian age when servants outnumbered the family they served.

Turning away from the kitchen and the house, she made her way down the path and out of the walled garden. On the other side of an arched door, turned silver by centuries of English weather, she found herself in a vegetable garden. A path led back round to the front terraces and she would have tried phoning again, but the greenhouses caught her eye.

They were huge but dominated by one in particular much bigger than the others. The greenery pressed thick and dark against the glass or plastic material that held it. Like plants from *The Day of the Triffids*, she thought, about to pull up their roots and escape.

Like the house, the place seemed deserted. Pots of fresh earth waiting for new bulbs or seeds for next spring sat on tables just inside the door. There were seed trays, specimen pots, cardboard boxes of plants, packets of seeds and bulbs pulled from the earth and nestling in brown paper bags tied up with string.

The smell of turned earth mingled with the stink of a compost heap. Mildewed cabbages leaves lay like a floppy hat on top the rotting pile.

Wrinkling her nose, she stepped past it and headed for the second greenhouse, then the third – the most interesting.

Sandbags were heaped around the door. She remembered they used to pile them around bomb shelters and gun posts in the Second World War. They were meant to protect a place from bomb blasts. A first aid box was nailed to a post which stood near to a jeep covered with a camouflage net – all terribly military.

The wall of sandbags hid a Perspex door. Sacks. She wondered if they had held something else before they'd held sand. There was no way she could check. Her attention turned to the door. It had a handle, and handles were meant to be used. Like Alice she pushed it open and entered Wonderland – of a sort.

Moist air hit her face like a damp blanket taking her breath away. The smell of vegetation growing thickly and roof high was so strong, the humidity was too thick to breathe – exactly like a jungle.

The effect was so real that she stopped and listened, half expecting the chattering of monkeys or the screech of parakeets.

'Me Jane. Where's Tarzan?' she whispered under her breath.

She looked up. Thankfully there was no sign of beefcake wearing nothing more than a pillowcase around his loins.

The humidity seemed to solidify as the door slid silently shut behind her.

The narrow path between the tropical greenery petered out just a few feet from the door. If she was to go on, she would have to part the thick foliage Great White Hunter-style; a machete would have been useful.

No, she decided stepping back. It was too dark in there. Too real.

It suddenly occurred to her that Charlborough might keep wild animals in here. The Marquis of Bath kept a whole menagerie at Longleat; lions, tigers and leopards prowled the grounds. Who knows what you could keep in a small jungle!

'Now's the time to panic.' She uttered the words in the weeniest whisper, and even that seemed too intrusive in this strange jungle hidden on an English estate.

Was it hidden? If so, why?

Backtracking was on autopilot. She could have turned round. Going forwards was always quicker than going backwards. But she didn't have eyes in the back of her head and she *needed* to see what was behind her. Just in case …

'Halt!'

Her breath stopped!

Her heart stopped!

Her feet certainly did. It was as though she'd backed into a barn door – one made of oak – big, hard and locked!

It took a big scoop of courage to make her turn round.

Facing this human barrier was worse than not doing so. Chiselled features, chiselled body, as though welded from sheets of steel and thus having no rounded corners. Being eye to eye with his pecs was disconcerting. Raising her eyes failed to improve matters.

'You're trespassing.' His voice was higher than she'd expected, like a voice is when the larynx has suffered a severe blow. The two didn't go well together. If her legs hadn't been shaking she might have laughed. Instead she played the trump card, the acceptable excuse.

'I'm working with the police with regard to the disappearance of an American tourist.' She chanced a grin and a casual shake. 'Just thought he might have wandered in here – you know how these Americans can be.'

She hoped he didn't detect the trace of the accent she'd inherited from her father years ago.

'What's happening here?'

A draught of fresh air heralded the arrival of Sir Andrew. Alarm flashed in his eyes then was gone. His smile was controlled.

'I thought you'd gone, Mrs Driver.'

Her heart stopped racing. Somehow she had no wish to tell the truth. A suitable excuse tripped from her tongue.

'Mr St John Gervais wished to take one last look at your clock. He's pretty upset about losing it. I said I would ask your permission. No one came to the door when I knocked, so I came around here. I thought I saw someone here ...' She threw a tight smile in the direction of metal man. 'And I did.'

'Trevor is my gardener, as well as my butler.' He turned to the man. 'That will be all, Trevor. Mrs Driver is just leaving.'

Sir Andrew took a firm grip on her arm. It wasn't quite frogmarching, but not far off. She took a last look over her shoulder at the gardener. Did jungles need gardeners?

The question was suddenly of no consequence. She'd been aware that Trevor was carrying something, but hadn't stirred up enough courage to look and see what it was. Now she saw him toss a small sack onto a pile of other sacks. It rolled off and something rolled out.

Trevor cussed.

Honey gasped.

Glassy eyes starred up at her from a severed head.

Her legs wobbled. Her head swam. She needed air. Fresh air. Right now!

# Chapter Twenty-one

Andrew Charlborough couldn't help chuckling at the woman's reaction to one of the many props they used in their war games.

Longleat had its wild beasts and extensive grounds in which to keep them. Most of the estate surrounding Charlborough Grange had been sold off years ago. War games complete with a pretend jungle and pretend bodies provided a decent income, besides which, he enjoyed them. It took him back to other times and other places. He'd explained all this to Hannah Driver. He'd seen her recover, seen her blush and then seen her off the premises.

Amateur sleuths were the least of his worries. His features hardened as he watched her car pull away. Once it had gone, he went back along the corridor to the study. From his pocket he took a neatly folded cotton handkerchief, the initials LTC embroidered in dark red at its corner. Gently he wiped the handkerchief over Lance's photograph before straightening it. He fingered its frame.

'I miss you, Lance,' he said his voice trembling with emotion.

Suddenly he became aware that he was no longer alone.

'You're an obsessive! Do you know that?'

Pamela's strident voice pierced through his sorrow and his skull. She sashayed toward him, hips rolling, blonde hair clipped tightly around her pronounced cheekbones.

Anger flushed his face. 'Get out of here!'

She dragged fiercely on the cigarette she was smoking.

'It's your own fault he stays away from here, you know. You're too overbearing. The boy wants to lead his own life. And why shouldn't he? What's it to you, darling? Eh? If you really, really think about it, what's it to you?'

Her husband's eyes followed her as she walked around the room purposely tapping the corner of each framed photograph so it no longer hung straight.

She laughed as she did it.

'You don't answer!' she said. 'I've heard how you talk to him, insisting that he tow the line, or else ... and the dear boy ... he so loves his father ... *his father*!'

She laughed like a gurgling drain.

If eyes could be knives, Sir Andrew's would have stabbed her twice.

She came closer and deliberately blew smoke into his face, then rested her hand on his chest. 'What if he knew the truth? I wonder how much he would love you then? Because I know you know. I met Mary's brother-in-law. He told me what you did. Now,' she said, a red-painted fingernail tapping the matching colour on her lips. 'Perhaps I should tell the police about this before I tell Lance. Or should I phone that woman and tell her?' Her expression hardened. 'What's it worth not to tell either of them, Andrew? Eh? Fifty thousand? One hundred thousand?' She shook her head. 'Chicken feed. And this chicken deserves more than that, I think.'

Andrew clenched his jaw as he gazed down into his wife's face.

'Marriage to you has been torture, Pamela.'

Her eyes opened wide with feigned surprise. 'What else did you expect? I didn't marry you because I loved you. It was all for money. For your beautiful, beautiful money! What else! And when we divorce, I'll take half of it with me.'

'Over my dead body you will!'

'Your dead body! Wonderful. Could you possibly

arrange your death and I'll forego a divorce. After all, I would much rather be a seriously rich widow, darling, than a moderately rich divorcee.' She patted his chest. 'How's your heart darling?' She laughed. 'Silly me. You don't have one. At least, not as far as your wife is concerned. You only love your son … if he was your son.'

'Pamela, have pity …'

She stopped and pouted. 'Pity has a price, darling. Think about it.'

She was still laughing when she left the room. Her husband stared after her, thoughts of what he'd like to do to her roaring through his mind.


Mark Conway looked up at the ceiling and tried not to breathe in her perfume. There was the smell of her and the smell of perfume. He preferred the smell of her. The perfume was too overpowering.

The room held only this bed, a chair and a low table. The rest of the house was divided up into flats. This was where they always met, where he would sate his physical desires and she would tell him of her contempt for her husband, his employer. He would listen but not comment.

Her fingers continued to trace circles over his chest. Her voice was low and huskily enticing. He knew the sex had been good for her. She'd told him so. Now she was saying other things, things that filled him with dread.

'I wish he was dead. How easy would it be to kill him? You could kill him, Mark. Just think …'

Her lips were full, but cold upon his. Strange he hadn't noticed that before.

'If he were dead, we could spend all day in bed. All day. Every day. How easy would it be to kill him do you think?'

'Easy,' he said, because he knew it was the truth. 'Very easy. But then, why should I? He's very good to me. He's always been very good to me.'

Her tongue flicked at his ear. 'Because, my darling, if he was dead you'd have me.'

'And you would have all his money.'

'That's right. Just me.'

'What about Lance?'

'What about Lance? No doubt he'd get something, but nowhere near what he's been used to. I'd get the lion's share.'

'You sound very sure of that.'

She smiled like a cat as her hand slid down over his loins and did delicious things between his thighs.

'Because I know something that you don't. I know that all Andrew's money could easily become mine.'

## Chapter Twenty-two

First she dropped Casper off. He'd thrown his head back and laughed like a drain when she'd told him about the plastic head and the war games in the greenhouse.

'My dear, never have I seen you so pale.'

She swore him to secrecy.

Placing his right hand on his heart, he adopted a suitably serious expression and promised from the depths of his soul. 'And in the interests of our continuing harmony,' he added.

After dropping Casper off she headed home and was surprised to see that Doherty was waiting for her.

Plastering a smile on her face, she trotted into the small lounge just off the main residents lounge, which she kept for business appointments.

A tray of coffee, brown sugar and cream sat on a tray in front of him.

She could tell by the look on his face that this was not entirely a social visit.

'I would have preferred a whisky,' he said, jerking his chin in the direction of the untouched tea.

'You could have asked for one.'

'I did. Your mother turned me down.'

'Oh! I'll get you one.' She vowed to have a word with her mother about making visitors welcome – even if you didn't approve of that type of man.

'Never mind.' He rose to go. 'I haven't time to hang around.'

'Really,' she said flippantly. 'Who's been murdered?'

His expression told her that she'd hit the nail on the head.

'Who?' she asked, ashamed she'd sounded so offhand.

'I told the chief constable I didn't have time for all this, but he insisted I inform you.'

His bluntness stung. And just when she was getting into this job.

She was just as blunt back. 'So inform me.'

'Mervyn Herbert.'

'In the river?'

Doherty shook his head. 'No. In his own garden under the rockery. There'd been a gas leak and the gas company dug up the garden. And before you ask, his head was bashed in and he had a sack over his head. A spice sack, same as before.'

'Do you think Mrs Herbert did it?'

'An obvious conclusion, but the lab boys tell us otherwise. We don't think he was murdered there, but Mrs Herbert is in a bit of a state. And there is that first husband to think about.'

'Oh yes. Loretta's father.' Her stomach rumbled. She'd been thinking of smoked salmon salad all the way back from Limpley Stoke.

'I suppose I'd better go along and see her.'

Doherty got to his feet. 'I'm fine with that, but I should warn you that until we've done a thorough investigation, we have to treat her as a suspect.'

'Even though the murder was done elsewhere?'

He shrugged. 'In the house, in the garage, or even outside in the alley. Who knows?'

'I take it you've already questioned her?'

'The doctor wouldn't let me. Said she was in deep shock.'

'There,' she said, swinging her bag over her shoulder. 'All the more reason for taking me with you. It might help calm the poor woman. Even if she is your prime suspect.'

'I didn't say she was my *prime* suspect.'

'An accessory with her first husband perhaps? Loretta's father?'

Honey had followed him out on to the street. He frowned. 'Are you by any chance a mind reader?'

'Only as far as men are concerned.'

'You needn't come with me to see her. You don't have to.'

'And you don't want me to.'

'I don't see the point. I never have.'

'Thanks a bunch.'

'OK.'

It was all he said. Honey decided it was about the best invitation she was likely to get from him.

Well just wait until I tell you what I know, she thought as she got in beside him. I'll surprise you. I'll make you *want* me to be with you on this.

On the drive to the Lower Bristol Road she told him about her visit to the vicar, but not about her snooping in the greenhouse. She'd never live it down.

'Elmer's wife's cousin was Sir Andrew's first wife. I think he went calling at the Grange, though everyone's denying it. Pamela Charlborough admits to meeting Elmer when he was wandering around the churchyard.'

'Is that right?'

'So says Mrs Quentin. I asked Lady Charlborough, but she's not the warmest heart I've ever met.'

'Useful person, Mrs Quentin.'

Honey made a sound of agreement and looked out of the window. The early morning rain had disappeared. A rainbow twinkled above the viaduct taking the railway line to London via Green Park. The air smelled fresh and new.

Doherty was thoughtful. 'Do you think he was having an affair with Lady Pamela?'

'Of course not! If he visited Charlborough Grange at

all, or if he talked over the church wall to Lady Pamela, it had to be something to do with his family. He was keen on what he was doing. Perhaps found an old family skeleton and got bumped off for it. You know how touchy some relatives can be.'

'Too melodramatic. OK, so he'd planned an activity holiday – if you can call it that. Believe me the root of the problem is at Ferny Down Guest House. Mervyn Herbert was a sleazebag – too fond of his stepdaughter from what I can gather. I want to know where her real father is. He's got something to do with this. I can smell it.'

Honey chewed at her lip rather than say outright that she thought he was talking out of the top of his head.

Doherty noticed. 'Are you worried or hungry?'

'I didn't have breakfast. Or lunch.' Pathetic excuse.

Doherty tutted. 'The most important meal of the day!'

Honey's head turned sharply. 'Did my mother ask you whether you were married?'

'No. She asked me whether I prefer carpet or hard wooden floors.'

Honey groaned. 'It amounts to the same thing.'

He was intrigued enough to take his eyes from the road. 'What?'

A blue double-glazing van veered away into the nearside lane. The driver gave a two-fingered salutation and shouted something about getting a driving license. Doherty's driving frequently attracted rude comments.

They reached their destination too quickly. Feeling as though her heart was somewhere behind her belly button, Honey held back, waiting for Doherty to get out of his car and ring the doorbell.

Two uniformed policemen were standing guard outside. They nodded in Doherty's direction as he got out of the car.

Honey took a deep breath.

'Nervous?' asked Doherty.

'No. Of course not.'

That was rubbish. The truth was that she'd never visited a scene of crime. She hoped the body had already been taken to the morgue. One fright per day was more than enough. She had to say something trivial to steady her nerves.

'That doorbell's been well polished,' she said.

Doherty looked at her as though her comment was just another cross to bear.

Loretta answered the door. Her clothes were basically as before; no sign of a black armband even and she had colour in her cheeks. The numerous rings she wore glinted as she shut the front door.

'Ma's out back,' she said brusquely. 'Straight down there.'

A single solitaire diamond flashed on her index finger as she pointed. Nice, thought Honey, and wondered why she hadn't noticed it before.

'Nice ring. Is it new?'

Loretta blushed. 'A present. From a mate.'

A male mate, Honey decided, and intimate. Only intimacy brought that bright a red to a girl's cheeks.

Cora Herbert was sitting in her favourite spot in the conservatory. A mug of tea and an ashtray sat on the table in front of her. Beyond the door men in jump suits methodically moved earth from one part of the garden to another.

The thick black lashes left traces of mascara on her damp cheeks. A pall of cigarette smoke rose and circled in the air. The cigarette trembled as she flicked the length of ash into the tray. She looked grim, tired, her eyes outlined in a red that almost matched her lipstick. Black roots ran like a basalt valley through her hair parting. The rest was dry, blonde and in need of a wash.

Honey's throat was like sandpaper. 'I'm so sorry, Mrs Herbert.'

Both she and Doherty took a seat. Tea wasn't offered. The room was stuffy and filled with smoke. The door was shut, the smoke seeking escape through a fanlight set in the plastic roof.

Cora nodded an acknowledgement.

Doherty went over the details again. 'When did you last see your husband, Mrs Herbert?'

'I've already told you that,' Cora snapped.

'Tell me again,' Doherty said slowly.

Listening to his line of questioning decided her. She nudged his arm. 'Can I have a word in private?'

Doherty pursed his lips. Yet again this was a different Steve to the one who let loose in a local bar. This was his profession. He'd trained for it, started at the bottom and worked his way up. Whereas she ...

His hostility was mild, but definitely existed. He looked as though he were about to refuse. What made him change his mind might have been the thought that two heads are better than one. Or did he really think he was in with a good chance of going to bed with her? Either way, they made their excuses and went out into the garden shutting the door behind them.

Not that Cora seemed to care. Smoking, staring at the floor, flicking ash and barking orders at Loretta. She didn't seem actually upset, just anxious, as though she wanted this to be over, and the quicker the better.

Skirting the heap of dug up earth, they made their way to the far end of the garden where a plastic garden gnome peered through a canopy of rhubarb leaves.

Honey folded her arms. 'What's this all about?'

Doherty adopted a blank look. 'I don't know what you mean.'

'Liar!'

He shrugged and spread his hands. 'What?' The innocent look just didn't wash.

Honey eyed him accusingly. 'OK. Don't explain. Let

me guess. Your last case was a shambles and so when the Hotels Association asked for a police officer within the force to work with them on their idea, you were ordered to volunteer. And then …'

He opened his mouth to protest.

'And then,' Honey went on, determined to have her say, 'when Elmer Maxted's body was found, you determined to hold on to the case. You saw it as a means to repair your reputation. That's why I'm here, isn't it? You don't like it, but I'm tolerated.'

He began to laugh, bending from the waist, lower arm across his belly.

Honey was unmoved. 'And now we have the laughing policeman!'

The look in his eyes contradicted what the rest of his body was doing. The eyes certainly had it, and that was what she would judge him by.

She headed back to the conservatory, satisfied that the air between them was at last clear.

All the same, she was feeling uneasy. The whole scenario had changed. This wasn't just about a misplaced tourist. It wasn't even about the likelihood that Elmer had been mugged and murdered purely by chance. Such things rarely happened in Bath. For the most part the city was peopled by the cultured, the civilised and the upwardly mobile. On the face of it this second murder had nothing to do with tourism and made her nervous.

'I've had second thoughts,' said Doherty from behind her as they headed back. 'Mrs Herbert has to be the prime suspect. Who else would plant their husband in their own garden?'

Although tempted to slam the door on him, Honey left it open. Irritating as he was, Cora's cigarette smoke was worse.

Cora was sitting in exactly the same position as when they'd left her. Goodness knows how many cigarettes she'd consumed in their absence. She was on a chain-smoking marathon and her eyes were watery. Despite the make-up, her complexion was greasy and white.

'I didn't do it,' she said before anyone had asked her. I didn't kill 'im and I didn't bury 'im in the garden. I loved that rockery.

'So how did he get there?' asked Doherty.

Cora's eyes popped like marbles. 'How the hell should I know?'

Honey was aware of Loretta leaning against the wall behind them, arms folded, her expression as dark as her mother's flaking mascara.

Doherty was sounding serious. 'I'm afraid you're going to have to come into the station for further questioning.'

Honey could find no words of sympathy and nothing helpful to say like, 'It's surely a mistake,' or 'I shouldn't worry if I were you.' The evidence was damning. Like Doherty had said, who else would plant their husband in the garden?

'I'll walk back,' Honey said once they were outside and Mrs Cora Herbert had been helped into the back seat of a police car.

Doherty shrugged. 'Please yourself.' He turned to Loretta. The girl's face was expressionless, as though she were still digesting what was going on.

'What about you?'

Loretta's bright eyes narrowed and her red lips twisted into a contemptuous snarl. 'I don't travel with pigs. I'll be down to visit her, give her a bit of moral support and all that.' She stood on tiptoe and shouted at her mother. 'I'll be down to see you, Ma! You can count on it!'

Honey caught the sob in her voice. 'Will you be all right?'

'I'll bloody well have to be. Mum would want me to take care of things.' She jerked her head back at the '*No Vacancy*' sign. 'We're expecting paying guests. Have to

161

look after them, don't I?'

'You're a good daughter. It must be upsetting. I think you're very brave.'

Loretta shrugged again causing the straps of her top to slide down over her thin shoulders. 'Not really. I know she didn't do it. There's no evidence.'

The statement was made confidently. She was standing with her arms still folded protectively across her chest, her head held high. Was that a smile Honey could see wavering around her lips?

Her smile vanished when she saw the enquiring look on Honey's face.

'Don't look at me like that!'

'I'm sorry.'

It wouldn't do to leave on a negative note. She forced a smile while her eyes dropped back to the flashing diamond.

'That's a pretty ring,' she said, trusting her instant change of subject didn't sound too contrived.

The comment lifted Loretta's heavily made-up face. 'Nice, ain't it?'

She flashed the ring. 'My dad gave me it,' she said in a strange and dreamy kind of way.

Honey's first thought was that Robert Davies had come into a nice sum of money to have afforded such a flashy ring.

'That's nice. Were you close to your dad?'

'Yep!'

'But not to Mervyn.'

Loretta's expression darkened into a deep scowl. 'A prime-time creep!'

Honey imagined the affect Loretta's skimpy attire might have had on Mervyn Herbert.

'Did he bother you?'

'No,' she said, her eyes blazing. 'He didn't *bother* me! He *raped* me!'

162

# Chapter Twenty-three

Honey stretched her tired body and plunged headfirst into sleep and a very scintillating dream. She was lounging beneath an azure sky by the side of a lagoon which in turn was fringed with waving palm trees.

The sound of surf brushing over a golden beach changed suddenly.

Funny, she thought languorously. The sea sounds just like my telephone at home ...

Just at the point when a gorgeous hunk was handing her a long, cool drink, the dream was broken.

Swearing under her breath, she switched on the light and reached for her watch. Twelve thirty-two. The phone was still purring.

Drawing her other hand from beneath the thick layer of sheet, blankets and satin eiderdown; an old-fashioned eiderdown; she so loved old-fashioned. She eased herself up against the pillows and reached for it.

'Hope you weren't doing anything special?'

Doherty!

'Just sleeping.' Well actually, the lean torso of her dream reminded her of him, but there was no way she would tell him that. His ego was big enough.

She rolled over on to her side, cuddling the phone against her cheek.

'I do sometimes go to bed before midnight!'

'Do you?'

He sounded genuinely surprised. The truth was she was

tired out after serving a party of history buffs holding their annual bash. History was sometimes viewed as dry; the historians ensured their throats were always wet. Dreaming of him had provided a little light relief.

'Look, Steve, running a hotel and being a sleuth …'

'Doherty. I prefer to be called Doherty.'

'OK. Doherty. Being a sleuth is quite burdensome. Anyway, what do you want?'

There was a pause. 'I've had a heavy day. You know, Mrs Herbert and all that. I thought you might feel the same.'

Honey pulled herself up into a more comfortable sitting position. She told him that she'd rung the station earlier to enquire what was going on. Cora was still being questioned.

She frowned at the thought of poor Cora ending up in a cell on a bed that wasn't her own.

'There have been developments.'

It was a case of 'pigs might fly' to hope that Mervyn Herbert had been a random killing. And did Doherty know that Mervyn had raped his stepdaughter?

'Steve …'

'Doherty. Call me Doherty.'

'Doherty. Loretta told me something, something that she may also have told her natural father that would make him real mad.'

She told him what Loretta had told her. 'I'm not sure whether her mother knows.'

'I didn't know that.'

He sounded genuinely sorry, almost as though he could really empathise as a parent. He'd mentioned having once been in a long-term relationship. He hadn't mentioned having children.

The likelihood of Cora killing her husband wasn't that far fetched. The option of her first husband, Loretta's father, having done the job, was also possible.

'Besides keeping me informed of developments and feeling mutually drained, what else did you want?'

'Company. How about we meet up at the Zodiac.'

'Now?'

'As good a time as any.'

'I don't know ...'

'The night's still young. And so are we.'

'I don't feel young.'

'I'll make you feel young.'

Something electrical steered a southerly course to erogenous areas she hadn't used in a long while.

She swung her legs out of bed. 'Give me twenty minutes – no – thirty. It's a pretty long walk unless I get a taxi.'

'No need to do either. I'm parked outside.'

'I could accuse you of being too sure of yourself.'

'I could accuse you of being out of your depth and say that I don't enjoy your company. But I won't.'

A pale green silk sweater, jeans and loafers, plus a quick brushing of her hair and she was ready. She popped on pearl earrings – a classy afterthought. Classy was good.

As he drove, she blinked at the impatient city where visitors still wandered taking in the atmosphere, and late-night revellers and theatregoers headed for nightclubs or a taxi home.

Doherty was driving extremely steadily. No van drivers were honking horns at him. Not that many van drivers made deliveries at one in the morning.

'How many have you had to drink?'

'Two small ones.'

A borderline case of drink-driving? She wasn't sure, but she wasn't chancing it.

'Can we go for a walk?' she said suddenly. 'I don't really feel like a drink.'

He gave in without a fight. 'OK.'

They headed for Pulteney Bridge, parked the car and

got out. He automatically offered her his arm. She automatically took it. Not a word passed between them. Honey was comfortable with that. She presumed he was musing over the day's events, but also enjoying making her wait for what he had to say.

She studied his profile. Strong silent type with well-chiselled features, a masculine smell and an aura of power. Leather jacket. Stone-washed jeans. Good thighs. Alpha male at his best.

They stopped at the water's edge, and looked towards the bridge and the river.

Doherty leaned on the parapet. He fixed his gaze on the lights reflected in the river.

'Mrs Herbert's out of the picture. Pathology confirmed a time of death when she was out at bingo.'

'So what next?'

'We're looking for Mrs Herbert's first husband. He's a dead cert for doing it.'

'Because of Loretta?'

'Could be. He's not long out of prison. There's nothing between him and the ex-wife, but he's very protective of Loretta.'

A breeze blowing off the river whipped her hair across her face. It was nice being here with him. Terrible circumstances of course.

Leaning forward, his hands resting on the parapet, he looked up into her face.

'You feel guilty you didn't tell me sooner about Loretta's accusation. I can see it in your eyes.'

'You can't see my eyes.'

'Do I have to beat it out of you? I can play good cop, bad cop if called upon.'

She sighed. 'Can I call upon you to buy me a coffee instead?'

'Yeah. Sure.'

His gaze turned to the other side of the river. 'Look at

166

the river. At its edges the current runs faster. I reckon Elmer came down on the current on this side. If the current on the river is just as strong upstream as it is here, then the body could have been put in anywhere along that stretch. But that piece of wood came down with it.' He stood thoughtfully for a moment.

'And Mervyn Herbert?'

He shook his head. 'Another sack over his head and traces of coriander. That's a spice, isn't it?'

She told him it was and thought of Jeremiah. The sacks had to have come from him.

Before she had chance to mention Jeremiah's spice stall and him being a personal friend, Docherty stepped in.

'We questioned a spice stall in the market about their sacks.'

'But not the stall owners. They wouldn't have a motive.'

'Not at this moment they don't, but who knows? Something may crop up.'

Honey thought of Jeremiah and Ade. No. There was no possible motive.

She rubbed at her forehead as she tried to work out where this was going. Being dragged out of bed for midnight walks didn't happen very often. Midnight walks were something lovesick teenagers did when they couldn't afford anything else after a lively night out.

'Are you insinuating that Loretta's father murdered both Elmer *and* Mervyn?'

'I think so. The spice sacks link them. And Davies has a record.'

'So do a lot of people.'

'Do you?'

'Not a criminal one. I just carry a lot of baggage – you know – failed marriage, widowed, raising a kid, mad mother ...'

'I wouldn't say you were mad.'

'I meant my mother!'

'No need to snap.'

'Sorry.' She rubbed at her frowning forehead again.

'Right. Now what is it you know that I don't?'

He sounded insistent. She wondered if he would drag her down to the station for questioning if she didn't spill the beans. Possibly.

'Loretta Davies was raped by her stepfather, her stepfather has been found with a spice sack over his head, and I know the bloke in the market who runs the spice stall. That's all.'

Doherty raised his eyebrows. 'Jeremiah Poughty?'

Honey looked at him. 'You know him?'

'Who doesn't?'

Honey frowned. 'I wonder if Loretta's mother knows about the rape?' Girls didn't tell their mothers everything. Neither did they always tell the truth.

'It happens. She might not have known. And who could blame the man? But Mervyn deserving what he got won't keep Loretta's father from prison.' Doherty grunted. 'At least he's used to it.'

Late-night revellers chose that moment to come skipping along the promenade like six-year-olds. Every so often they leapt up at the flower baskets hanging from the lampposts, hitting them with their hands and sending them swinging.

Doherty waited until they'd gone by before explaining.

'Mrs Herbert told us at first that Mervyn had gone to the pub. The Green Park Tavern, a favourite of mine, it so happens.'

Honey nodded. The Green Park Tavern was a fair walk from the guest house towards the viaduct and the train station.

'She told me that,' said Honey. 'He did it quite regularly apparently.'

'When did she tell you?'

'On the first occasion I went there when Mr Weinstock, as he was then, went missing. Mervyn shot off at the same time. I presumed he was avoiding me – you know – just another busybody to blight his days. Obviously that wasn't quite the case.'

Suddenly the scene that day came back in full clarity. 'Oh my God!'

'God's not here. Just me. What's the problem?'

'He was helping some men from the council take out a large chest freezer. It was being dumped. I never saw him after that.'

'The chest was checked when our American friend went missing, then left unattended and unoccupied. Just enough room for Mr Herbert – if only temporarily.'

Doherty flicked open his phone, punched the shortcut button and immediately introduced himself and what he wanted.

'Check the file. Where's Davies working?'

There was a pause as the lowly police officer on the other end obeyed and checked the particulars.

Something was said that she couldn't hear. Doherty didn't look too pleased.

'That's all it says? The council? Didn't anyone think to check which department?'

Obviously not. He slammed his phone shut.

'Chimps. The lot of them. Qualified by a bit of paper and they're all bloody chimps!'

'Never mind. You already know that there's nothing in the freezer now.'

'Absolutely. But there could have been.'

Doherty's arm brushed around her back. She took it as a signal to resume their walk. He was surprisingly serious as he talked, his eyes now fixed on the ground in front of them. If he was being 'fresh' as her mother used to say, he showed no sign of it apart from the encircling arm. He was into his subject, recounting what had happened – as related by Mrs Herbert.

'Sometimes, when he'd had enough of Bath and tourists, or when her former husband was threatening to bash his head in, Mervyn used to jump on a train.'

'Where to?'

'Anywhere. Two days or so and he returned. But not this time. Then Davies turned up and was more than pleased that it seemed he wasn't coming back. Offered to move back in. Loretta was all for it. Cora didn't seem too bothered about it. They could have worked in collusion.'

'What makes you think that?'

'He's scarpered! That's a sign of guilt if ever there was. Probably in Mervyn's Volvo estate. We haven't found that either.'

'So the murderer could be driving around in a Volvo estate.'

Doherty pulled a face. 'Some people have no taste.'

# Chapter Twenty-four

Honey smiled as she greeted diners arriving for dinner in the restaurant of the Green River Hotel. Most were guests, but Smudger the chef knew his stuff, so there was always a smattering of locals wanting to sample his seafood thermidor or his heaven-sent white chocolate mousse with orange liqueur.

Mary Jane came floating in wearing strawberry pink chiffon, her long feet encased in Roman-style gold sandals the straps of which finished in a knot halfway up her shins.

A look of contentment suffused her gaunt features and her eyes glittered with a far-seeing look – quite suiting a woman who claimed to number ghosts among her friends, Honey thought. The incumbent of her regular room had left and she immediately changed rooms. Once again it was left to her and Sir Cedric.

Her usual room was spooky; there was no other way to describe it. Honey disliked the high wooden ceiling and the silly closets that were lacking in depth and had no room to hang clothes. She planned to renovate during the off-season. Sensing her plans would not be welcome, she had not yet mentioned it to Mary Jane.

'Sorry I'm a little late coming down,' said Mary Jane in a lazy Californian drawl.

Close up, her eyes shone with unworldly brightness. Honey guessed what was coming.

'I have been conversing in the most intimate terms with dearest, darling, Sir Cedric,' she said, her eyelashes fluttering, and her long fingers resting on her ribcage. Her voice dropped to a whisper. 'He has confided some really scandalous family secrets.'

Honey feigned awe struck interest and adopted the same hushed voice.

'Is that so?' At the same time, she guided the elderly and very tall lady to her usual table where the long legs and torso folded obediently into a chair.

'Indeed. He had three wives you know!'

She tittered like old ladies are prone to do when salaciously delicious sex is mentioned – though, it had to be said, Mary Jane did not quite fit the image of a comfortable old lady.

Honey handed her the menu. 'He didn't chop off their heads did he – you know – like Henry the Eighth?'

'Oh, no,' came the adamant reply. Her expression was deadly serious. 'It was very naughty, and I've been sworn to secrecy.'

'Then I won't pressurise you,' said Honey smiling.

'But I must tell you,' said Mary Jane, her fingers locking over Honey's arm. 'I'm going on one of these fabulous Ghost Walks this evening. It visits some of the places Sir Cedric has told me about. Would you like to come along?' she asked, eyes of periwinkle blue youthfully bright in her wrinkled face.

Honey eyed the steadily filling restaurant and shook her head. 'I can't see I'll have time for that.'

Mary Jane looked crestfallen. 'I quite understand, my dear. Now let me see,' she said, rummaging in her solidly square bag. 'I have a bus timetable here somewhere ...'

'No need for the bus. I can't come on the walk, but I could spare ten minutes to give you a lift.'

'Oh good.' The voluminous bag was snapped shut. 'Your mother said you would.'

Honey maintained her smile through gritted teeth. It galled to find out she'd already been volunteered before she'd had chance to offer.

She might have stayed prickly if her eyes hadn't clapped on to John Rees. He was wearing a smart but casual cream linen shirt with shoulder tabs. It gave him a soft military kind of look.

'How are ya?' he said, getting to his feet and shaking her hand.

She wanted to say, 'All the better for seeing you,' but she didn't.

'I'm very well. And you?'

She held the professional smile. He might be here just to sample the food and not to see her. Once she came back down to earth, her gaze strayed to his dinner partner.

The woman was slim; not just in a *thin* way, but glossy, as though a copy of *Vogue* had fallen open and the model had stepped out fully fleshed.

She was sipping water and her eyes were downcast. The latter were perfectly made up; dark smudges in all the right places, lashes as thick as furry caterpillars.

'Miriam,' he said by way of introduction. 'This is Honey Driver who owns this fantastic place.'

Miriam nodded, murmured good evening, but didn't look up.

Honey resisted clenching her jaw. After all, what did it matter if she'd been fantasising about their assignation at his bookshop? The stuff he'd wanted to adorn his walls beside the artworks and books had already been collected. OK, so although it was by invitation only, it was still basically a public event. Anyone could go in and buy tickets.

'I'm looking forward to the open evening,' she gushed, keeping her smile trained on gorgeous John.

'So am I.'

There was something about his manner that was different. He smiled but his features were stiff. She guessed he was coping with tension and Miriam, his glossy, bronzed companion with her black hair and red lips, was the cause of it.

Honey excused herself. Waltzing around the restaurant, she was a picture of solicitous charm. Waltzing around in her head was the same recurring thought. Why were all the best guys already spoken for?

Lindsey was supervising the bar. As usual she dispensed drinks and opened bottles of wine swiftly and efficiently. She never mixed up orders and neither did she panic.

She was tipping a measure of Harvey's Bristol Cream into a schooner, the largest of the sherry measures. Honey knew without being told that it was for Mary Jane. She'd developed a passion for the very English drink. No doubt a little spirit inside would prepare her for the spirits she might encounter on her Ghost Walk.

'I see that your friend the bookseller has company,' said Lindsey.

Honey resisted the urge to grit her teeth, rested her elbow on the bar and sighed. 'And there was I thinking I might get the opportunity to eat him alive.'

'You don't mean that. Personally, my preference is for the rugged, silent type. I like the cop.'

'Don't let Gran hear you say that.'

'The fact that I'm giving my mother the benefit of my experience?' Lindsey leaned forward, arms resting on the bar. 'You need youth on your side, mother. Grandma's talking marriage; I'm talking about having fun.'

'Your grandma's old-fashioned.'

'No she's not. She's a control freak. She doesn't really want you to remarry. I've seen how she works it. Take that businessman who used to come in here. First she pushed you in his direction, and when you did take an interest she told you he was like a sailor; a girl in every port.'

'He was.'

'I think she lied.'

174

Lindsey was telling the truth. It was strange, it was annoying and it was also plain bloody-mindedness. The kind of scenario Lindsey referred to had happened more than once. But not now. She was now Crime Liaison Officer for Bath Hotels Association and had acquired street cred; and a policeman friend.

Honey asked, 'So who's the supermodel dining with out bookseller friend?'

Lindsey checked the reservation register, running her finger down the page until she found the right time and name. 'Mr and Mrs Rees.'

The restaurant was full and compliments to the chef were coming thick and fast. Honey knew she should have felt supremely smug that things were going so well tonight, but John Rees had punctured her balloon. Steve Doherty was still a contender, but that ego ... John Rees didn't have one. Or baggage. At least she hadn't thought so; until tonight.

She was almost glad when the customers thinned out and Mary Jane came tottering over to claim her lift to the Ghost Walk.

'I hope I'm not inconveniencing you,' she said, her bony fingers light as swan's feathers on Honey's arm.

'Of course not,' Honey lied, her eyes sliding sidelong to Mr and Mrs Rees. Their heads were almost touching across the table. Their expressions were intense, not with desire, but with something else. They could have been talking about their marriage; they could just as easily be disagreeing over the colour scheme for a new kitchen.

Mary Jane folded herself into the car in much the same way as she had her seat in the restaurant; basically in three parts; lower legs, upper legs and torso.

A finely crocheted grey cape was draped around her shoulders and fastened with a pin at the front.

Mary Jane chatted all the way, recounting how often she'd contacted Sir Cedric in the privacy of her room. By

the time they'd reached Queens Square and the Francis
Hotel, Honey knew all about Sir Cedric's wives and which
one Mary Jane was related to.

'Fanny,' she pronounced emphatically. 'Fanny
Millington. Bob the Job actually located a picture of her;
just a sketch but enough to tell me she was a handsome
woman. She bore Sir Cedric six children. His first wife
didn't have any. Apparently she was fragile. I suppose
we'd say that Fanny had good genes.'

Honey couldn't argue with that. She knew Mary Jane
was at least seventy-five and still looking good.

'What about the third wife?'

'I don't know anything about her genes. Apparently she
ran off with the coachman and the marriage was annulled.'

Beaming broadly, she shrugged her square, bony
shoulders. ' Isn't family history just wonderful!'

Quite a crowd had gathered at the bottom end of
Queens Square, just along from the Francis Hotel.

Crocheted cape billowing in the breeze, Mary Jane
strode to join the other tourists. The merry band chattered
like magpies, full of excitement at the prospect of seeing
what few had ever seen, and pleased to pay for the
privilege.

Honey turned the steering wheel meaning to head back
to the hotel, when Loretta Davies emerged from Charlotte
Street at the top end of the square. She was wearing a
white blouse and a black skirt, regulation uniform for a
hotel waitress.

Honey hit the horn and opened the passenger side
window. 'Do you want a lift?'

Loretta opened the door and got in. 'Thanks. I've just
finished my shift. Working helps keep my mind off things.
I've made sure our place keeps going, but you just have to
get out, don't you?'

Honey agreed with her.

Despite the uniform, three gold earrings dangled from

Loretta's right ear. The white blouse was long enough to cover her belly button.

It was now nine-thirty. She calculated that Loretta had been on duty since mid-afternoon to be going home this early.

'Where do you work?'

'La Traviata.'

Honey recognised the name of an up-market Italian restaurant situated behind the world famous Royal Crescent.

Loretta slid her feet from her shoes.

'Me feet are killing me. I've been on since two.'

'Poor you. I didn't know you worked in the catering trade. I presumed you did a bit for your mother and had something else ... you know ... like an office job.'

'Not bloody likely. My mum likes things done her way. She gets Marge in to clean and do the laundry and ironing when it's busy. Especially now. I've hung around and looked after things, but it's only temporary. I had to get out. Honest I did.'

Her voice seemed to nose dive on the last two words. Honey decided that she was not quite as confident as she made out. She was hurting. Under the circumstances, it wasn't surprising.

The smell of trees bathed in darkness drifted into the car. So did the aroma of fast food joints; hamburgers, kebab shops and tacos bars.

Now was as good a time as any to ask the most difficult question. I might even get an answer, thought Honey. Either that or she'll tell me to bog off.

She decided it was worth the effort.

'What did your mother say – you know – about your stepfather ... doing what he did? I presume you told her.'

'Fat lot of good it did. She didn't believe me. Couldn't live without 'im, but could live without me.'

Honey bit her lip and kept her eyes on the road ahead. She felt so sorry for this girl, not just because it seemed her mother had not believed her. While being questioned, Doherty had asked Cora Herbert outright about her daughter's accusation. Her response had been casually indifferent, stating that her daughter could lie for England. In the next breath she'd declared how devastated she was.

They were fast approaching the Lower Bristol Road.

'I'll come in with you if I may,' said Honey. 'Just to see how your mum is bearing up.'

'Why?'

Loretta eyed her suspiciously.

'It's OK, isn't it?'

Loretta chewed her bottom lip. 'I suppose you can.'

To Honey's eyes Loretta was no longer the girl with the hard eyes and the blatant attempt to be sluttish. She was a little girl and vulnerable. How must it have felt to be raped by her stepfather and being too afraid to tell her mother, and when she did, not being believed?

The porch light was still on when they got there. Loretta had a key. Honey followed her along the passage leading to the rear kitchen and the small sitting room adjoining the conservatory.

Dishes were heaped in the sink. An empty tin of ravioli sat on the draining board. The place smelled of bacon fat, old teabags and Guinness.

Honey averted her eyes from a frying pan containing rashers of bacon – tomorrow's breakfast for residents.

'Mum?'

'I'm in here.'

The response came from Mervyn Herbert's 'den'.

Cora was on her knees tidying up, repacking what the police had unpacked, and putting it away. Her backside wobbled against her meaty calves as she did it.

'I hope I'm not interrupting anything.'

Cora stopped what she was doing and glared over her

shoulder. 'What do you want?'

'I saw Loretta and gave her a lift. I just thought I'd see how you were. It must have been quite an ordeal down at the station. Is there anything I can do to help?'

'Well you could start by finding a landscape gardener. My rockery's a right shambles.'

'Sorry. Can't help.'

Cora Herbert threw her a sneer before going back to what she was doing.

'Everything's a mess,' she grumbled. 'Bloody coppers! Mucking my place up like this. I've got a business to run. It's got to be a bit tidy, you know.'

'Yes. I know.'

Honey made a snap decision. If she was going to get this woman to trust her, she had to bend. Literally.

She knelt down beside her on the moss-coloured carpet. 'Let me help you.'

'Mervyn's watch collection,' explained Cora.

Honey took a look. Each watch was individually wrapped in old newspapers and repacked in a cardboard box.

'They look quite valuable,' she said.

'I wish,' muttered Cora. 'We'll let Bonhams find that out. The whole lot's going to auction.'

'I hope you get a good price for them. I'd put a reserve on them if I were you. Just in case.'

Cora's response was mumbled and begrudging.

Honey tried again.

'Honestly, Mrs Herbert, specialist collectors who are looking for certain items might give you quite a bit more than you'd get at auction. I can ask around if you like. In fact, there's a certain name that springs readily to mind. You might know him. Or perhaps Mervyn knew him. Casper St John Gervais?'

Cora shook her head in a vague manner as though not only didn't she know, she didn't really care.

'Never heard of the bloke.'

She'd had a similar response from Casper when she'd first seen the watch collection and wondered at the connection.

'I collect clocks, not watches,' Casper had said imperiously. 'And I never, ever frequent establishments along the Bristol Road!'

The flaps of the box were slapped firmly into place.

'Well that's that,' said Cora with an air of finality.

Honey noted that she got no thanks for her pains, but doubted Cora was ever grateful or gracious to anyone.

Honey got to her feet. 'I'll see myself out.'

Loretta was in the porch next to the conservatory swigging Coke from a can and staring out into the garden. There was something vulnerable about the girl. There was also something about Cora's behaviour that made her ask a further question.

'The police said your mother was surprised that you'd told me about your stepfather raping you. Why was that?'

The teenage shrug again, the sort of shrug that's meant to signify indifference but in fact conveys deep concern.

'She didn't want me to tell you. She didn't want me to tell anybody.'

It was like a gate closing. Not much of an answer, but she sensed it was the only one Loretta was prepared to give.

Outside the night sky had blurred to slate grey, it was that time in June and July when darkness never quite takes hold.

Honey took deep breaths and looked up at the sky as she tried to clarify her thoughts about the clues and the people. Some said that a crime was like a jigsaw puzzle; one bit fitted into another. It was just a case of gathering up the right bits and putting them into the right place. Trouble is, she thought, you have to find the bits in the first place.

For a start, there was Loretta's father. His motive for killing Mervyn Herbert was understandable. But Elmer Maxted? Everything began with the lone American here to trace his family tree. Surely Davies could not have had anything to do with killing him? Could he? The watches and clocks situation was also puzzling. Was it just a coincidence that Mervyn collected one and Casper the other?

She flicked open her phone and selected Casper's landline number.

'How well did you know Mervyn Herbert?'

He sounded taken aback at first, but quickly recovered. 'My dear girl, as I've already told you ...'

'I don't believe you. So! Who are you going to speak to? Me or the police?'

This was all instinct, a long shot. She sensed his unease. She'd asked quickly even before he'd had a chance to say hello.

There was a pause, a period when she felt she could almost hear his brain ticking over. If she closed her eyes she could even see his throat tightening.

'You'd better come on over.'

# Chapter Twenty-five

Pamela Charlborough drank deeply from a lead crystal wine glass while eyeing her husband over its rim. The wine tasted good but did nothing to make him look more appealing.

Once again she imagined him lying still and white instead of sitting at the same table with her, his hair almost white, his face mottled with broken veins. If he were dead she would get to keep the lifestyle and the wherewithal to maintain it. In her mind she blessed Sun Alliance and Royal Life. What a boon they were to modern living and the plight of the recently widowed.

Unfortunately, she wasn't widowed. For better or worse – mostly worse – she was still tied firmly to Andrew.

She breathed deeply as the aftertaste of the wine tantalized her taste buds and fumed upwards into her brain. She opened and closed her eyes as she took deep breaths. Each time she opened them her gaze alighted on things in the room she would keep and things she would throw out once he was dead. It was something she'd done a thousand times, her mind changing as things were added or taken away from the house according to how Andrew's dabbling in antiques – more notably clocks – was going.

The stuff from the Far East would be first to go, though she really couldn't see anyone bidding much for those dreadful bits of bamboo that fell over if you brushed too close. There was a table made of it, a coat stand and a matching umbrella stand complete with bamboo handled umbrellas and walking sticks.

She sighed. It was really all too much. The only flimsy things she adored were made of silk, edged with lace and extremely expensive. She still looked good in silky underwear. She smirked to herself. She looked pretty good out of it too.

The pristine white porcelain clock on the sideboard struck eight. Both her eyes and those of her husband went to it before looking at each other. A slow smile crossed her husband's face that made her glower. He was laughing at her, crowing because he'd got it back and grabbed the money she'd been paid for it from her luggage.

Simmering with rage, Pamela raised her wineglass in a mock toast. 'All right darling! You've got it back. Well bully for you!'

Andrew was drinking brandy. He swilled the amber liquid around his glass as he regarded her. His smile was contemptuous.

'Really Pamela. You have no taste and your propensity for seeking out the seedier side of society is really phenomenal. Fancy selling it to a second-rate clock dealer like Simon Tye. The man's a crook.'

'Necessity!' she snapped. 'I needed the money.'

'You spend too much.'

'You give me too little!'

'My dear, I must have been mistaken. I thought it was cheap to live in Spain. That's why it suits cheap people.'

Pamela sprang up from her chair sending it toppling backwards.

'I'm not cheap, Andrew! I'm normal!'

Her husband raised his eyebrows and glanced at her over the day's headlines. He read the newspaper in preference to conversing with his wife. Conversation was confined to necessary subjects. Like money.

'Now don't lose your temper darling. It emphasises your wrinkles.'

The lead crystal wineglass flew down the table. Andrew ducked.

'You bitch!' Andrew sprang to his feet.

Pamela stood her ground on four-inch mules, the soles of cork, the uppers made of interwoven pink and blue silk.

Andrew was on her before she could run. The back of his hand hit her face and sent her flying across the table. Hair tousled, eyes blazing and blood trickling from her lip, she glared up at him, her fingers gripping the table edge.

Her look was full of hate. 'Why did I marry you?'

Andrew was no less disdainful. 'Hah! Why did I marry you is more to the point?'

Her lips curled into a sneer as she pushed her hair back from her eyes.

'But I know why you married me. I was the barrier between your first wife's family and you and Lance. If they probed too close they'd find out the truth. As a widower you would still have attracted their attention and occasional visits. Marrying again put them at a distance. And I know, Andrew. He told me. Elmer Maxted told me!'

She laughed at his sudden pallor, knowing she'd hit the mark.

Clinging to the table edge, she struggled up from the floor her eyes shining.

'I know what you did. I know about Lance and who he is – who he really is.'

Andrew's jaw tightened. 'Shut your mouth. Or I shall shut it for you!'

Blood trickled into Pamela's mouth when she smiled.

'I can ruin you any time I like. But it won't cost you much to keep my mouth shut. I like Lance. I wouldn't want to ruin his life.'

Andrew said nothing, his pale eyes darting between her, the drinks cabinet and Mark Conway. Unheard by his wife, Mark was standing in the doorway, listening and waiting. Andrew threw him an unspoken message to stay.

Pamela, the worse for drink, carried on with her tirade.

'Lance, the real Lance bled to death. Haemophilia. He had haemophilia. Only men suffer from it you know. Yet it's passed on to them by their mothers. The American told me Lance had it – or at least the Lance he knew. But our big, grown-up Lance doesn't have it does he? Oh no, most certainly he does not. In fact, he's an extremely healthy young man. I wonder what his DNA would prove if they took swabs from you and him? But then, you already know the answer to that, don't you?'

'You're drunk.'

Pamela laughed. With half a bottle of Chateau Talbot sloshing around inside her, she staggered to the door, pausing to throw him a mocking wave.

'Spain here I come! And I don't give a hoot if I've got to crawl there!'

Gripping the banister, she dragged herself up to her room.

'Spain, sun, sea and sex! Here I come!'

She turned round when she got to the top, her eyes hovering over the scene beneath, the lush carpeting, the antiques, the smell of wealth and centuries of arrogance.

'The sex especially,' she shouted, her voice echoing over the pale cream walls where paintings of long-dead ancestors looked down on her and what the family had become.

Nothing could stop her now from saying what she wanted to say and would say even more. She wanted to hurt him. She wanted to pay him back for making her feel cheap. More than that; a marriage of convenience to someone he thought to control. And all she wanted to do now was to hurt him.

'Good sex happens with young men, not old has-beens like you!'

Trevor, her husband's butler and part-time gardener was also at the top of the stairs.

Pamela glared at him. 'What the hell are you staring at?'

'Nothing, madam.'

'Nothing, madam,' she mimicked. 'Nothing, madam!' God, but she hated these old retainers of his. Even they looked down at her, treated her with deference but also disdain.

She saw Andrew standing at the bottom of the stairs and swayed slightly.

'I bet you want me to fall down the stairs,' she shouted at him.

He said nothing. He didn't need to. She knew that was what he wanted.

'Be a good little husband, Andrew, and transfer some money into my account. Fifty thousand to start with.'

'I don't know that I can. Not that quickly.'

'Then sell a few things. Especially that clock! Yes! I insist you sell that clock in order to buy my silence. Now! Immediately.'

Although her vision was blurred, she saw the hatred on her husband's face. So what?

She began to laugh then tapped Trevor on the shoulder.

'Your master awaits you – Fido!'

She swayed again before staggering off to her bedroom.

The sound of the door slamming ricocheted around the landing.

Sir Andrew beckoned Trevor to follow him. 'I need to talk to you.'

'A rare example of a late eighteenth-century mantle clock. Can we start the bidding at one thousand pounds?'

Eleven-thirty in the middle of an auction room was not the best place for asking questions and getting answers. Honey assumed Casper had done it on purpose, especially when their meeting coincided with lot 75.

To her eyes the clock looked incredibly plain, but the

tense atmosphere in the saleroom confirmed its importance.

'Its provenance is indisputable,' whispered Casper as though he were in pain.

'It's plain.'

The auctioneer's voice filled the room. 'One thousand three, one thousand four, one thousand five …'

Casper was bidding. He did it casually, as though he didn't really care whether he bought it or not. But anyone who knew him would not have been easily deceived.

'It is said to have belonged to Jane Austen's father, sold to pay for his burial.'

'I didn't know Walcot Street church charged that much, seeing as he's buried next to the road.'

It was a joke. The graveyard had been peaceful back then. Now visitors could almost do a drive past, it was that close to the main A4.

Casper hissed at her to be quiet.

'Sorry. I'll wait for you outside.'

She slipped into the store opposite and purchased a chocolate muffin. Casper wasn't into eating in company so it was a case of grabbing what she could and eating it before he came out.

The traffic was heavy around Queens Square. The bin hanging from a lamppost received her food wrappers. She had time to brush the crumbs from her chest before Casper came strolling out of the auction house looking mighty pleased with himself.

'I take it you were successful?'

He nodded. 'Did you doubt that I would be?'

'I wouldn't dare.'

'Now, my dear girl. This fellow Herbert. He is, or rather was, very friendly with a clock and watch dealer named Simon Tye.'

'You never met him yourself?'

He shook his head. 'Absolutely not. But if anyone

knew him and his collection, it would be Simon Tye. Indeed, I do believe he referred to him once or twice.'

Honey thought of the watches and described them to him.

'They sound quite exemplary.'

'Do you think they could be stolen?'

'Ask the police.'

'That's him,' Casper said, pointing to where two men were manhandling a grandfather clock into the back of a dark blue Volvo estate. 'I'll introduce you.'

# Chapter Twenty-six

A Volvo estate. She just couldn't take her eyes off it.

'Is this your car?' she asked the man pointed out as Simon Tye.

Simon answered her a split second before Casper was about to butt in that he thought she was going to ask about watches.

'As matter of fact, no. It belongs to a friend.'

'Mervyn Herbert?'

He grinned. 'I know, I know. I should 'ave give it over to the coppers, but I was after this clock and me own jalopy is off the road.'

His blatant honesty astounded her.

'I wanted this clock,' he said on seeing her expression. 'The price was right, and for the mo I had the transport. OK?'

It sounded a reasonable excuse, but clues were stacking up. He'd known Mervyn. He'd known he'd collected watches. He also knew that his body had been found and here he was loading his latest purchase into the back of the deceased's missing car.

He caught her eyeing him with curiosity. 'Tell them I'll drop it round.'

His cheek amazed her. Her first priority had been to ask Doherty about the watches. Now she would first tell him about finding Mervyn's car.

'He lent me it prior to me buying it off him. He was off on one of his train trips and didn't want the car and said I could borrow it until I could scrape the money up together. You knew he liked trains, didn't you?'

She could hardly deny the fact, so nodded in agreement.

'If they want a look at it, they can. No prob.'

'No prob,' said Honey, flicking open her phone. 'I'll tell them you've got it.'

The desk sergeant showed her into an interview room. He also provided her with tea and biscuits.

Honey sucked on a chocolate digestive that she'd just dipped into her tea. Chocolate muffin followed by a chocolate digestive; not the healthiest diet in the world, but snatched on the hoof. That meant it didn't count towards consumed calories.

Through the window she could see the Georgian buildings at the back of Manvers Street. Her eyes travelled slowly over the back yards where weeds grew and stray moggies mated and fought. Down under the houses were deep cellars. Some stretched out under the road, with rough workshops behind iron grills. Some were damp, dark and musty. Others had been transformed into very nice basement apartments, or workshops and studios. The best, abutting the main thoroughfares, had become trendy wine bars and up-market restaurants.

Doherty looked as though he hadn't slept all night. 'Complicated,' he said in answer to her enquiring look.

'I left a message on your phone. I saw Mervyn's car this morning.'

He suddenly seemed to wake up. 'Where?'

She told him. 'A chap called Simon Tye said that Mervyn had lent him it prior to him raising the cash to buy it. He also said that Mervyn was going off travelling again.'

'You're kidding!'

She shook her head. 'You'll catch him unloading a

clock on the double yellow lines on the road closest to his shop if you want to give it the once-over.'

'You bet I do!'

She waited as he opened the door and shouted instructions to have both the car and Simon Tye picked up.

After he'd slammed the door shut, he scraped the chair back from the table, and sat astride, arms resting on the chair back.

'I take it from your lack of excitability that he wasn't too nervous about the murder.'

'No, he wasn't. You can never tell, though, can you?'

'Simon Tye is hardly whiter than white – call him pure as the driven slush. That would be about right.'

He went on to tell her that forensic were adamant that the number six ingrained on the rotten wood must refer to a house close to the river. But which house? Which street? There were a lot of houses and streets with access to the river.

'Does Simon Tye have a house close to the river?'

'I don't think so, but we'll check.' He eyed her as though not quite sure of what to say next. 'Tea OK?' He took a slurp of his own.

'Mmm,' she muttered, unable to get rid of the feeling that something was going on here. 'You sound as though you know where he lives.'

They both fell to comfortable silence.

Doherty suddenly surprised her. 'Are you free next Wednesday evening?'

She shook her head. 'Sorry. I've been invited to an open evening at a bookshop.'

'Please yourself.'

Tiredness. She could see all the signs.

'I will.'

She sensed that he wanted to ask her if she was going alone, but had curbed himself.

However, something was brewing, and it wasn't just

tea. He was fidgeting, rubbing his hands together, and his eyes were unblinking when he looked at her. It struck her as odd that he wasn't showing that much enthusiasm for pursuing enquiries regarding Simon Tye and the Volvo estate.

'OK,' she said, sensing he wanted her to ask what was afoot. 'You look as though you scored with a supermodel last night. What's up?'

'We've got him,' he blurted.

'And this is a celebratory tea?'

She raised her mug. It had a motif on the side saying *I Love Bath*. She flashed that side at him.

'Nice to see that the police are promoting tourism, if only in a small way.'

'I'm being serious. Robert Davies is in custody. We found him living with a girlfriend on a narrow boat at Bathampton.'

'I'm pretty serious too. Why do you think the Hotels Association are getting involved in police work? It's not because we've got nothing better to do.'

'We can't celebrate just yet, not until I've got a full confession.'

'You haven't got any evidence have you?'

His cheeks did a funny sucking in and out, as though she'd slapped him.

'Don't look at me like that.'

'Like what?'

'As though I'm not doing enough.'

'Are you being persuasive enough?'

'You mean, slap him around a bit, burn him with lighted cigarette ends or attach electrodes to his meat and two veg?'

'Is that what you do?'

'Nah! The Bill of Human Rights put a stop to all that. Anyway, I don't smoke so the cigarettes are out. And I'm not a qualified electrician. You know how it is with Health and Safety these days.'

'I see your point. You act within given guidelines. But I don't. You're the professional. I'm the amateur.'

'You Jane, me Tarzan.'

'Let's not be silly. Now. Important question. We can understand why Robert Davies would kill Mervyn.'

'Loretta's confirmed that she told him.'

'Right. But why would he kill an American he didn't know?'

'There is another possibility. Mervyn Herbert and Elmer Maxted were about the same build, same height. It's possible that the first killing was a case of mistaken identity.

Honey sniffed. 'A bit overdramatic in my book!'

'Look,' he said, mimicking her stance, knuckles on the desk and facing each other so that their noses were only inches apart. 'Trust me on this. Davies did both murders. I guarantee it.'

One look into those baby blue eyes, and her thoughts hit the buffers. It took some effort to get the wheels back on the line, but eventually she got everything – including her pole dancing hormones – back on track.

'What about the watches? Were they stolen?'

'Mrs Herbert provided receipts.'

Honey eyed the backs of Georgian houses through the window behind him. The view verged on the ugly. The crescents and squares were beautifully symmetric at the front. The backs of the properties were a different matter, carbuncles of varying shapes and sizes added in Victorian times.

'Steve, it doesn't make sense. How could one be so easily mistaken for the other? OK, I know they were the same height and build, but their features were so different. Their hair colour for a start.'

She'd only seen a passport photograph of Elmer Maxted, but she'd seen Mervyn Herbert. There were more differences than similarities.

'Clothes could make them look similar.'

'It's been warm this month and neither would have been bundled up in coats. People can disguise themselves if they're dressed for winter wearing scarves and mufflers, and thick padded jackets, but hi there, just in case you didn't notice, it's summer.'

'An English summer, though I'll grant you it's been fairly warm, but I still believe that he did it. The first victim was a case of mistaken identity. The second – well – I think we all know the reason for that. The bloke had it coming to him.'

'And the piece of wood? And the spice sacks? The wood had to come from somewhere, a house close to the river. And why spice sacks? Whoever killed these men had to have had access to a source. Otherwise, why not coal sacks or hay sacks, or even plastic bags?'

Honey glanced at her watch. 'Got to go. I've still got a hotel to run.'

*And maybe that delicious John Rees might have dropped by.*

'I'd really like to see you again,' he shouted after her as she headed for the door.

Her footsteps slowed then she thought of John Rees and they quickened again.

'I'll be in touch,' she called over her shoulder.

# Chapter Twenty-seven

Back at the Green River Hotel, things only *appeared* to be running smoothly.

Honey walked into the dining room and instantly felt an undercurrent of something askew.

Her mother was standing in front of a table, taking linen squares from one side of the table and folding them into table napkins.

Straight from the laundry and stiff with starch, they usually stood crisply upright. Today the folds were haphazard and the fan shapes they were supposed to represent flopped this way and that.

Normally meticulous about presentation, it was obvious to Honey that her mother's mind was elsewhere.

'Lindsey didn't come home last night. I don't think it's right.'

Lindsey's movements and behaviour continued to be a bone of contention between them. Honey thought Lindsey should be allowed free rein to make her own mistakes. Her mother thought she should have more boyfriends and even be thinking of getting engaged.

Honey had got into the habit of playing the problem down – because really there was no problem.

'Oh, I don't think she was that late. She was out with friends and told me she would be late coming in. It's no big deal.'

Her mother threw her an accusing look. 'Hannah, I may be on the downhill run to the time when I receive the centenary birthday card from the Queen, but I am not gaga. I still have all my marbles and I know that my granddaughter did not come home last night. I know this because I went in to make her bed this morning, but didn't need to. It hadn't been slept in.'

'She slept at Sam's,' said Honey.

'Sam? Who's he?'

'She. Samantha.'

She wasn't too sure whether Lindsey had a friend named Samantha, but it was as good an excuse as any.

A friend made up is a friend indeed.

The truth was that Lindsey had phoned and left a message on the answer phone saying she was sleeping at Sam's place. She didn't know of a female friend named Sam. No way was she telling her mother that.

The pinched lips straightened. 'That's all right then.'

Her mother's next subject was that Mary Jane was organising a séance in the hope that Sir Cedric would manifest himself on a more visual plain.

'I think she's nuts,' said her mother. 'But there. What can you expect from a woman of her age who dresses like a refugee from a Cindy doll factory?'

The phone burbled against her hip. She eyed the caller's number, didn't recognise it, but pressed receive anyway.

'Hi. This is John Rees.'

Flip went her heart. The day was turning brighter. What was it Lindsey had said? Better to be desired by two men rather than one.

'Just a minute.' She turned her back, her feet heading for the far corner of the restaurant.

'Who's that?' her mother called after her.

She took the phone outside where sun-dappled leaves rustled against a powder blue sky.

'I thought we needed to finalise things regarding the Victorian evening.'

'Of course.'

Swooning time. His voice reminded her of the southern guys in Elvis Presley's backing group – the sort of huskiness that comes down the nose rather than out of the mouth. Her legs turned to jelly.

'How about we meet up this evening. Have some dinner. Talk about all things Victorian?'

'Especially underwear. And foundation garments in general. The historical perspective.'

'Yes. The historical perspective. Nice angle.'

They arranged to meet at the George at Norton St Phillip, an ancient hostelry a few miles outside the city.

Both a brewery and inn for close on a thousand years, the place was a living museum. Leather harnesses, old flintlocks, rusty farm implements and bright brass lanterns hung from every beam, every spare bit of ceiling space. A pile of leaflets stating that the hostelry had been brewing since the fourteenth century steadily dwindled. A Japanese group were in, cameras strung around their necks, faces full of enthusiasm. One after another they went to the bar, scrutinised the leaflets and took what they wanted.

North American accents blended easily with those from Canada, Australia, New Zealand and South Africa. French, Italian, German and Dutch gabbled alongside Japanese and Spanish. The place was busy – as usual.

'Wow! Can you beat this!' John exclaimed, head back and eyes wide with wonder. 'Everything is so … old! Don't you just love it?'

'England's like that. Old, I mean.

'No point in visiting England if you don't like old,' he said, his smile warming parts some people's smiles couldn't possibly reach.

'Are you interested in history …?' she asked, then felt stupid. 'Sorry. Of course you are. That's the whole point of the exhibition, isn't it?'

If she'd been younger she would have blushed. The

thought was whimsical and fluttered around her mind pushing aside the remaining impetus to go knocking on doors bearing the numbers six and nine, at least for now. It wouldn't go away completely. She felt an affinity with Elmer Maxted. He'd come looking for his roots. She understood that. Daughter of an American father and an English mother, she'd floated between the two worlds not knowing quite where she belonged. Once he'd blotted his copybook her mother had blocked out her father's memory.

Like Carl and me. Could behaviour towards men be hereditary?

John was ordering food. She'd been running on automatic when she'd told him what she wanted – King Prawn salad in Cajun spices.

They were both driving so they stayed with soft drinks. Once that was done they got down to serious conversation – or as serious as it needed to be.

'So how long have you been running the hotel?'

She fingered her glass then took a sip.

'Two years now.'

'You must enjoy it.'

'Sometimes I enjoy meeting people. Sometimes I want to hide away from them.'

He made a so-so kind of face.

'Understandable. I suppose you don't get too much time off.'

'Not nearly enough. At least this police thing gets me out of the place. It's an interesting other dimension to the hospitality trade. She surprised herself by burbling on about the murder case and what Steve had said, and what she had said. She stopped herself when she thought she was giving too much away.

'I met your mother and your daughter.'

Honey smiled. 'The sugar and spice in my life – though don't ask me which is which.'

'Your daughter looks like you. Your mother ...'

She held up a warning finger. 'Please don't mention anything about broomsticks! OK?'

He grinned. 'I was going to say that she's quite a character.'

'That's a thought-provoking description.'

'Hey! You make her sound like Cruella de Ville.'

'No, my mother would never make a coat of puppies, though she might make a stew.'

He eyed her speculatively. Speculation and truth-seeking about her family was the last thing she needed.

'Only joking. She's just getting old and cantankerous,' she said lightly lowering her eyes as she sipped her drink.

Heaven help her if she ever found out she'd said that.

Over plates of magnificently pink prawns speckled with spice, their conversation turned to the exhibition. She watched his lips move as he told her about the guest list. They were strong lips, supple with words. And kissing, she thought. I bet they're good at kissing.

He told her the names of the wines he'd chosen and the fact that his sister-in-law had taken charge of the catering. She wanted to ask why his wife, the ice queen he'd brought into the restaurant, wasn't doing it, but it was none of her business. Keep to the facts, she thought to herself.

*Be a pleasant girl, Hannah!* Her mother's voice again. On this occasion she decided to take her advice.

'So what other historical artefacts have you managed to get hold of?'

He finished chewing a particularly fat prawn before he answered.

'A suit of armour, a sedan chair and a clock. Each represents a certain aspect of history. The suit of armour represents military history, the sedan chair represents the history of transport and the clock represents industrial history – the crowning glory of the industrial revolution.'

Her hair tickled her shoulder as she tilted her head to

one side.

'So where do Queen Victoria's unmentionables fit in?'

'Simple. They represent women's rights, the march towards emancipation.'

Honey coughed into her drink.

John looked surprised. 'Have I said something funny?'

Regurgitating her drink and in danger of having it come down her nose, Honey pinched her nostrils quite fiercely. It took a few seconds before she could answer.

'I can't quite see the connection between a massive pair of crutch-less bloomers and the onward march of women's emancipation.'

'Big underwear. Big skirts. Women's movement was restricted by their clothes. Then came the twentieth century and – WHAM – everything changed.'

'Though not very quickly.'

'OK, no. Not very quickly, well not until the twenties, the Charleston and the flappers. But it happened. Women finally escaped big skirts, tight corsets and big underwear.'

'So my pair of bloomers are the before part of the equation.'

'Right.'

'Imagine all the things you wouldn't be able to do if you wore a big skirt.'

She was thoughtful as she watched him mop up the remains of his meal with a piece of granary bread.

As she raised her glass to finish off the last of the wine, she caught sight of a familiar face. Loretta Davies saw her, pushed back her chair and marched over.

Loretta was drunk. The smell of wine fell from her mouth and her eyes were bright with too much of it.

She was wearing an embroidered tunic and green leggings. Rings still adorned her fingers and dangled from her ears. Honey gave silent thanks that her pasty belly was covered.

'You know they've arrested my father.'

Honey half rose. 'Yes, I'm so sorry, Loretta.'

'He didn't do it.' She shook her head slowly as she said it, each individual movement coinciding with each spoken word. 'He didn't,' she added defiantly, as though those two last words confirmed everything not contained in the evidence.

Other diners cast looks in their direction.

Honey looked across in the direction Loretta had come from to check who she was with. Cora had kicked back her chair and was on her way over.

'Come away, girl. You're making a scene. No point in doing that, and anyway, Mrs Driver can't help you. She's not police. She don't carry any weight at all.'

Loretta calmed down. Cora took hold of her hand and began to guide her away.

She paused suddenly and eyed Honey over her shoulder.

'They've told me not to touch any of Mervyn's stuff until you lot take another look at things. Robert didn't do it. I know he didn't.'

Honey couldn't think of a single solitary thing to say that would help. But somehow she felt Cora deserved some help; she deserved it, married to the likes of Mervyn.

She sipped at a glass of water as she thought it through. What piece of evidence was there that could possibly let Robert Davies off the hook?

The only thing that sprang to mind was the impression of a number in a piece of wood.

John's voice suddenly invaded her thoughts.

'Judging by the look on your face, I guess we'd better call it a day,' he said.

'I'm sorry.'

Her gaze strayed to the heavy oak door shutting behind Cora and her daughter.

'They need support as much as sympathy.'

And I have plans to make, she told herself.

201

First she had to go back to Charlborough Grange and ask if Elmer Maxted had visited the house itself, not just the church or talking to Pamela Charlborough over the wall.

She sighed. Not this afternoon. She still had a business to run. Tomorrow would do, and she didn't need to go alone.

She was aware that John Rees was studying her closely, a slight frown feathering his brows.

'Are you doing anything tomorrow?' she asked him.

A lock of fair hair fell over his eyes as John shook his head.

'Fancy a drive in the country?'

He grinned. 'Sure. Where to?'

'Charlborough Grange. Do you know where it is?'

'Sure. Of course I do. That's where the guy lives who's loaning me this very clock, one that was first shown at the Paris Exhibition.'

# Chapter Twenty-eight

A summer shower had come and gone and the sun had stepped out from behind a pink puffy cloud.

The main A36 that ranged out of Bath and up through Freshford was as wet and shiny as a docile river. A rainbow stretched from one side of the valley to the other. The road, the valley, the river and canal snaked towards it.

'It's not really true to say that this is an afternoon drive,' she said to John Rees.

To her surprise he agreed with her.

'It's a great opportunity to finalise arrangements for the loan of the clock. Business and pleasure; what could be better?'

Her phone rang just as they pulled up outside. It was Steve Doherty.

'Guess where Davies has been living?'

She didn't want to guess. From the moment she'd squeezed into the bucket seat in John Rees's Austin Healey, the real world and her concerns had folded in on itself – a bit like the way she'd folded into the seat, skirt thigh high and knees slightly apart and pressed against the dashboard. Elegant she was not!

The warmth of John's thigh was pressing against hers. Who cared that the day was warm? A little more heat of this type was perfectly acceptable.

She thought about hitting the 'busy' button. Doherty pre-empted her action.

'Honey? Are you there?'

Too late!

'Go on. Hit me.'

'Prior to the narrow boat, Davies was living in a flat in Charlotte Terrace. Right next to the river. Number SIX Charlotte Terrace! We've got him!'

She could imagine his face, the wide-open eyes, the smile fixed like that of a painted clown. No. Clown was wrong. He was a man doing his job in a straitjacket. He had rules and guidelines, the media and a demanding public to deal with. He was also quite dishy, an uninvited thought that had the effect of making her remove her thigh from that of John Rees.

'Did you find any evidence?'

'Circumstantial, but enough. See? I told you he was the right man.'

Doherty was cock-a-hoop that he'd found the culprit. Either he hadn't latched on to the note of misgiving in her voice, or he'd ignored it. The inclination to tell him she was still unconvinced played second fiddle today. He deserved support.

Once she'd conceded that he was right, the connection was terminated.

'All set?' said John.


Rose petals disturbed by the wind were blowing across the gravel driveway at the front of Charlborough Grange.

Mark Conway was standing in front of the main door. He looked as though he'd been expecting them.

There was hostility in his eyes, but, my, he certainly knew how to control it, Honey thought. His mouth smiled independently – almost as though they were long-lost friends.

He listened attentively as John explained why he was there.

'The clock ...' He expressed himself eloquently and was straight to the point. Mark Conway nodded.

He nodded. 'Ah, yes, sir. I am aware of the arrangement. Please come this way.'

If Mark Conway had recognised her as having visited before, he did not acknowledge it.

They were shown into the conservatory and invited to sit on Lloyd loom chairs. Gratefully they sank into cushions covered in heavy cotton on which huge roses flourished. Mark went off to alert Sir Andrew.

'It's pretty hot in here,' said John, wiping the back of his hand across his forehead. He looked around pop-eyed. 'Hey. Look at this. A genuine Victorian conservatory.'

With Honey it wasn't so much the history that made the impression.

'This place gives me the creeps. Don't you think those plants look like refugees from *The Day of the Triffids*?'

He eyed them sceptically. 'I have to say that this place grows on you. Like moss might grow on you if you were dead. It's probably just its age.'

'Come on. It's creepy. Admit it.'

He gave her a direct look.

'Sure. I think I'm picking up vibes.'

'Please. No paranormal stuff.' She explained about Mary Jane. 'One doctor of the paranormal is enough for one day!'

Charlborough chose that moment to make an impressive entrance.

Honey could hardly bear the look on his face; the confidence with which he strode towards them, his face a picture of patrician bonhomie.

'Good day to you both. It's about the clock of course. Pleased to help out.'

Today he was casually dressed in pale green lambswool sweater and matching trousers. The collar of a checked shirt showed above the 'V' neck of his sweater.

'John Rees, isn't it? How are you, my dear fellow?'

'I'm good. Real good. I thought I would drive out and

go over the final arrangements with you – if that's OK with you. If it's not inconvenient that is?'

'No, no, my dear fellow! Not at all!'

Perhaps it was the way John said it, or perhaps the way he looked, but Charlborough seemed unable to say no.

Charlborough turned his attention to Honey. John leapt in with an introduction.

'This is Honey Driver. She collects antique clothes,' John explained.

They shook hands. Recognition clouded his eyes then was gone. His smile was tight, his grip limp.

'I came here in my capacity as liaison officer for the Hotels Association. I asked you about Elmer Maxted.'

'Ah, yes,' he said with a stiff nod of his head. 'I seem to recall that you'd mislaid an American tourist.'

The terminology irritated.

'He was not mislaid. He was murdered.'

'Ah! And the police have arrested the perpetrator?'

She couldn't help but get the impression that he already knew. News travelled fast – the 'old boys' network was rife with senior police chiefs and crown court judges.

'They have arrested someone. Whether they make the charges stick is, as always, a different matter.'

'Quite so.' He turned immediately to John. 'Now about my clock …'

Honey's gaze wandered to the gardens and grounds beyond the thick foliage and the stifling conservatory. A church spire pierced the sky above a row of rustling poplars. The humidity, all for the benefit of the monstrous plants, was unbearable. She began dabbing at her glistening cheeks with the back of her hand.

'I'm sorry,' she said, interrupting their conversation, 'would it be all right if I went outside for some fresh air?'

For a moment she detected indecision on Charlborough's face, as he weighed up the consequences of granting or refusing his permission.

'Sorry for boring you,' John said as casually as you'd like. 'We're rambling into the realms of history.' He grinned across at Sir Andrew. 'Not everyone is as fascinated by the subject as we are. A little fresh air helps blow the cobwebs away so they say.'

Charlborough's expression veered between arrogance and pained forbearance. 'Of course.' He turned to Honey. 'Please keep to the garden area. I have projects under way in the rest of the grounds.'

'Not more decapitations,' she said laughingly.

'No. Not real ones anyway,' he smiled back.

Her sweat cooled once she was out in the fresh air. Steps led down from the raised area outside the conservatory. Red and orange nasturtiums trailed from weathered urns. A balustrade of moss-covered stone ran around its perimeter.

Manicured lawns of epic size and decorous design swooped between the flowerbeds and trees, like a river running towards the sea. Unlike a river, these lawns ran up against a red brick wall. The mortar joining the bricks was white and smeared, the bricks uneven and irregular, signs of age and aging. An arched wooden door, the sort found in churches and medieval castles, dissected the wall just before it disappeared behind a laburnum. Nothing of a gardener, she vaguely remembered that laburnum flowers were poisonous.

The door might not have beckoned so strongly if Charlborough hadn't ordered her – yes – *ordered* her to stay within the garden. But there it was, a cast-iron ring hanging there, waiting to be touched, turned and pulled.

The door opened. There again were the huge greenhouses thick with greenery, far more profligate than the huge specimens thronging the conservatory. And the size … a football pitch? At least. It was huge!

The roof curved like those on wartime structures, now disintegrating under the onslaught of the years and the weather. Sandbags piled a dozen or so high protected its entrance. A shovel stood upright in a pile of sand beside a wooden fruit box – the sort used for storing oranges.

Just like the last time, no one was around. She wondered when they actually held these war games that people paid to fight.

The only sound was of birds and bees. Just as she'd hoped there were a few loose sacks on the ground next to the sand.

Sacks!

She grabbed one and shook out the sand. Holding it with both hands, she scrutinised its size. It looked too big. Just to make sure, she took a deep sniff. It smelled of new sacking and the tangy sea smell of sand.

Still clinging to the sack, she turned to leave, her heels sinking into the damp earth.

Suddenly the door to the greenhouse made a wheezing sound. Humid air poured out tainting the freshness of a day after rain.

The fact that someone had come out with the tepid air did not register as quickly as it should have done. The sandbags were piled high and hid him until they were facing each other, each taken off guard, each unsure of how to proceed.

'You.'

The same man as the time before. The man Sir Andrew had referred to as Trevor. Some kind of butler. Some kind of nightmare. Big, broad-shouldered and seemingly devoid of coherent speech.

She brazened it out. 'It's OK for me to be here. I got a little hot in the conservatory. Sir Andrew said I could go outside.'

He had a square face, a down-turned mouth, deep-set eyes and shoulders that, although wide, totally lacked muscle definition. It was as though they had been cut out of stone and the sculptor had not as yet chiselled in the bodily details. Eye colour was hidden in the dark hollows beneath his brows.

He scared her. It was like coming across Frankenstein's monster on a dark and dirty night, except that it was daytime.

She sensed for her own protection, that she was the one who should first offer an explanation.

She held the sack behind her back, letting it fall slowly to the ground.

'I'll make my way back now. I was promised a pot of tea.'

Not the entire truth, but close enough.

The man standing before her shifted his weight on to the opposite leg; either his tension was dissipated or he was about to make a grab for her.

Discretion immediately became the best part of valour. Her legs propelled her back to the door and the manicured lawns, the house and the overpowering heat of the conservatory.

Hidden behind a sweet-smelling bush, she took the opportunity to catch her breath, daring to look behind her when she was sure no one was following.

Sir Andrew had said that Trevor was just a gardener tending the greenhouse. But the unease remained. Was it really only for war games, or was it something more sinister? Drugs were the obvious answer if she cared to take a jaundiced view of Sir Andrew. But what sort of drugs grew to that height?

'Better now?' asked John when she got back.

She forced a casual smile, the sort that worked well with pink cheeks and being slightly breathless.

Sir Andrew eyed her with distrust. 'I'm so glad you feel better.'

'Yes. Thank you.'

She wondered if he had guessed that she'd disobeyed his orders, but wasn't given the chance to find out.

The sound of a woman's voice seemed to splinter the beams of weak sunlight that had managed to shine through the canopy of plants.

'Darling, I didn't know we had visitors!'

Pamela Charlborough's hair was Helsinki blonde. Her face was Bermuda bronze. She wore a red silk dress that rustled when she walked and her perfume smelt of money.

Her bare arms were covered in freckles and her toenails were painted the same colour as her dress and the high-heeled mules she wore. A gold chain glistened around her ankle.

Gold and good make-up wasn't all she had on board. Flushed cheeks and a saucy swaying of her whole body betrayed that she'd been drinking.

'Booze for breakfast, booze for lunch and booze for dinner,' she said raising a very full wine glass. 'It's basically replacement therapy. It replaces sex. Can't get any of that in this house, can I, darling?'

'Pamela, you're drunk,' growled her husband.

Pamela appeared not to have heard him, her flushed face turned to the American bookseller.

'And who might this be? Another of your little soldier friends? My, but he's out of uniform! You should reprimand him at once, darling. Bend him over your lap, pull down his trousers and smack his tight little bottom!'

Her attention transferred to Honey.

'Oh! A little woman soldier perhaps?' Her features screwed up like discarded paper as something occurred to her. 'Don't I know you from somewhere?'

'Pamela!'

The broken veins in Charlborough's cheeks spread over his face like a raging forest fire.

Lady Pamela looked surprised. 'Have I got the wrong end of the stick, darling?'

Sir Andrew's face was like thunder. 'Go away, Pamela!'

John was looking embarrassed.

Honey found herself feeling embarrassed that she was of the same sex as the sun-tanned blonde.

Once she was within range to see Honey's face more clearly Lady Charlborough's eyes narrowed.

'Didn't you come here before? Yes! I'm sure you did.' She turned to Sir Andrew. 'Oh, my dearest, darling, what have you been up to now?'

These two were far from being dearest, darling to each other.

Sir Andrew looked daggers. 'You are drunk!'

'Oh, am I, darling? Then I'd better stop at once.'

She laughed, took a few steps forward then poured her wine into a potted plant. The wineglass followed its contents, the bowl breaking from its stem.

Her husband was far from amused.

'Pamela! For God's sake, that's Waterford Crystal!'

Smirking stupidly, Pamela Charlborough hid her mouth behind her hand.

'Silly me. Should not have said those dreadful things should I. Naughty, naughty things.' She laughed again.

Although Charlborough looked thoroughly embarrassed, Honey found it hard to pity him. The role of being lord of the manor was ingrained in him. This was hardly the first trophy wife to end up feeling trapped and disappointed with the older, richer man she had married.

'I apologise for my wife's rudeness.' Sir Andrew's voice dropped an octave or two and his apology seemed sincere.

'We get on best when we're apart,' said Lady Pamela. 'In fact I'm off to Spain tonight. My husband is footing the bill. Aren't you darling?'

'I trust they won't have run out of Sangria by the time you get there,' said Honey, her smile and tone as sarcastic as she could make it.

Pamela wagged a perfectly manicured finger. 'Aren't

you presently playing at being a detective? I recollect you mentioned this when we met before.'

'Yes.' Honey maintained her smile. 'I probably recollect it more clearly than you do.'

The inference was obvious but took a while to sink in. Once it did, the insincerity of her ladyship's smile was echoed in her eyes.

'Well that's the way it is with trade, isn't it? I presume one has to do everything one can to make ends meet.'

They left with arrangements fully made for the loan of the clock, Lady Pamela inviting John to stay at her private villa if ever he came to Spain. Honey was ignored.

'Bitch,' muttered Honey once they were in the car and heading back to Bath.

'I think her husband is of the same opinion,' said John.

'A divorce in the making?'

'You bet. I've been lucky in that respect. My ex-wife is very convivial.'

The slim, gorgeous creature? Honey had to find out. 'Was that her ...'

'In the restaurant the other night? Yes. We're still good friends. When either of us has a problem, we talk it through together.'

Honey's interest in John Rees was instantly resurrected. He was just her type; good-looking, pleasant and available.

'Your wife sounds like a decent sort – a lady in fact – which is more than I can say for Lady Pamela Charlborough.'

# Chapter Twenty-nine

The stables surrounding the yard to the rear of Charlborough Grange had been turned into garages years ago. Where past members of the family had kept their hunters, carriage horses and children's ponies, the present incumbents kept their Mercedes saloon, their four by four and a variety of sports cars, all with dents in the bodywork, some complete write-offs. Lady Pamela loved speed almost as much as she loved men, money and booze.

Mark Conway was servicing the engine on Pamela Charlborough's Mercedes Sports, which was presently the one with fewer dents than the others.

Slick with sweat, he pulled his T-shirt away from his body, pulled it up from his belly, and mopped at his face. The action hid his smile and even went some way to masking the smell of her perfume.

He knew she was watching him; had seen his bare torso, the line of hair that dipped down below the waistband of his jeans.

Her heels made a clicking sound as she crossed the concrete yard. Even without looking he knew her hips were swaying provocatively as she sashayed towards him.

She came up close, her hip brushing against his.

'Darling,' she breathed. 'You are coming to Spain with me, aren't you?'

The raised bonnet of the car threw a shadow across his face. It also went some way to hiding him from the house.

'I'm wanted here,' he said without taking his attention

from the engine.

Despite his resolve not to cave into her, his blood raced when she touched him. She licked her lips as she ran her hands down his back, tracing his muscles beneath the thin fabric of his T-shirt.

'I want you in Spain,' she said. 'I want you all ways and which ways in Spain.'

His bare biceps were hard beneath her hands. She sucked in her breath. 'You have such a beautiful body, Mark.'

'I'm busy.'

Although he tried to shrug her off, she clung on. Her fingertips tantalised the nape of his neck. He smelled alcohol when she whispered in his ear.

'Imagine making love on a deserted beach or high on a cliff top overlooking the sea.'

He turned his back to her while wiping his oily hands on a rag.

'Your husband might not like that.'

'I would like it,' she breathed. 'You know I would.'

Her fingers travelled along his jaw.

'I thought you loved me,' she said in a silly doll-like voice.

'Then you got it wrong. I've made love to you. If you can call it that.'

'Whatever. It's enough for me. And I thought we'd agreed … you know … that afternoon. You agreed to get rid of him.'

'I thought it was down to you to get rid of him – you know – divorce.'

'The money, darling. The money. If you want to share the money with me, you have to get rid of him good and proper.'

He fancied she was mocking him, talking as though she hailed from the East End of London – like his family, coming to Somerset to settle for the good life.

'And how do I do that?'

'Fix his brakes,' she whispered. 'Make it look like an accident.'

He stared at her wishing he'd never given in to her, but also wanting her again. And again.

'You really mean it.'

'Of course I do. You look appalled, my darling boy.' She sounded surprised.

With a look of disdain fractured with disbelief, he shrugged her hand from his arm. 'I can't believe you're saying it. I can't believe you'd want me to do it.'

She stroked his face and kissed him.

'Believe it.'

Honey checked herself in the mirrored doors of the dining room. This evening she'd chosen to wear a white linen suit with a blue-and-silver rope belt and a dark blue silk top. Casual but classy, her favourite words when it came to fashion.

'These earrings,' said Lindsey who had insisted on helping choosing her clothes, had made up her face, and was now choosing her accessories. 'And this bracelet.'

'Whatever you say.'

Having someone make all the decisions was unbelievably wonderful.

'And remember to be home before twelve,' said Lindsey with a crafty grin.

'Will I change into a pumpkin if I don't?'

'No, but you'll be locked out if you forget your key.'

'I promise I won't sleep over.'

'Just knock the handsome prince off his feet.'

'Is there a sure-fire way to do that?'

Lindsey shrugged. 'How would I know? You're the one with the experience.'

'You would tell me if there was anyone special in your life?' Honey asked her. 'As in Sam? Who is he?'

Lindsey tutted and shook her head. 'You couldn't resist, could you? You had to ask.'

'I worry about you.'

'Just take it from me that he's a great guy. There's a lot between us. Just how much, only time will tell.'

'How old is he?'

'I think that's enough information for now.'

'I know when I've been shown the red card.' Honey held up her hands in mute surrender. 'I am off to meet Prince Charming.'

'Are you going out?'

Her mother's voice! She'd arrived wearing Donna Karan and smelling of Chanel N° 5.

'Yes,' replied Honey through gritted teeth.

'With a man?'

'Yes.'

'Do I know him?'

'Not really.'

Gloria Cross sucked in her breath.

'It's that bookseller! Or is it that policeman? Please don't let it be that policeman.'

She made it sound as though going out with him would be tantamount to going out with Frankenstein's monster.

It wasn't easy, but Honey kept her cool.

'It's one of them. Possibly two in the same night.'

'And what shall I tell Mr Paget?'

'Mother, are you talking about the dentist?'

'He earns a very good living.'

She said it as though pulling people's teeth was as important as overseeing the International Monetary Fund.

'And that, my dear mother, is reason enough not to be interested. I'll look him up when I need a tooth pulled. Is there a specific reason for this visit?'

Her mother pouted her apricot lips. 'Mary Jane's séance.'

'I forgot!'

'Yes, you forgot, Miss Know All!'

She marched off.

With a sigh as heavy as a sack-load of old horseshoes, Honey slumped over the reception desk.

'Come on, Mum. You're going out.'

Honey raised her head a few inches off the desk.

'Why does she make me feel guilty?'

'It's her way. Now come on. Your prince awaits you.'

Lindsey took hold of her shoulders and guided her to the door.

Her mother reappeared having merely paid a visit to the ladies room.

'So you're not coming to the séance. Well, how cruel is that? Mary Jane will be so disappointed.'

Honey looked at her daughter and whispered, 'Mary Jane or John Rees? Should I flip a coin?'

'You're off. Never mind the séance. Grandma and I will go. Won't we, Grandma?'

Gloria Cross glanced from daughter to granddaughter.

'You're conspiring against me. Don't deny it.'

'Grandma! I'm going to the séance with you. We'll have fun. Let's see if Grandpa comes through.'

Her grandmother rolled her eyes. 'Heaven forbid!'

Union Passage is a traffic-free thoroughfare of specialist shops with narrow frontages; some unchanged since Beau Brummell was a lad.

Street musicians and jugglers rub shoulders with tourists looking for a bargain and office workers looking for a lunchtime sandwich. Despite the shops selling video games, mobile phones and computer graphics, it has retained its Dickensian charm.

Ideal for a bookshop, thought Honey, walking with confidence through the gathering dusk on a balmy July night.

John Rees had been lucky enough to lease a shop still

retaining an old-fashioned frontage of Art Deco design. The theme of the framework supporting the window was taken across the glass in the form of a transparent Beardsley-type woman. Typically she had flowing tresses and gown, her willowy arms framing the central display.

A hum of conversation and the tinkle of glasses drifted out of the open door. With luck the night air would drift in. Few shops in Bath boasted air-conditioning and although linen was cool it creased easily.

Making up in depth what it lacked in breadth, the shop was choc-a-bloc with people jostling as if in a queue, wine glasses held tightly to chests.

Cut glass voices droned on about the meaning behind an author's work or the reasons why women were forced – *forced* – into wearing corsets.

'It was a man's way of keeping a woman submissive,' the dreaded Audrey Tyson Dix was imparting to a politely attentive John Rees.

Honey stood on tiptoe to ensure that their eyes met.

John saw her and smiled, swiftly introduced Audrey to someone else and eased himself in her direction. He managed to grab a glass of wine en route.

'Glad you could come.'

'It's a tight squeeze,' she said. As she said it a woman with a bookshelf bosom and belly to match squeezed between them. Despite the fact that she'd eased through sideways, Honey ended up with her wine glass pressed against her nose.

John grabbed her hand.

'Follow me.'

Holding her wine glass high, she did as she was told.

'There's steps here,' he said over his shoulder. 'Three steps.'

She tottered forward, feet unseen.

'And some more.'

Her feet seemed to sprout eyes and feel their way.

'Another three.'

Eventually, they were at the back of the shop and had room to breathe.

John nodded towards the area where the crowd was thickest. 'Never mind the culture, you can see what they've really come for.'

Sadly, he was right. The wine and food had been placed on a table at the front of the shop on the lowest level. That was where the crowd was thickest. From where they were standing at the highest point at the far end of the shop, they could see it all.

She smiled up at him and clinked her glass against his. 'There are always exceptions.'

He smiled back. 'I'm glad to hear it. Would you care for a look at the exhibits?'

'OK.'

First stop was her own property.

'Yours of course.'

'Not literally,' she said, shaking her head. 'They might have been OK for Queen Victoria. Passion killers, still they can't have put Albert off. They had nine kids I believe.'

'I suppose it all depends what turns you on. Big though.'

'You're right there. I barely saved them from one of my foreign waitresses who presumed they were a tablecloth. My mother calls them *Harvest Festivals*. All is safely gathered in.'

'Can't say I'm surprised.'

Her eyes strayed to Sir Andrew's clock. John followed her gaze.

'He insisted I insure it.'

Honey frowned. 'I've only met the owner a few times, but already I get the impression that it's the love of his life.'

John tilted his head to one side as he observed it. 'Not

exactly. I hear he idolises his son, Lance.'

'Is that so? I haven't met him.'

'He's at Harvard, though, I get the impression, unwillingly. It was his grandfather's wish and a provision in his will that Lance finished his education there. The old man left all his money to his daughter, but when she died everything went to him. Seems he was only a kid at the time, not much more than a baby.'

'I wonder what she was like in comparison to Lady Pamela?'

'A bit more of a lady, I think.'

'I can believe that. I don't see her here, I thought she might put in an appearance seeing as there's free wine on offer.'

'I understand she's leaving for Spain. Sir Andrew phoned me earlier. He's promised to show up later but made apologies on his wife's behalf.'

Honey's gaze slid to the horde of hungry guests.

'He'll have to squeeze himself in.'

John looked at his watch. 'He did promise.'

'Well I doubt that he's accompanying his darling wife to Spain. I think he must hate Spain as much as he does her.'

John shrugged and took a slug of wine. 'Understandable. He was living there when his wife died in a car crash. Head-on, just her and the boy. Luckily Lance survived.'

They moved slowly along the exhibits: the books, memorabilia, lace mittens, bonnets, old tools, etc.

'Look at these,' he said. He indicated a few sheets of newspaper preserved behind glass. 'Do you know it's only in the last hundred years or so that newspapers were available to everyone? Facts were shouted out by town criers and passed mouth to mouth. Truth could be mighty distorted between source and target audience back then.'

Honey squinted to read the tiny print of the oldest

newspaper he had there. 'It's a wonder any news ever got through.'

'Great battles and occasions; it all got through OK. My dad kept old newspapers covering the war years. He used to bring them out now and again just to remind himself of what he'd gone through.' John's voice took on an aura of sadness. 'It's surprising how reading an old newspaper can jog the memory.'

'Yes,' she murmured, still squinting. 'Old newspapers can be ...' Suddenly it hit her. Old newspapers. Old news, forgotten by some but interesting to others.

'That's it!'

John frowned at the glass she'd shoved into his hand.

She felt elated and guilty; elated at what should have been obvious – newspapers. Old news. And having to leave the party.

'I have to go.'

'Was it something I said?'

'Yes,' she groaned, touching his face with her fingertips. 'John, would you think I was too forward if I told you that I wanted to take you to bed?'

He shook his head. 'No.'

'Oh, that's wonderful. But I can't hold you to that just yet. There's something I've got to do. Can you keep it warm for me? I can't say I'll be back tonight, but imminently. What do you say?'

'That's good for me.'

He looked happy when she kissed him on the cheek. 'A consolation prize,' she said to him. 'Bear with me.'

Every step to the shop door was painful, not just because it was slow but because business was overriding pleasure.

She had to get to where it had all began, and clocks had nothing to do with it. A few steps along Union Passage and she recalled what she'd said to John Rees and almost flipped at how forward she had been. You're a mature woman, she reminded herself. You can do anything you want.

She didn't hear him following her. She wasn't meant to. That was the good thing about wearing trainers. OK, your feet might end up stinking, but no one heard you following.

He saw her take her phone from out of her pocket and tap in a number. Judging by the brief moment the phone was next to her ear there was either no signal or the battery was flat.

He'd expected her to return to the hotel. Instead she headed for the taxi rank outside the Abbey.

Swearing beneath his breath, he pushed his way through the crowds strolling around, recording their visits to the city on digital camcorders and cameras and stopping to sniff the aroma of up-market cuisine wafting on the evening air.

His eyes followed her as she wove through the crowds. He saw her get into a taxi.

Suddenly a text came through to him on his own phone. He read the message quickly. He was wanted. It wouldn't take long. He'd catch up with Honey Driver later.

# Chapter Thirty

Lady Pamela Charlborough snapped shut the clasp of her Gucci handbag and, turning to her husband, put on a confident front.

'My car's broken. Mark will have to drive me to the airport. I've booked a hotel. He can stay overnight.'

Her husband took quick strides across the room, caught her wrist and squeezed hard.

'You expect me to believe that? But don't worry. I'm not jealous. Sorry for the poor sod. That's all.'

'Stop it! Stop it! You're hurting me.'

He tightened his grip.

'Good. I want to hurt you.'

He smiled at the thought of her feeling pain, the discomfort as her veins filled up with trapped blood.

He brought his face close to hers.

'Let me go!'

'How can I let you go my little darling, you who think you have the right to dispose of my possessions even before I am dead, things that I prize, things that have been in this house for years.'

'I needed the money!' she snapped.

His face closed on hers. His hand encompassed her neck before his thumb pressed on her windpipe.

'You need!'

She tugged with both hands at his fingers, eyes wide with fear as she struggled for breath.

He was doing this with only one hand, still holding his

brandy glass in the other.

The feel of her squirming against his strength excited him. Her mouth was open. He knew she was trying to scream but no sound came out.

Such was the strength and tension in his fingers, that the hand not compressing his wife's throat snapped the stem of the brandy balloon.

Pamela's eyes were bulging, her face changing colour.

Feeling an incredible surge of excitement that he hadn't felt for years – not since he'd left active service; not since he'd come home from killing people, he brought the jagged edge of the stem close to her face.

She mouthed all the most profane words she knew yet no sound came out. But he understood. She could see from his eyes that he understood. It had been years since she'd been this close to him and it scared her. He looked as if only part of him was in the room. The rest was somewhere else.

Suddenly he let go. Staggering and gasping for air she ran for the stairs.

Once the bedroom door was safely locked, clothes, shoes and toiletries flew into her luggage. Lingerie was wound into balls; shoes were shoved haphazardly amongst delicate laces, silks and cashmere.

Passport and essentials were thrown into a tan leather bag with the famous Gucci symbol on the side. Her mobile fell onto the silk and satin counterpane.

Her enhanced breasts heaved and she coughed a little before regaining control, before even being able to speak.

She stared at the passport. Revenge was like an ice-cold knife between her ribs. It was not in her power to destroy Andrew, but she could make things difficult for him – swine that he was.

She phoned the police, asked for whoever was in charge of the case and told him that the murdered American HAD visited Charlborough Grange.

'It would be very worthwhile if you questioned my husband.'

Doherty noted what she said. 'We do already have someone helping us with our enquiries. I'll let you know if we need to speak to you or your husband again.'

Frustrated by his answer, she slammed the disconnect button. Someone had to be interested.

Her! The hotel liaison person! She'd left her card.

Honey answered on the fourth ring.

'My husband lied. The American was here,' she said once the initial introductions were taken care of.

'That's interesting. Thank you very much.'

Lady Pamela's mouth remained open. This was not the response she'd hoped for – from either of them.

'Interesting? Is that all you can say?'

'Look, I'm a bit busy at the moment, but if you'd like to jot down all you remember ...'

'Surely what I know deserves a little time?'

'All right. Tell me something.'

Pamela paused. 'Elmer Maxted. Do you know where he died?'

Honey was currently in the back of the taxi, en route to Cora Herbert's establishment.

Still, information was information. She answered Pamela's question.

'As far as they know, he was killed in the cellars of one of the houses with access to the river. They think the house he was murdered in was numbered six or nine.'

Silence ensued before Pamela spoke.

'I see.'

She sounded a lot less intense. Again silence. Honey gave her a nudge.

'What did you want to tell me?'

'Never mind. I'll put it in a letter.'

She slammed the phone shut. Razor thin, it slid from her hand and into her suitcase.

Nothing was going quite as she'd wanted it to. Even her car was refusing to start. 'Give me an hour and I'll take a look at it,' said Mark.

'Half an hour!'

He turned his back on her temper. 'Mark, I think you should come to Spain with me.'

He said nothing.

She wanted to say so much, but couldn't. He might not approve of what she was about to do.

The maid had left today's *Bath Chronicle* on the dressing table. The headlines caught her eye. SUSPECT RELEASED. She read on. The police had raided the wrong house, the wrong terrace. What was more, the suspect, Robert Davies, had been released due to lack of evidence. She shivered.

Her room was an oasis of tranquil pale lime and deep pink. She sat down at her desk, took out a pad and began to write. Once finished, she read what she had written. Her fine eyebrows arched with satisfaction. Yes. This would do the trick.

Frances Tolly, housekeeper at Charlborough Grange, came in to tell her that Mark had failed to fix her car.

'Then tell him to get the Rolls out, and tell him I need a driver. I'm not driving that bloody great thing! He'll have to stay overnight at the airport hotel.'

*And come with me. Yes, he must come with me!*

Pamela smiled at the prospect. Although she had told her husband that she wanted Mark to drive her and stay overnight, there had been no guarantee that he would. But the car was big. Perhaps there would be time to get together en route.

Perhaps it was just as well that the sleek little Mercedes would not start. The thought of Mark's youthful body sent a shiver of excitement down her spine. There was so much potential in that young man. She'd tempted him into having sex with her. She hadn't managed to persuade him

226

to kill Andrew, but there was more than one way to skin a rabbit.

Frances turned to go.

'Wait a moment. Can you post this for me, Frances? It needs a stamp.'

After sealing the envelope, she passed it to the maid.

That, she thought, closes the last chapter in a loveless marriage.

Her luggage was transferred into the trunk of the Rolls Royce.

To her dismay she found that Trevor was driving.

'Mark's gone on an errand,' he told her.

She wasn't sure that he was telling the truth. But she had a flight booked. She wanted to go before the shit really hit the fan.

She didn't look back as they drove off. She never wanted to see the place again.

The main gate loomed up before them. Suddenly, Trevor stopped the car.

'What's wrong?'

'There's something wrong with the brakes. We'll have to go back.'

He swung the car round and headed back down the drive. Out back in the old stable yard, he left the car running. She tapped her fingers impatiently, watching as he went into the garage to find what he needed.

Trevor hadn't liked lying. The fact was that Sir Andrew had ordered him to drive his soon-to-be ex-wife to the airport.

Damned nuisance with the brakes, but soon fixed.

He cocked his ear, thinking he'd heard the engine rev up then disappear. Perhaps it had cut out?

Never mind. It would soon start up.

Whistling to himself, he opened the top tier of the toolbox, found what he was looking for and went back outside.

Swinging the tool from his hand, he went back to where he'd left the car – but it wasn't there.

'What the bloody …?'

Thinking her ladyship had driven it round the front – perhaps because she'd left luggage behind – he ran round the front to check. No car to be seen.

'What the hell! Sod her. Let her drive her bloody self.'

Arms hanging listlessly at his side, he shrugged and walked back to the house. It wouldn't be the first time she'd shot off to meet a secret lover. Either that or someone from the house had taken over.

He didn't care which it was. He had the greenhouses to contend with. He had war games to prepare.

# Chapter Thirty-one

Cora's hands shook as she placed the cereal packets along the sideboard in the dining room, the granola next to the bran flakes; the Cornflakes next to the Rice Crispies, then the Weetabix, the Shreddies and the Sugar Puffs.

Honey watched silently, a picture of calm professionalism. Things wouldn't be done like this at the Green River, but in a guest house it was perfectly acceptable. The lines were straight, the crockery gleamed and the cutlery sparkled. None of this seemed enough for Cora. Again and again she realigned the packets. Her hands shook and for once her fingers did not reach for cigarettes.

Feeling as though she'd won the lottery, Honey tried to contain her excitement. She could be wrong about the newspapers being the key to everything, but her instinct told her otherwise. Her instinct also told her to tread carefully; be nice.

'It must be very difficult – losing your husband and trying to keep things going.'

'Two husbands actually, and when it came to charm and reliability, both were interchangeable.'

It wouldn't be right to add anything about Mervyn having abused his position as stepfather to Loretta. How would I feel, she wondered. A pair of large pinking shears – the heavy and very sharp sort that dressmakers use popped into her mind – something else she mustn't voice!

'Our Loretta's a help. She's given up her other job to

229

give me a hand.'

'That's good of her.'

Cora stopped the obsessive moving of cereal packets and glared at her.

'She's a good girl! I won't have anyone saying anything else. Neither will Bob.'

Robert Davies! The impression came over loud and clear that Cora and her former husband were shoulder to shoulder in this.

'You don't think he killed Mervyn?'

'Of course he didn't! Though at times he was tempted, mark you!'

'It has to be admitted that your first husband did have a motive for killing your second husband. But why the American? It doesn't make sense to pin that one on him as well.'

Cora shook her head emphatically. 'He didn't do it! Neither of 'em!'

And Andrew Charlborough lied. Once she was finished here, he was next on her list – once she'd informed Doherty.

Sitting at a table with an instant coffee, Honey watched as Cora resumed her fussing along the sideboard, straightening servers, smoothing the lace-edged cloth covering the polished wood. The intricacies of the case slid around in her head – a bit like pieces of scrabble – a bit like Cora rearranging the cereal packets.

Move that bit there, this bit here, and approach from another angle. She could have come straight out and said, 'Hey, can I have a look at the old newspapers those watches are wrapped in?' Best to tread softly, she'd decided. *Softly, softly catchee monkey,* or in this case a motive and a murderer.

'Do you think Mervyn was capable of murder?'

The question was out before she could put on the brakes.

Cora was like a figure on a TV screen when someone hits the pause button on the video. She didn't seem surprised, more confused as though the thought had never, ever entered her bleached blonde head.

Eventually, she came to herself. 'Mervyn was a first-class creep. And that's putting it mildly! Bob was never like that. An out and out tea-leaf, but never a scumbag.'

She picked up a duster and began flicking it at imagined specks around the bay window. The windows rattled as a heavy truck trundled past heading along the main A4 towards Bristol.

'But him murder that nice Mr Weinstock? No. Like our Loretta said, Mervyn invited him into his den. He didn't do that very often, I can tell you. Even me and our Loretta weren't allowed in there.'

Something clicked in Honey's brain. Cora had just called her first husband Bob. No! Could it be Mary Jane's Bob the Job?

'Did err ... Bob ... meet Elmer?'

Cora stiffened.

'Bob the Job?'

Cora stopped fussing. Her doughy figure turned doughier.

'That was his interest, you see. He started doing it in prison years ago. He'd put adverts in magazines about helping people trace their roots, and they'd write to him. Got hundreds of replies he did.'

Mouth dry with excitement, Honey curbed her enthusiasm. She didn't want to alienate Cora. The poor woman had gone through enough.

'Is there any chance that you and Bob might get back together?'

Cora shrugged. 'There may be – if we get through this bother that is. It would be good for our Loretta.'

Honey put down her coffee mug. 'So. Tell me about Mervyn's watches. He was quite a collector.'

'That's right. Rubbish most of them from car boots and junk shops. But that was his hobby. Mended them and got them going, he did.'

'Do you think I could have another look in there?'

Cora made a whistling sort of noise as she drew in her breath. 'I was going to put it all to auction. I've been advised to keep them all together as one lot.'

'That's good advice. You can come in with me if you like, though I'm not into collecting watches.'

'Can't understand why people collect old junk. What is it you collect then?'

'Underwear.'

'Get on!'

Cora looked flabbergasted.

'Old corsets, stockings, liberty bodices …'

'Knickers?'

'Especially knickers. So you see I'm not going to steal your deceased husband's watches. You never know. I might pick up on something that the police have overlooked that might help your first husband get off the hook. Perhaps then the two of you might have a future together.'

Cora pursed her lips then flicked at a cornflake packet with her duster.

'Why not?'

Mervyn's den smelled of dried rubber and stale beer. The blink of a computer terminal caught her eye. The unit was old and smudged with dirty finger- and palm-prints. Having a frugal attitude to energy waste, she turned the screen off and looked for the box.

Cora had placed it beneath the ancient desk on which the computer sat. She pulled it out. As she unwrapped the contents from their newspaper, she became aware of Cora watching her from the doorway.

Wishing she had a camera, she placed each watch on top of the desk. None of them looked particularly valuable, but you could never tell.

'Do you have a camera?' she asked Cora. 'Only I think it might be a good idea for me to photograph the whole collection and pass them to a friend of mine who's an expert on timepieces. He could advise you of the best way of disposal.'

'I could do with the money,' said Cora.

'That's what I thought.'

Cora disappeared and came back with the required object.

Pretty soon all the watches had been photographed.

One of the newspapers tore as she started to rewrap each watch as she'd found them. Her hands shook. This was the real reason why she was here. If she was right, there was something here that caused Elmer Maxted to pay Sir Andrew Charlborough a visit.

Various headlines caught her eye. They were interesting, some downright dramatic, but what exactly was she looking for?

The odd thing about the newspapers was that most of them were Irish, none so far from Bath. The tragedies of the world were there in black and white. Robberies, murders, and children left motherless following a fire.

She read on about the motherless children. One of the boys had been abducted and never seen again. The other had been given a home by a wealthy landowner in the southwest.

Honey sat back on her haunches and sighed. 'These newspapers are next to useless.'

Cora misunderstood. 'I'll go and fetch some more.' Cora turned to go.

'No. Best not,' said Honey. 'The police might get uppity about us disturbing things.'

As far as she could see, the newspapers said nothing. The sudden idea at the bookshop wasn't as good as it first seemed. None of these articles could possibly be the reason behind the murder of two men of two different nationalities. Except …

There was a son … he'd survived an accident in which his mother had died. The only Bath newspaper there carried the story, but why was it wrapped up with the Irish national?

She eyed the orphans whose mother had died in a fire.

One of the boys looked quite a bit older than the other. The age of the younger one was the same as that of the child whose mother had died in a car crash.

She frowned. And this means something. But what?

Once the watches were rewrapped, Cora went with her to the front door.

'It's a nice night,' said Honey.

Cora sighed. 'It'll be a better night once all this is sorted out. It's unsettling having people think you've done away with yer husband. Bad for business.'

Honey wasn't so sure. Having a murdered husband found in the back garden attracted the ghoulishly curious. A murdered American was a different matter. The national press had got hold of the story. OK if it had stayed local, but national could syndicate the news to international. She thought about this more deeply as she walked back along Bristol Road. She got a taxi as far as Widcombe Basin. A little evening air would help the thinking process.

'I'll walk from here,' she said, got out and paid the driver.

She took a left turn along the towpath, enjoying the smell of water, the colours of a narrow boat moored in the lock. Lights from the restaurant of a nearby hotel lay like fallen stars on the water.

Veins of purple stretched from the western sky, the air just cool enough to invigorate the brain without chilling the skin.

She passed a troop of tourists undertaking yet another Ghost Walk. The tour guide, a leggy chap wearing learned glasses above an acme-covered chin, sounded full of enthusiasm.

'There are many legends and many buildings supposedly haunted by a "Grey Lady". One of the most famous has to be the one who haunts the Theatre Royal.'

A low murmur of interest rustled through the listeners. 'Have you ever seen her?' someone asked.

'I didn't exactly see her,' said the guide, his eyes brilliant behind the wire-rimmed specs. 'But I did feel her presence. It's a bit like turning round quickly and fancying you've just seen someone out of the corner of your eye.'

Perhaps it was the tone of emphatic belief that made Honey do just that.

Was it her imagination, or had someone ducked into a doorway? She'd caught a glimpse of white trainers. Ghosts didn't wear white trainers; did they?

Under the circumstances, she joined the crowd following behind their guide like a clutch of spring ducklings.

Someone nudged her elbow. 'Have you ever felt someone was trying to get in touch with you from the other side?' The woman spoke in a thick New York accent.

Honey grimaced. 'Yes. Mostly my bank manager when I've gone on the wrong side of my overdraft facility.'

# Chapter Thirty-two

The sun streamed into the dining room of the Green River Hotel. The clattering of cutlery against crockery drowned the sound of butter knives grating against toast. Guests conversed across white damask tablecloths and the smell of grilled bacon and fresh coffee drifted like a friendly wraith around the room.

Mary Jane sat at her usual table in the farthest corner – her favourite spot. From there she had a panoramic view of the breakfast room and everybody entering it.

A starburst of wrinkles spread out from her lips as she smiled.

Honey raised the coffee pot. 'Coffee?'

Mary Jane's eyes stayed unblinking on Honey's face.

'Sorry you missed the séance.'

'I am so sorry. Previous engagement.'

'I quite understand. But I have to tell you, you're being watched,' she said in a hushed voice.

Honey was taken aback.

'Well that certainly puts the egg and bacon into the shade.'

She wondered if he wore white trainers.

'I saw you waltzing along the Royal Crescent the other day. He was right behind you.'

'Are we talking about a ghost?'

Mary Jane leaned backwards, cricking her head to an awkward angle. 'Not a ghost. I mean the guy who looks like that film star who ended up getting butchered in

Gladiator.'

Smiling, Honey put the coffee pot down on the next table. 'Help yourselves,' she said to the four Australians sitting there.

Pulling up a chair, she leaned over the table and looked up into Mary Jane's wise old face. 'Make my day. Am I being pursued by Russell Crowe? If so, I'll slow down and let him catch me.'

Mary Jane went all vague. 'It might have been Spartacus I was thinking of. You know, fair-haired and a broken nose.'

Honey's elation vanished. Kirk Douglas and a Zimmer frame came to mind.

'Now this guy, he wasn't wearing white trainers by any chance?'

As she considered the question, Mary Jane's pink lips pursed on the rim of her coffee cup. A perfect pink imprint was left behind.

'I didn't notice his feet. Just his face.'

'Ugly?'

She meant ugly as in dangerous. Police mug shots clicked through her mind.

'Rugged,' said Mary after much consideration. 'But then, I might not have noted his features in detail. I wasn't concentrating too much on him. I was watching the sheep feeding on the grass in front of the Royal Crescent.'

'There aren't any sheep grazing in the Royal Crescent.'

Mary Jane's expression of total belief was undiminished. 'Not now, but there used to be.' She nodded at a picture on the wall of the Royal Crescent as it had been in the eighteenth century.

'See? If you go to the Crescent and narrow your eyes, you can see them gambolling there just as they used to.'

'Amazing.'

As she rose from the chair, Mary Jane caught her arm.

'Before you go,' she said, her voice falling into a deep

whisper. 'I thought you should know that Sir Cedric reckons your life is in danger. He saw blood and a lot of trees – like a forest he said, only worse.'

'Really?'

'The other night at the séance. He came through you see. He was terribly specific. You should have been there.'

In the past she had always taken Mary Jane's prophesies with a pinch of salt. Suddenly she felt vulnerable.

'Perhaps that what comes of being a detective,' she said with a hint of sarcasm. 'Jane Marple,' she added with a laugh that she thought sounded convincing.

'I'm sure that's got something to do with it,' said Mary Jane. 'And that's why I've decided to assist you.'

She wondered what the cop shop would think when they saw Mary Jane, dressed head to toe in a pink caftan and wearing silver sandals. Probably that somebody had put magic mushrooms in their tea.

'I'm supposed to do this by myself.'

'Yeah. Sure. I know. But that isn't what I meant.'

She sat back as though about to deliver a eulogy fit for a king.

'I have a private income, thanks to my dearly departed mother, so I've decided to move in here permanently.'

Honey's jaw dropped. 'You're not going back to California? Not ever?'

'Why should I? I've found my roots and I'll be buried here in the land of my forebears. What could be better? Can we agree a special rate?'

The shrewdness of age shone in her eyes. No doubt the funeral parlour would also be tied into a discounted deal when the time came.

'Leave it with me.'

Uncertain about the advantages of having the gangly woman as a permanent guest, Honey gathered up greasy plates and headed for the kitchen.

Her mother was putting the bacon away and Clint, complete with cobweb tattoo, was dealing with the washing up.

'Hannah,' said her mother once the fridge door had slammed shut. 'Mr Paget tells me you have not returned his calls.'

Each time her mother's dentist had called, she'd got someone to tell him she was out. The Eastern European girls were quite wonderful at it. Trying hard not to giggle, they adopted thicker accents than they actually had.

'Mother, I'm rather busy at the moment.'

'You sound just like your father. He was always busy.'

'That figures. He ran a multi-million dollar industry,' she muttered while scraping bits of sausage and bacon rind into the bin.

'And left me almost destitute!'

'Hardly that. He allowed you what he could. After all, he only *managed* the company.'

Her mother grimaced. 'Keep your voice down. Think of my image.'

Honey rolled her eyes. Rumours that her mother's former husbands had all been millionaires were exactly that – rumours put about by Gloria Cross herself. Image, as she insistently reminded her, was everything.

'Well there you are! No one could blame me for finding solace in the arms of another man! Nothing can beat good and frequent sex for keeping a woman looking young. You should do more of it yourself.'

Hearing this, a soapy plate slid from the washer up's fingers. The top plate from the greasy pile followed it.

Gloria Cross jerked her chin at the smashed plates. 'Two plates. That's bad luck. Everything should come in threes.' A hand encompassed in pink rubber reached for a plate.

Before the deed could be done, Honey had grabbed it with both hands.

239

'Plates cost money.'

'Yer mother may have a point,' said Clint, his shaved head wreathed in steam from the dishwasher. 'It's Friday the 13th today. Unlucky for some,' he said with a smile, and winked.

What with Mary Jane deciding to move in and now this!

Accepting she was surrounded by weirdos, she shook her head and left the kitchen.

Making out bills in reception and dealing with the morning mail would make things right again.

It didn't!

The quality envelope smelling of perfume intrigued her. It did more than that once she'd opened it. Pamela Charlborough had kept her promise. Honey's jaw dropped. She'd forgotten all about the phone call.

Stuffing the letter back into the sweetly scented envelope she addressed the girl on reception.

'The bills are done, the phone's quiet and I'm off out.'

'And if anyone wants you?' asked a surprised-looking Olga, her cheeks pink with youthful energy.

'If they want to reserve a room or a table in the restaurant, write it down. If it's a man and he sounds reasonably endearing, give him my mobile number.'

Olga's face burst into a grin. 'And Mr Paget? Your mother told me he wishes to marry you.'

'Tell him I've gone to work in a leper colony.'

## Chapter Thirty-three

A stilted silence hung over the incident room and the aroma of stewed coffee clogged the air. Coffee got colder in half-full cups and no one seemed to have much of a laugh in them. Even in the direst of circumstances somebody usually came up with a corny gag or dry pun to break the gloom of the occasion.

Clutching the letter from Lady Charlborough, Honey peered in through the glass door at the glum expressions and lacklustre postures. Some of the officers were slouched in their chairs, others bent over their desks, heads resting on arms. Steve Doherty was using a pencil to tap at a Santa Claus mug.

Honey took a deep breath. Boy, was she going to lift their spirits – she hoped.

A few pairs of eyes looked up to see what nosey so and so was disturbing their grief.

'Our person from the Hotels Association,' said Doherty, his chin resting on his hand, his elbow resting on the desk. The corners of his mouth were wedge-side down.

He flashed her a grim reaper grimace before shifting his glance on to something less unsettling. He chose the paperclip dispenser.

Honey sensed discomfiture. Severe discomfiture.

'OK, OK. You've had to let Robert Davies go and you're peed off about it!'

Doherty's overly wide mouth twisted into a snarl. 'You come to gloat?'

'No. I am the bearer of glad tidings, oh sad-looking shepherds!' She held up the letter.

'What is it?'

'A letter from Lady Pamela. It explains a lot.'

He eyed it suspiciously.

'Go on,' urged Honey. 'It won't bite you. Though she might have taken her teeth to you given half the chance,' she added with a grin.

A wave of sniggers circled the room.

Doherty glared the sniggerers to silence. 'You lot got nothing else to do? How about a bit of door-to-door? Better still, traffic duty. Savvy?'

His colleagues turned back to their individual tasks: sieving evidence files, playing solitaire and drinking tea.

As Doherty devoured the words, his dour expression brightened.

'So! She's accusing this bloke Trevor Spiteri of being a psycho.'

'Hmmm.'

'What's hmmm supposed to mean?'

'I thought she'd accuse the person she hates most.'

'Her husband?'

She made that 'hmmm' sound again. 'Someone dedicated to her husband. And with the right address.'

'This is enough for me!'

Sensing a shift in Doherty's mood, a few of his team eyed him like dogs about to be let off the leash.

'Braden,' he barked.

A dark-skinned female detective with shiny black hair bolted upright.

'Get a fix on a bloke named Trevor Spiteri.'

'Yes, guv.'

Her fingers pounded the computer.

'Fleming?'

The man named Fleming was already on his feet, leaning towards his boss as though ready to snaffle up every word.

'Get a warrant issued!'

The excitement was tangible. Honey could almost taste the surge in testosterone. It was as though she had entered a different room, certainly not the one she'd come into just a few minutes ago. Everyone was animated. Everyone was keen to replace one arrest with another.

She basked in their praise.

'You're one of the team!'

'We got him now!'

'You're a doll.'

The corners of Doherty's mouth went sunny-side up. 'You'll be wanting a job here before long.'

Honey shook her head. 'Let's not get silly. Though I did prove myself right, but there, I'm just an amateur.'

His eyes said bitch! She didn't give a hoot. She told herself it wasn't gloating, just setting the record straight.

'Don't rub it in.'

'You owe me.'

'Dinner?'

'OK. But more than that. I want to come with you. I want to be in on the arrest.'

He hesitated.

'You owe me,' she repeated.

He made the decision.

'OK. And let's hope he'll be there.'

His attention jerked to the glossy-haired woman. 'So what do we know, Braden?'

Glossy hair leaned back from her console. 'Grievous bodily harm – ten years back. He's ex-army. Born in London, stationed in a few foreign conflicts before ending up in Warminster …'

Doherty jabbed a finger in her direction. 'Print it off!'

Honey took a deep breath and began to read.

Charlborough's batman, Trevor Spiteri, lived at number 6 Rathbone Terrace, a stone's throw from Charlotte

Terrace where Robert Davies, Bob the Job, lived. As with other properties in the city, its cellars went under the road and had doors opening on to the river. In the past the rich people who lived in the houses had moored shallow leisure craft on the river which ran along behind. The rich people were gone, the elegant houses divided into equally elegant apartments, rented at roughly the same price per month as each house had cost to build way back. She wondered if Trevor Spiteri wore white trainers.

'Got it!' Fleming shouted, an arrest warrant flapping in the air. Up went the cheer. Cars were organised. The plan discussed. Honey ran out behind them, her heart thudding with excitement. Without waiting for a specific order she got into the car beside Doherty.

He opened his mouth to form the words 'shove off', then seemed to have second thoughts and changed his mind.

With a screech of wheels they were out of the car park and on to Manvers Street, Doherty aiming the car like a missile homing in on its target.

The terrace was not as elegant as some in the city, its architecture originating at the beginning of the nineteenth century. Gone were the Palladian pillars each side of a wide door, the carved pediments over long, light-filled windows. The refined features had been replaced by the more business-like style of a swiftly moving industrial age. Aprons of black and white quarry tiles sloped from threshold to pavement in front of each house, worn down by countless thousands of footsteps.

Car doors slammed in unison. Uniformed and plain-clothes officers tumbled out of cars.

'I'll take the front door with you two.' Doherty pointed a crooked finger at two of the passengers of another car. He turned to Honey. 'You get around the back with these two. And keep out of the way.'

Hair flying and face flushed, Honey followed the two

policemen, the heels of her black suede boots scattering gravel behind her.

They came face to face with a blank wall. The two policemen looked baffled. One lifted his helmet and rubbed at the redness left behind on his forehead.

'The guv'nor must 'ave got his facts wrong, miss. There's no entrance round here.'

Honey bit her lip. The place fitted in with everything required to make this work, but not entirely. The river bounded the rear of the houses but the side wall prevented them from going any further. There was no back alley, no way of slipping from one back yard to another.

Honey looked in the direction of the river. Doherty hadn't wanted her to come. He'd got his way and sent her in the wrong direction. Bloody man!

Doherty's name was mud.

Back in Rathbone Terrace, heads were appearing at windows, figures at doors. As insistent as plague, speculation crept from one flat, one house, one doorway, to another.

By word of mouth, it passed the black railings protecting the drops to narrow basements. Sash windows shaded with Venetian blinds, or the braids and tassels of traditional design, became open.

Honey barged through the cordon at the entrance to number six. The entrance was narrow. Four uniformed bods were plenty enough to keep the curious at bay.

'Nobody's allowed in,' said a young constable with a ginger moustache.

'I'm not a nobody.'

Braden, the dark girl with the glossy hair, chose that moment to come running out.

Honey homed in on her. 'What's going on?'

'I'm sorry, Honey. Spiteri's barricaded himself in his flat. Steve – DS Doherty – is talking to him. He says that until this is resolved no one is allowed inside.'

The sound of a sash window being pulled up was followed by a head appearing out of a third-floor window.

The two women looked up.

'I suppose that's him,' said Fleming.

Honey agreed.

'I'll jump if you smash my door in!' Spiteri shouted.

Honey recognised the hushed voice coming from a broken voice box.

'We only want to talk to you,' Fleming called back.

'If I jump and hurt myself, I'll claim police harassment,' Spiteri shouted back.

Without being invited, Honey joined in. 'You might not be able to claim a single penny.'

'Name one reason why I couldn't.'

'The fall might kill you. Your head and guts could be splattered on the pavement or speared on the railings and the bill for cleaning up would be set against the compensation.'

A posse of police dropped jaws turned in her direction.

Ignoring them, she kept her attention fixed on Trevor. Even from this distance she could see his perplexed expression, now the horror had been spelled out to him. To jump or not to jump. No contest.

Things seemed to have come to a halt so Honey tackled Braden. 'Doherty sent me round the back on purpose!'

'Um. Yes,' said Braden, torn between loyalty to Doherty and disgruntled sisterhood.

'He's a pig!'

Fleming managed a lop-sided grin. 'We all are, aren't we?'

'He's miffed,' said Braden.

'He's toast,' grunted Honey.

After confirming that Honey was definitely not to be allowed in the house, Braden summoned more assistance on her radio.

Honey found herself melting into the small crowd of watchers as though she never had been of any consequence. Mentally she was sticking pins into a real-life Doherty. She'd been part of the investigation and now she was not.

She hardly noticed the dusky young woman in the business suit come out of the house next door. Only when she spoke did it occur to her that the woman had moved like a panther, silently, swiftly, and making an instant impression.

'What *is* going on?'

Her voice was as dark as her hair.

Honey turned and took in the details. The crisply white collar of a starched blouse lay flat against the lapels of a navy blue business suit. She carried a briefcase – or perhaps it was a laptop. The heels on her shoes were business-like, built for daywear. It was easy to believe that at night those long legs appeared even longer in four-inch heels. She was beautiful.

'The police are trying to arrest the man next door,' Honey explained. At the same time she wished she'd been blessed with sooty lashes and flawless skin.

Intelligence shone in the dark, kohl-lined eyes.

'But not very successfully.'

'Par for the course. Nothing to do with me.'

'Do excuse me for saying so, but I got the impression you were with them.'

Honey grimaced. 'So did I. I think they'd decided that I'd outlived my usefulness.'

Blurting it all to a stranger seemed ridiculous, but she couldn't help herself.

'The annoying thing is that I obtained the evidence. Not them.'

The lovely lady from next door tutted and shook her head.

'Poor Mr Spiteri. And only just back from visiting his

family.'

Honey's interest slackened. 'Really?'

'Yes. He was away most of the summer and has only been back two weeks.'

'Two weeks?' Honey was counting back the days to Elmer's disappearance.

Honey turned to face her informant. 'Is that a fact?'

The young woman's complexion was to die for. Honey felt a tinge of jealousy for her youthful skin, dark eyes and confident manner.

Her perfect teeth flashed pearl white. 'I was told this by a nosey parker that I know very well. My own grandmother in fact.'

The thick lashes flickered as she checked her watch.

'Your being treated so offhandedly annoys me. Sisters have to stick together! Now if you wish to confirm all I have told you, go into my house and up the first flight of stairs. My grandmother is home. The rest of the family are out at work all day. Don't tell her that I called her a nosey parker, but I can confidently assure you she can tell you everything that happens in this street. She doesn't get out much and sees everything.'

Out of gratitude, Honey felt a need to show interest in such a helpful young woman.

Honey made an assumption. 'Your family is in business?'

'My parents, along with other members of the Patel family, run various businesses. My brothers and I have professions.'

'And what is yours?' Honey asked adopting the warmest of smiles.

'I'm a tax accountant.'

Honey's smile froze.

The young woman saw her look. 'I said tax accountant, not tax inspector.'

'Ah, yes,' said Honey taking a deep breath and fanning

her face with her hand. 'Thank goodness for that.'

'Please. Tell my grandmother that Zakia said you should speak to her. Like a lot of elderly people, she has an obsession with security.'

Like most Georgian houses, the property had once been home to just one family and their servants. Now it was divided into individual homes for the members of one family.

After the third knock at the Patels' door, it opened inches and a pair of dark eyes appeared over the tight restraint of a brass security chain. The perfume that wafted out through the gap was immediately recognisable. Chanel. Honey instantly thought of her mother. Grandma Patel and Gloria Cross had something in common.

'Mrs Patel? I'm working in conjunction with the police. Your granddaughter Zakia suggested I speak with you.'

'Will she get to work on time?'

'I see no reason why not.'

'Oh. That is good.'

Her dark eyes darted from Honey's head to her toes and back again before the door closed, the chain rattled and the door reopened.

'Please. Come in. I will put the kettle on. You'll have to excuse the mess. I'm researching my thesis for a degree with the Open University.'

'Oh, really? What subject are you studying?'

'Computer Science, though I am not sure I have picked the right aspect. I think I need to enrol for a City and Guilds-type of qualification. I'm more interested in stripping them apart rather than understanding the mathematics and the science of the subject.'

Honey was suitably impressed. 'You mean you can actually take a computer apart and put it back together again?'

Mrs Patel grinned. 'Oh yes. I can strip it down now, thanks to my grandson's instruction.' She frowned as a thought occurred to her. 'The trouble is that neither of us are any good at putting it back together again. That is what I need to learn.'

Mrs Patel was dressed in a swathe of rich green silk banded with gold. Grey hair spread like a halo framing her face. She was elegant and oozed confidence. Nothing, thought Honey, had ever been allowed to stand in the way of anything she'd ever wanted to do.

'Come. Follow me. We will make ourselves comfortable.'

She limped as she led her to the back of the house overlooking the river.

'This is my private little flat where I go when I wish to be away from the family,' she explained.

Her eyes shone as she spoke. Arm outstretched, she indicated a row of family photographs including one of Zakia wearing mortarboard and gown, and clutching her degree. Pride shone from Mrs Patel's eyes.

Honey guessed she did not frequent this room when the family was home.

'Sit here. Make yourself comfortable. I will make tea.'

She limped off into the adjoining kitchen. The sound of a kettle being switched on and crockery being laid out rattled into the living room.

The Georgians had favoured high ceilings and big windows to let in the light. This room was no exception. A Bentwood rocker packed with silk-covered cushions was placed in front of the high window. Beyond the yard was the river.

'This is where I sit and watch the world at the back of the house,' Mrs Patel explained on coming back with the tea. 'Sometimes I watch the world at the front of the house. I have another chair just like this one in front of that window. But I prefer back here. It is so quiet. So deserted – most of the time.'

'You have very nice views. I bet you see all that goes

on.'

Mrs Patel sighed, her fine wrinkles deepening, as she eased herself into her chair.

'I see a lot. Sometimes it is very interesting. Sometimes it is tiring. I sit here a lot, you know. It is my hip you see. The pain it causes interferes with my studies. I am waiting for an operation. I am waiting until the end of the month and then if I have not got an appointment my son says he will pay for me. I can get it done in France if I have to. One can do that now we are in Europe.' She rubbed her hip as she said it.

'I hope you get it sorted soon,' said Honey politely. 'Let me help you with the tea.'

'That is very kind.'

There was a clear view between the trees to the parapet at the rear of the yard and the river.

'I wish I had a view like this.'

Mrs Patel smiled.

'It is a joy. I see all life from here even though I find difficulty getting around nowadays. There is little I miss.'

She suddenly looked worried and the smile dropped from her face.

'No one has complained about me being a nosey parker, have they?'

'No, Mrs Patel. In fact, because of your habit – and your pain, you might be of some help in solving a murder.'

'A murder!' Her face brightened. 'A real one? This is a real case, not just for television?'

Honey thought of poor Elmer Maxted and Mervyn Herbert. 'I'm afraid this is for real.'

Mrs Patel clapped her hands. 'All the years of watching murder mysteries and now I might actually be a witness in a real-life murder.'

'Possibly.'

'So,' said Mrs Patel, her face beaming. 'How can I help you?'

251

Leaning forward, Honey rested her elbows on her knees and clasped her hands together in front of her.

'I understand that Mr Spiteri next door has just come back from abroad. Is that right?'

Fearing she might frighten the old girl, she spoke softly, but clearly.

'Is he a suspect? What did he do? How did he do it?'

Mrs Patel, despite her obvious age, didn't appear to be frightened at the possibility that a murderer lived next door. On the contrary, she seemed to relish the prospect.

Honey had to disappoint her.

'I actually think that his guilt or innocence rather depends on what you've got to say.'

Mrs Patel's mouth dropped open. Her brown eyes glowed with excitement.

'Do go on, do go on!'

Mrs Patel was the witness a good policeman dreamed of; clear-headed and committed to giving a good account of all she knew.

'Was Mr Spiteri away for some time?'

Mentally, Honey had her fingers crossed. The correct answer would win Spiteri his freedom and Doherty a big slap of mud on his face.

There was no baited breath about it; Mrs Patel came straight out with the answer.

'He came back about two weeks ago on a Thursday at about five in the morning. I don't sleep that well, you see. That's the trouble with getting old.'

'And how long was he away?'

Her heart thudded against her ribs. Everything depended on the answer. If Spiteri had been away at the same time as the murders were committed, then he was in the clear. Doherty was not.

'He was away for about two months visiting his relatives on some island in the Mediterranean. It's near Sicily I believe.'

A map of the Med surfed through Honey's mind. 'Malta?'

Mrs Patel nodded. 'I think that is the name of it. He did tell me this but I was never very good at geography.'

'Fantastic!' Honey clapped her hands. She couldn't wait to slap the details around Doherty's dumb face.

Mrs Patel smiled. 'I am so glad I was able to help. Although he looked a little intimidating, he was really quite a nice man. So friendly. Not like the other man who used to stay in the basement flat. You would never think that they worked together for the titled gentleman.'

Mrs Patel's nosiness was reaping rewards beyond belief. Honey's feet had been itching to be up and away, confronting Doherty with the fact that Spiteri could not have murdered the two men. But this other man. A sneaking suspicion invaded her mind.

'What other man was that, Mrs Patel? Do you know his name?'

She shook her head. 'No, I cannot remember.'

'Would you recognise him again?'

'Of course.'

'You definitely saw him arrive next door?'

'Most definitely.'

Honey got to her feet. 'I have to tell the policeman next door. Will you come with me to confirm this, or shall I get them to come in and take a statement?'

For someone with a dodgy hip, Mrs Patel got to her feet in double quick time. Her enthusiasm had more effect than the discomfort.

'I am right with you! I will put up with my hip.'

'I'll take these into the kitchen for you,' said Honey reaching for the tray.

'No! No!' Mrs Patel pushed the tray back on to the table. 'Never mind that. This is the most exciting thing that's happened to me in years. Come on. We must hurry.'

Honey paused. 'Mrs Patel, I can't thank you enough.'

The dark eyes sparkled impishly. 'I used to be a journalist, you know. I used to gather and write factual features on a freelance basis. That is why I am so sure about times and dates and the comings and the goings. Besides, I keep a diary.'

Champagne bottles popped and sherbet fizzed; or at least that was the way it felt. Things couldn't get much better than this.

'A diary?'

Mrs Patel smiled and her eyes sparkled like the teenager – and possibly rebel, Honey thought – that she'd once been.

'I like to write down what I have seen. Sometimes I write a line or two of poetry about the night scene – you know – the lights and everything, people hurrying by, lovers strolling, the river – anything that catches my eye.'

'May I see it?' Honey asked. 'If you don't mind that is.'

'Don't worry,' laughed Mrs Patel. 'My diary does not contain the personal secrets it once did. There,' she said, opening a drawer and bringing it out.

It was bound in pink plastic. Red plastic lips stood proud of the cover.

Mrs Patel placed it on a brass-topped table, the sort that's no more than a big plaque on turned legs.

'If you don't mind getting that for me,' said Mrs Patel.

Honey took it with both hands, placed it on her knees and opened it up to the first page.

The fluidity of the writing was far more beautiful than what she had to say. Her entry for each date read almost like a shopping list.

There were times of the comings and goings of her son, her daughter-in-law, the postman and even the traffic warden and what colour cars he'd booked. The entry for Trevor Spiteri coming home was there.

Just as she had stated, there were a few lines of poetry

added which reflected what she had seen that day.

*Green leaves, black road, grey river swirling swiftly by.*
*People walking, people talking, green, green grass and*
*crisp blue sky.*

Mrs Patel followed her down the stairs. At the bottom
Honey turned to make sure she was all right.

'I am fine,' said Mrs Patel, her face glowing. 'Just wait
until I lock my door. I am right behind you.'

Having been at the back of the house, it came as
something of a surprise to see that the police presence next
door had diminished.

Honey addressed a remaining constable. 'Where is
everyone?'

'Gone back to the station with the accused.'

Honey swore under her breath. Doherty and everyone
of importance had flown the nest.

After finding that her phone battery was flat, Honey
sighed and turned to Mrs Patel. 'I'm sorry but we'll have
to go to the station and report this.'

'No worries,' Mrs Patel said brightly.

'Can I keep the diary?'

'Of course you can.'

Honey's gaze slid between the two front doors, the
number six of next door, and the number seven of Mrs
Patel. She frowned. After that, the numbers leapt from
seven to nine. Number nine had a For Sale notice outside.
The frontage of seven was wider than each of the
properties to either side of it.

'Where's number eight?' she asked.

'We are six, seven and eight,' answered Mrs Patel.

The door of number six was still open to allow the
comings and goings of the forensic people.

'I would dearly love to look inside that basement flat,'
said Honey, eyeing the stone steps leading downwards.

'I have the keys.'

Mrs Patel began rummaging in the tan leather handbag she had insisted on bringing with her.

'You do?'

Though of short acquaintance, nothing about Mrs Patel should have surprised her, but the old girl was still capable of springing the unexpected.

'My other son owns next door. I keep the spare keys.'

Three cheers for Mrs Patel. D minus for my bloody phone, thought Honey. If it had been working Doherty would have had to eat humble pie. She'd make him regret not including her in the real action.

After deliberating about whether they should impede the legitimate key holder, a remaining police officer, left to guard the house where Trevor had threatened to throw himself out of the window, watched as they descended the steps.

'The basement flat has its own private entrance,' said Mrs Patel. She winked. 'Very discreet.'

The basement flat consisted of two bedrooms, a bathroom, a kitchen and a ground-floor living room. A pair of French doors opened on to a tiled patio at the back.

Even after modernisation and damp proofing, some basements retained a mouldy smell. Not this one. Painted white and lit by recessed spotlights, the flat was crisp and clean. Perhaps too crisp, too austere. There were no books, no magazines, no television set or the slightest evidence that anyone sometimes lived here. And yet Mrs Patel had assured her that someone did.

A familiar smell was also prevalent – not greasy bacon or chemical cleaners like you find in old bed-sits – perfume, very expensive perfume hung in the air.

Mrs Patel smelled it too. 'Quality perfume. Not a cheap tart,' she said with a saucy wink.

Honey laughed.

'I have remembered the name of the man who rented

this flat. Conway. Mr Conway.'

'Conway!'

Honey recalled the polite young man who'd brought the tea.

'Did you ever see the woman he came here with?'

Mrs Patel rolled her eyes suggestively. 'Oh, yes. Very blonde and trimmed with gold. Expensive, though slightly less than tasteful. Not a cheap tart. An expensive one.'

'I couldn't have described her better myself.'

Lady Pamela Charlborough. It couldn't be anyone else.

'So! It was a love nest.'

'Indeed. He wasn't here all the time.' A concerned frown crossed Mrs Patel's cheery face. 'Just the one woman of course. It is not a knocking shop, as you call it.'

Honey shook her head and controlled the grin. 'No, of course not, Mrs Patel.'

'He did not always come with her. Sometimes he came alone.'

'What did he do there – when he came by himself?'

'Mostly he used the workshop. Through there.'

She pointed to a door beneath the stairs. 'It leads to the cellars. He makes heads from plastic and clay down there. He told my son this when he began renting the flat. My son said he could not do such things here in the flat itself, so he must use the cellar.'

'I should think not,' said Honey approvingly. Their surroundings were pristine. It made sense to keep them that way.

'Anyway I do not like dolls,' said Mrs Patel.

'Neither do I,' said Honey recalling the heads in the greenhouse. 'How come you managed to get a look at them?'

'He wanted something to cover them with. He asked my son if he could save him the small sacks the spices come in. My son did this and asked me to give them to him.'

Sacks! So whoever made the latex heads for the war games, used spice sacks to keep them clean. And got them from Mrs Patel's son.

Honey mentally slapped herself around the head. She'd been barking up the wrong tree thinking the sacks might have come from Jeremiah's market stall. And they hadn't come from the pile outside the greenhouses either. They'd come from Mrs Patel's son and were used to cover latex heads. Perhaps the murderer had got so used to covering latex heads with the sacks, that he'd not been able to resist doing the same with his victims.

Finding out the truth about something as perplexing – and stupidly simple – as those sacks, was like breathing frosty air. It wasn't just refreshing, it invigorated.

'So,' she said, trying hard to control her racing heart, 'when's he expected back?'

'He's not. As you can see, my son is selling both this house and number nine. Mr Spiteri had agreed to move out at the end of the week. He's been offered accommodation with his employer who I believe is moving abroad. In the meantime my son offered Mr Conway the basement of number nine in which to keep his heads. I did not see him move his things there, but I presume he did.'

She phoned Doherty from Mrs Patel's phone before leaving but was told he was interviewing a suspect.

'Tell him he's got the wrong man.'

'I wouldn't dare,' said the female voice on the other end.

'Well I will. I'm on my way over.'

# Chapter Thirty-four

Doherty was being stubborn. They wouldn't let her in, so she phoned him from the reception line in the Green River Hotel.

He listened, grunting in places as though he really was taking it on board.

'You need a search warrant for number nine.'

'No I don't. I've got our man.'

'No you haven't. He was abroad at the time.'

'He'll have to prove it.'

'There are witnesses.'

There was silence.

'What's that? I can hear something mechanical rattling into place. Must be your brain. Use it before it goes rusty.'

She hoped the sound of the phone being slammed down burst Doherty's eardrum. Stubborn cuss!

For the rest of that day, she played the same game, refusing to take his calls, pretending she was out, doing anything rather than speaking to him. At the same time she was considering what she could do herself to sidetrack him and get the right man arrested.

Lindsey caught her cleaning the glass in the front door.

'You don't have to do that.'

'It's surprisingly therapeutic.'

'You're taking long enough.'

'You bet I am.'

Three times she'd sprayed the glass, and three times she'd pushed the polishing duster around.

'How's Sam?' she said lightly, though in all honesty all she wanted to do was stop Lindsey from interrupting her thought process.

'Coming on nicely. By the way, I told Grandma you were practically engaged.'

The polishing stalled. 'Why?'

'She wouldn't stop asking me questions about the other night when I slept at Sam's.'

'So I was thrown to the lion.'

Lindsey looked contrite. 'Sorry. I needed to do that. She wouldn't let go.'

Honey smoothed Lindsey's hair back from her forehead. 'Poor darling. I shouldn't have mentioned it. I'm sorry.'

'Don't be. It's not you giving me hassle. It's her. Grandma would have been great in the days when young girls were presented at court as debutantes.'

'I think she would have been better as a wife of Henry the Eighth.'

'He cut off three of his wife's heads.'

'Yes. One of those.

Honey's gaze went through the glass to the white trainers standing on the other side of the street.

There was a flash of white as whoever was wearing them did his best to hide behind a green wheelie bin.

'Does he look familiar to you?' she asked Lindsey.

Lindsey took a bite of the cold toast she'd snitched from kitchen leftovers and shook her head.

'What's he doing?'

'Following me. I think.'

Lindsey frowned. 'Perhaps he's a hotel inspector from the tourist board or something.'

Honey blew a mental raspberry. 'Hotel inspectors don't wear Lee Cooper jeans and white trainers.'

Lindsey peered out of the window. 'How do you know they're Lee Cooper? Have you seen his butt?'

'They just look that kind of quality, and no, I haven't seen his butt.'

'By the way, Doherty's just called again.'

'Was he apologetic?'

'He asked you to phone him. He's brought Sir Andrew in for questioning and is now looking for Mark Conway.'

'Ah!' Honey tapped her smiling lips. My, but it was good to be right. She became aware that Lindsey was giving her the incisive, *what have you been up to, mother,* type of look. Honey knew it well. She often used it to stump her own mother.

'He wanted to solve this case all on his own,' said Honey.

'But he didn't.'

'No. His call means that he's been out to Charlborough Grange, but Mark Conway wasn't there. Mark Conway is the murderer, not Trevor Spiteri, the man he hauled in for the murders of Elmer Maxted and Mervyn Herbert.'

'Right. And you know where he is. Yes?'

'I'm working on it.'

In her mind she was the Lone Ranger hunting down the baddy alongside a bumbling lawman. The truth was that crime wasn't like that at all. Leave it to the professionals, said a small voice in her mind, you know it makes sense.

The trouble was that there were *two* small voices. The other one was feeding her ego, telling her, *sure, babe, of course you can do it. You're cleverer than him!*

'What are you doing now?' asked Lindsey. Not for the first time in her life, she sounded nervous about her mother's intentions. The way her chin was jutting reminded her of the time they'd lived in a brand new house in a village. The locals had opposed the development. They'd also insisted that a footpath still ran through the backyard of the house they'd bought. One day Honey had caught their ringleader relieving himself against a bush she'd just planted.

He did it three days on the trot, insisting he was entitled.

On the fourth day her mother had been ready with a piece of brown paper smeared with thick, dark molasses.

Taking him unawares, she'd slapped the brown paper onto his exposed loins. The stuff was a devil to remove without help. His wife would have to help him. Likely as not, he'd also had to explain how molasses had got tangled in his pubic hair.

Honey was heading for the door and the man across the street.

'I want a word with you,' she called out as she ran across the road, weaving in and out of the cars.

A bevy of car horns blew in quick succession. Brakes screeched and a truck driver let loose with a whole host of expletives that did nothing for Bath's cultural heritage.

Her attention was fixed on the man in the trainers. She'd half expected him to leg it, but he didn't. Instead he hesitated, shifting his stance and drawing his hands from his pockets.

Flight or fight, that was the choice he was facing. Flight meant darting off through the evening rush-hour traffic. Fight was facing a middle-aged woman who was wide enough to keep him pinned behind a wheelie bin.

'Why are you following me?' she demanded.

He had chocolate brown eyes and corn-coloured hair. Mid-twenties and made to be admired. She'd seen him before. But where? It would come to her, but first the explanation.

'I didn't mean to frighten you.'

'So! Apologise!'

'I … I … apologise.'

Shifting from one foot to the other, he looked preoccupied, gazing into the distance.

Suddenly she was back in Charlborough Grange, studying the family photographs hung in a line on one wall.

'You're Lance Charlborough.'

'I found out,' he said, as though those three little words answered everything she might wish to know. 'I found out that my real mother died in a fire.'

The fuzzy photographs in a copy of the *Irish Times* sprang into her mind.

Suddenly the articles in the old newspapers pointed in the right direction. One in the *Irish Times*. One in the Bath newspaper.

'How?' she asked.

'Mark had always tried to keep the truth from me. He's older than me. He wouldn't let anyone hurt me. No one.'

'Mark Conway?'

He nodded.

'We're brothers. He's older than me. When our mother died, he ended up in an orphanage. I disappeared, fostered out so he was told. But I wasn't. Not really. Money changed hands. I become Lance Charlborough. Mark ended up in London and went looking for me. He saw my photo in a newspaper with my father at one of his military things.'

There was an intense sadness in his eyes.

'So! What happened?'

Lance swallowed as though he were having trouble coming to terms with what he'd learned and what he wanted to say.

'Our father couldn't cope when our mother died. He abandoned us. Sir Andrew took me in. He'd lost his son. He wanted another. A lot of money was involved, but it wasn't only that. He was devastated. His real son was a haemophiliac. He died in a road accident miles from anywhere. Mark was fostered with some people Sir Andrew knew. It was them that got him the job with Sir Andrew after he came out of the army.'

Initially, she had been going to berate him for

following her, but not now.

'How did you find out?'

'She told me. My stepmother. She got it from the American. Apparently the first Lady Charlborough was his sister-in-law.'

'And your father? Sir Andrew? Does he know that you know?'

He nodded. 'He does now. When I left home a few weeks ago, my father – Sir Andrew – cried out after me that he'd make everything right. That there was no need to worry about my inheritance.'

He shook his head, his eyes brimming with unshed tears.

'But it isn't my inheritance, is it? Not really.'

Honey felt a compunction to cuddle him, pat him on the back as though he were a little boy again, a little boy who had lost his mother.

'I don't know the details. I can't comment.'

'I never knew anything about it until she told me. Mark knew, but he'd kept it from me. He'd protected me. He's always protected me.'

Despite his age, Lance Charlborough had a waif-like quality about him.

'Come and have a coffee.'

Over coffee he told her that he'd got a job as a voluntary prison visitor. That was when he'd met Robert Davies – Bob the Job. It was him that did the tracing and came up with Elmer Maxted, related by marriage to Sir Andrew's first wife. Lance had contacted him. He'd insisted on coming over right away. Lance had begged him not to use his real name, just in case his adoptive father sussed what was going on.

'I wish I hadn't started this. I feel so guilty about Elmer getting killed.'

'Do you think your father did it?'

The chocolate pools looked into hers before he nodded.

'But I couldn't turn him in. I love him as a father, so I couldn't do that no matter what he's done.'

She thought of her mother and nodded. 'I know what you mean.'

'I wanted to know what was going on, so I followed you.'

'Why not follow the cops?'

He shrugged. 'They're the professionals. They might have noticed me.'

It hurt. But never mind, she told herself. You're proving them all wrong. The professionals adhered to strict guidelines. Her enquiries were less stringent and carried out between the shenanigans of a domineering mother and a dozy dishwasher.

They parted company once she'd promised she would let him know when someone was actually arrested. He gave her his phone number, but no address.

'Just in case you cave in under torture. I don't want my father – my adoptive father – to know where I am.'

*Your father's liable to torture me?*

She didn't voice the comment, just in case he confirmed it was true and she gave up sleuthing to take up line dancing instead. You couldn't line dance if your legs had turned to jelly or your toenails had been pulled out one by one.

After he'd gone, she felt a need to talk to someone about the nuances of the case, but not the police. They were busily looking for Mark Conway, Lance's brother.

She phoned Casper. He answered within seconds.

'What now?'

'I thought you'd like to know what's going on in the world of crime fighting.'

'Not really, my dear. I just want things tidied up for the sake of next year's profit ratio. I trust you are swiftly putting this problem to bed. Are you doing that, Hannah?'

Honey failed to suppress a surprising shiver. Only a

man like Casper could sound like her mother.

She bounced back, her mood was reflected in her tone. 'Well you know what they say, Casper. If you want a man to do a good job, get a woman to do it.'

He made a snorting sound. Disdain was Casper's middle name.

She carried on, wanting to tell someone involved – even if only on a moderate level – all that was going on.

'The police arrested the wrong man. His name's Trevor Spiteri.'

'That's a foreign name.'

'Being foreign isn't an indication of guilt.'

'That's a matter of opinion.'

'They'll have to let him go. And by the way, I think I should tell you I'm being followed.'

'A psycho?'

'No. Just sad.'

She explained about the basement flat and the expensive perfume. She also explained about the newspapers the watches were wrapped in being the clue and reminded him of the photos she'd sent to him.

'At least the newspapers were of some value,' he said sniffily. By that Honey presumed he meant that the watches were not.

She stuck to the subject in hand.

'It all ties in. Lance wrote to Elmer who was murdered because he knew it was virtually impossible that his nephew was still alive. The real Lance died in a road accident way out in the Spanish interior, far from any city. Drugs to speed blood clotting in haemophiliacs weren't so widely available then. Mervyn was showing Elmer his watch collection, but Elmer's attention was drawn to the old newspapers. First the report of a fire, and then the photograph of father and son at a social event, plus Mark Conway. The two boys were doubles for the two boys whose mother had died in the fire. Both Elmer and Mervyn put two and two together. I think Mervyn tried a touch of blackmail.'

'And now?' Casper's tone was only slightly less disdainful than it had been.

'I'm going to try and speak to Lady Pamela. She's a cow but I think she's willing to drop her husband in it.'

'Not a happy marriage?'

'Far from it.'

Casper taken care of. Doherty was next.

'Are you now ready to hear more?'

'Tell me.'

'The next door neighbour kept a diary of the comings and goings in Rathbone Terrace.'

'And?'

'I think I know where Mark Conway is.'

'I want that diary.'

'I'll bring it to you, but not yet. Not until I'm satisfied that every stone's been turned.'

# Chapter Thirty-five

It might have been sheer instinct that made her swerve into the car park in front of the church. On the other hand, it could have been fear. Confronting Charlborough filled her with dread.

She watched as two women armed with bunches of gladioli, roses, lupins and delphiniums disappeared through the arched doorway. Keeping the church clean and placing flower displays in dark little alcoves took on a sudden – and safe – attraction.

Why do you suddenly want jam and Jerusalem? she asked herself. Surely you knew before you started this that being a detective isn't like doing a crossword puzzle?

Summer was in full swing, the trees groaning in the breeze under the weight of dark green leaves, the grass bowing in waves.

Once the coast was clear, she got out of the car, locked it and followed the path through the churchyard.

Passing along the side of the church and around the back, the grass was longer and the earth lumpy. She stopped and kicked at a mound.

'Moles,' said a voice.

The muddy face of a gravedigger was regarding her from an empty grave.

'Well I didn't think it was somebody trying to sit up.'

He bent back to his job. Honey went back to hers.

Wispy heads of uncut grass tickled her legs as marble headstones gave way to pock-marked stone from centuries before. The names of the departed had flaked away. Lichen blemished the faces of granite angels and ivy smothered the last breath from a rose bush planted on a child's grave.

In the distance sunlight flashed on the windows of Charlborough Grange.

Swiftly, before she could change her mind, she followed the overgrown path to the stone stile and climbed over.

The footpath on the other side of the stile led her beside the canal before veering off towards Charlborough Grange.

The smell of wood smoke curled lazily up from a well-stacked bonfire. There was no one in sight.

The huge greenhouse lured her onwards. She remembered the heads, the very ones Mark Conway made from wax, clay and latex.

The sandbags were still piled around the entrance and because of their height would hide her from anyone.

The door made a sucking sound when she opened it and the humidity gushed out like a warm wave.

Leaving daylight and fresh air behind, it took time for her eyes to adjust to the gloom and her nose to the smell of rotting vegetation. Worse was the humidity. Within seconds her clothes were stuck to her back and the silence was oppressive.

'Anyone here?' she called. Her voice was lost in the greenery.

There was no neat path down the middle, no trays of seedlings waiting to be planted. Huge leaves fanned out from plants whose more natural habitat was Borneo or Sumatra; somewhere further south and east than North Somerset.

Jungle was the only word to adequately describe it. Just as she thought it, the sound of insects, monkeys, and all the other strange noises associated with a tropical rain forest burst into being.

*Don't be scared. It's no different from being in Kew Gardens. Though clammier.*

And there wasn't the possibility of latex heads being scattered around at Kew.

Her hair clung stubbornly to her face.

'Is anyone there?' she shouted again. The sound of insects and monkeys drowned her out.

A tape. It was only a tape.

All the same she kept her eyes open.

Bravely she made her way beneath huge leaves, stepped over thick roots. A flash of colour to the right caught her attention. An orchid. Just one. For some stupid reason she was curious to know whether it was in a pot. She stepped closer, the thick foliage closing behind her.

Looking everywhere except down at her feet, she suddenly fell over.

'Damn!' she muttered, then checked her ankles, then her knees. Nothing broken. Just caked with mud.

But who had turned on the tape? It hadn't been running when she'd first entered – had it?

With trembling fingers, she parted the leaves and peered out.

At first she saw no one, and then there he was.

His face was blackened. He wore fatigues, carried what looked like an AK47 under one arm, not that she knew much about guns, only that they scared her.

His hand rested on a long leather sheath hanging from his belt.

Her nerves jangled. Suddenly, she wanted to pee.

In the bushes? Hardly ladylike and in this heat she could probably sweat it out.

Putting her trust in her metabolism, she melted into the undergrowth.

The soil she slid into was soft and damp. She inwardly groaned at the obvious. Footsteps would be seen.

She sank back as far as she could without making a

noise. What would Charlborough – if it was Charlborough – do if he caught her?

Swallowing fear was like swallowing cornflakes without milk. It stuck and was sharp in her throat.

More rustling ensued around her. Another figure joined the first one.

She heard someone sigh. 'Christ, I've had enough of this.'

Peering cautiously through the undergrowth, she saw the recent arrival take off his balaclava.

'Still, it has been quite a team-forming weekend,' said the other man.

She didn't recognize either of them. Peeing was still a priority. She just had to break cover.

'Gentlemen!'

They looked taken aback to see her emerging from the bushes.

'Are you with us?' asked the Johnny-come-lately.

'No. I'm with the Tourist Board. We're doing a survey on customer satisfaction. Are you totally satisfied with your weekend here?'

She dragged Mrs Patel's notebook out of her bag just to make the lie look a little more authentic. Her hand wasn't really big enough to hide the pink plastic cover and the bright red lips; only King Kong could do that.

'I'll just make a few notes,' she said as more weekend soldiers tumbled out of the bushes. 'How do you rate the course on a scale of one to ten?'

She pretended to note down the series of numbers called to her.

'Thank you,' she said, shoving everything back into her bag. 'You've been very helpful.'

All thoughts of confronting Charlborough went out of her head. Hot and sweaty, she ran all the way back to the canal.

The sobbing branches of a willow tree dipped into the

water on one side and on the bank the grass beneath it looked soft and green.

Her legs protesting that they hadn't done cross country running since she was fifteen, she flung herself beneath its shade.

Her bag flopped open and Mrs Patel's notebook fell out. The red plastic lips looked incongruous amongst the greenness.

Birdsong and the sound of a brightly painted narrow boat heading towards Bath made her want to linger.

Castles, roses and impossibly blue birds decorated the vessel's full length. The bright colours even outdid the cover of Mrs Patel's diary. But the cover made her smile.

'Nice day,' she called out. 'Lovely boat.'

'Thank you.'

She looked along the canal in the direction the narrow boat had come from. There was a white boat moored fifty yards away. The sign fastened to it said, PRIVATE MOORING. CHARLBOROUGH GRANGE.

So! Sir Andrew owned a luxury river boat made of shiny fibreglass and stainless steel. It must surely have a large engine, another mechanical device for Mark Conway to look after.

She picked up the diary and began to read. It was strong stuff – at least as far as the case was concerned.

Mrs Patel reported Mr Conway coming in but not going out. She also mentioned activity at the river's edge; someone clearing out their cellar and boats coming and going.

The dates were clear. Mrs Patel was very observant. She described what looked like a rolled-up carpet or a piece of furniture being turned out into the river. The phraseology reflected her obvious indignation. It looked to come from number nine, she had added.

'But number nine's empty,' murmured Honey.

She lay back in the grass. The peace of the old canal

was disturbed by yet another boat. Opening her eyes, she raised herself on to one elbow and looked.

The river cruiser was white and long. Its owner/captain stood proudly at the wheel with a blonde woman beside him. They were both in their fifties, just about the right age for indulging their dreams.

Suddenly she sat upright. Sir Andrew Charlborough could afford to indulge himself. The canal, not the river ran through the grounds of Charlborough Grange. Via a series of lock gates, the canal led into the river ...

As one piece of jigsaw fitted into another – and all based around the canal – she dialled Steve Doherty's number.

'Have you interviewed Mrs Patel?'

'Honey!'

He sounded pleased to hear her.

'Yes, I have. Very interesting, but we need a bit more. Best of all would be finding Mark Conway.'

'He's our man. I told you. He killed both men.'

'We confirmed with Sir Andrew that his wife had been having an affair with Mark Conway. He didn't seem unduly worried about it.'

'Did she deny it?'

'She wasn't there. Her husband says she's gone back to Spain.'

'And I don't suppose he's worried about that either.'

'Not at all. You don't seem surprised.'

'I met her twice. Enough to form an instant opinion.

'She wasn't that bad.'

'She was blonde, Steve, and you're a man which means you're biased.'

'I prefer brunettes – like you.'

'Smoothie!'

'We're trying to find Mark Conway,' said Doherty.

'He's in number nine! It's empty! Mark Conway was used to slipping in and out unnoticed and I know how he was doing it. Sir Andrew has a boat. Mark Conway maintains it just like he does the cars. Anything mechanical, he said. Are you going to do anything about it?'

'Yes.'

She heard him shout at someone to get hold of the key holder before coming back to her.

# Chapter Thirty-six

It was eight o'clock in the evening. A mist was rising from the river when they eventually got the keys.

The estate agent had insisted on accompanying them.

Although the key was in the lock, professional habits – as well as bad ones – are hard to kick. The policeman with the key heaved his shoulder into the door.

The estate agent turned pale.

'Go carefully! This is a very valuable property. It has great development potential,' he protested.

'Search the whole house,' Doherty ordered. Four burly detectives rushed into the ground-floor hall.

The estate agent had a shiny tie and a surly attitude. 'I hope you don't expect me to accompany you. There's no electricity on. You'll be in pitch darkness in some parts of the building,' he added.

Honey headed towards the front door when Doherty grabbed her arm. 'Not you. This is police business.'

'No way! I've been with this case all the way through. You can't blank me out now.'

'Yes I can. I'm a policeman,' he said after frogmarching her back out on to the pavement.

Doherty headed back towards the front door.

Honey leaned on the railings and looked down into the basement courtyard. There was another door down there, one that led directly into the basement flat.

The gate hinges creaked as she pushed it open.

Doherty chose that moment to reappear.

'Get back up here,' he shouted down at her.

Doherty raced after her down the slimy green steps. The small courtyard wasn't big enough to swing a cat – even a kitten, but it still smelled of cats pee.

'I'm going in whether you like it or not,' Honey told him.

He shook his head. 'Honey, I just can't resist an angry woman.'

The door to the cellar area had multi-coloured diamond-shaped glass panels in it.

It wasn't locked. Doherty pushed it open.

'I say again, the electricity is not switched on,' said the estate agent who was leaning over the railings above them.

Doherty switched on his flashlight. 'No need to concern yourself, sir. Boy scouts are always prepared.'

'So are girl guides,' said Honey and did the same with her mobile.

They passed into gloom; the light from their torches showing that whoever bought the place had a lot of work to do. It didn't hold a candle to Trevor's flat in number six. Nevertheless, they were likely to make a fortune. This was probably the last house on the block ripe for conversion to flats.

A passageway led to the rooms at the back. He opened a latched door and discovered the steps down to the lower level. At the bottom of the steps was a small hall. Honey raised her hand to her nose. The smell of damp and mould was overpowering.

Doherty moved off to her right.

Doherty motioned for to stay behind. She did as she was told, though not because he'd ordered her to. She'd heard something and fancied he had not.

The light from Doherty's torch moved away. Her own light began to dim. Drat. Why hadn't she thought to recharge it?

Telling herself that she wasn't in the least bit nervous,

she moved sideways to her right, thinking she had passed through a doorway, although she couldn't be sure.

It was dark now. Doherty and his flashlight were far away.

She guessed she was in one of the small, square cellar rooms close to the river and beneath the road to the rear of the property. This was where provisions were kept in years gone by. Not now. Now there was only decay and damp and darkness.

She moved sideways again thinking she heard someone, something. Not Doherty. Doherty was behind her. The noise came from somewhere ahead. In the hope of not being seen, she turned off her phone light.

The smell of mud and a rush of air told her she wasn't far from the river now.

Suddenly she could see the orange lights shining from the other side of the river. She turned her light back on and told herself that it was probably only a rat she'd heard earlier.

Was that rats she could see moving about on the river? If they were, they were a strange shape and very large.

Her foot brushed against something. She flashed her phone at the ground. Her mouth went dry.

A pair of staring, dead eyes were caught in the flashlight's gleam. Not one of the plastic heads she'd found in the war games greenhouse. This was real, the flesh blackened and falling away from the face. Probably eaten by rats.

The flashlight picked out the glint of gold earrings. Expensive earrings.

Pamela Charlborough was not in Spain!

Her stomach churned. Sickened at the sight, she put her hand over her mouth and tried not to breathe.

Something knocked against her knees causing her to bend. An arm thick with muscle wrapped around her neck. Her legs buckled as he jabbed his knees more forcefully into the back of hers.

His arm was tight against her throat.

'Do you see them?'

His breath was moist against her ear. 'Do you see my trophy? My father told me how to kill. That was the other reason Andrew stepped in when our mother died. Our father served with him in Malaya. Did you know that? The Gurkhas used to cut off their enemies' heads. My dad learned how to do it from them. And Sir Andrew. Him too.'

A cold chill ran down her spine. Even before she felt it against her neck, she knew it was coming.

'This is my friend,' he said.

Because the steel blade rested on her neck, he loosened his grip on her throat. Obviously he guessed she'd be too scared to do anything silly. He was dead right.

'I'm not a police officer,' she said, trying not to sound frightened.

'I know. You're just like the others. You want to upset everything. Can't have that, can we?'

She closed her eyes, prayed it would be over quickly, then thought of her mother and Lindsey. Which one would have to identify her?

*YOU ARE NOT GOING TO PANIC.*

'Please!'

Her voice sounded small.

She managed to peer over his arm. She could see the river and the waning light of sunset glowing around the opening and the city lights across the river. She prayed for Doherty to come. He was *bound* to come.

Fifty yards away, Doherty's flashlight had failed. Muttering to himself, he edged his way back over the slimy flagstones.

The walls crumbled silently as he felt his way back. Some instinct told him to be very quiet as he retraced his

278

way to where he'd left her. The muted light from the world outside shone somewhere ahead of him. He looked to his left and suddenly there she was, held tightly, silhouetted against the light coming from the river. It glinted on the knife at her throat.

His first thought was to rush Conway. Not wise! She'd be dead by the time he got there. Somehow he had to catch Conway off-guard and get him away from her. But how?

He saw her tense and knew she'd seen him. Perhaps Mark Conway had not; he didn't turn.

In the little light there was, he looked for anything that might help him take Conway out. There was nothing on the walls, nothing on the floor.

All he could see were iron hooks and bars ranged along the ceiling. Before refrigeration was invented this was where meat would have been hung. One of the bars was hanging from the ceiling like a giant pendulum, one end fallen from its bracket.

Honey had indeed seen him. She kept as still as she could, very much aware that the strong arm holding her could break her neck if it chose.

So he wouldn't be heard, Doherty kept his breathing under control. Sweat ran down his face and into his collar as he calculated the weight of the pendulum and how hard he'd need to swing it. Honey's life depended on him getting it right.

Judging by the consistency of the walls, the ceiling would be equally crumbly; he hoped it would hold. The iron bar was huge. Everything depended on Conway's position if he was to get it right.

Honey saw him, little more than a shadow, looking at the long, thick iron bar that hung from the ceiling.

She saw it was loose and guessed that if it was swung in the right direction Conway would get the full impact – if she could get him closer. If she could turn him so the iron bar hit him and not her.

*Keep him talking. You have to keep distract him!*

'I spoke to your brother. He told me everything. I can't blame you for what you did. I mean, you were just looking after your brother's interests ...'

'The American should have kept his mouth shut then none of this would have happened. Stupid bitch ...'

Honey closed her eyes thinking at first that she was the stupid bitch he was referring to, but he went on with his diatribe and the reference to Pamela Charlborough became obvious.

As he ranted on, Doherty gingerly tested the movement of the bar.

Honey listened as he muttered about Charlborough and what he'd done.

'He was my brother, you see. Our mother was dead. Our father didn't want us. That's what hurt the most, but Andrew made up for that. He gave us a home – as long as Shaun became Lance. That was the deal.'

'And he paid your father off,' she said, glancing at Doherty and praying she'd get the timing right.

'That's right. Very handsomely, but then, look what Sir Andrew was gaining.'

Honey swallowed. The knife was sharp against her throat. The tiniest movement or the wrong word and her crisp white shirt could be the wrong shade of pink. And yet she had to move, and not just a little. Violently, so that his body would be facing Doherty.

She braved herself to ask a few more questions.

'So you hate him for that?'

'Of course not. He's treated us well.'

'And Lance didn't know that Sir Andrew was not his real father?'

'He didn't! Not until she told him. That bitch! That harlot!' His arm tightened around her. 'I won't have anyone – *anyone* – spoil his life. And she did. Though I tried to be nice to her. I really did.'

Honey thought of the crisp, clean love nest next door. 'Yes. Of course you did.'

'First that American trying to upset the applecart, and then that slime-ball Herbert begging for money.'

'He tried blackmail?'

'Yes. That's the only way his sort ever gets money – by leeching off others.'

'So you buried him in the rockery hoping that Mrs Herbert's first husband would be blamed?'

'That's right! Bob the Job. Lance had been having a fling with that little slut Loretta. He told me all about it.'

His laughter echoed off and around the damp ceilings.

'Bob Davies deserved to be blamed. It was his fault that the Yank came visiting in the first place. Him and his stupid hobby. Maxted had the money to check things out. Detecting was his hobby. He didn't need to do it. But he wanted to see the boy, and then that stupid bitch told him the truth.'

Mark told it all. The real Lance had inherited haemophilia from his mother. He had died in the same car accident as her. Sir Andrew hadn't been too well-off at the time and was determined to hold on to the fortune his wife had brought to the marriage. Without an heir it would have reverted back to her family. So he'd bought – it was the only way she could describe it – *bought* Shaun from his father. The deal was struck on the condition he took Mark as well, though only loosely, not as a family member.

'So a kidnap was contrived, the boy never found?' Her voice sounded shaky.

Mark continued to be forthcoming. 'That's how it worked. Shaun – Lance – never knew any different.'

'But you killed Lady Pamela. Surely she was trying to protect you?'

'And make sure she got her husband's money. That's why she accused Trevor and not me. Bitch! Dishonest bitch!'

Honey licked the sweat off her lips and tensed her muscles. She could see Doherty was almost ready. His arms were gripping the bar, moving it backwards.

With an almighty effort, he heaved it back as far as he could, then let it go.

The pendulum made a grating sound as it swung.

Just before it reached the lowest point of its arc, Honey jerked back sharply from the waist, twisting her hips. Conway was taken off balance. To regain his hold on her, he turned sideways towards Doherty – and the iron bar.

Honey was flung forward as the force of the great iron bar sent Conway crashing towards the wall.

She lay winded, breathing in dust and dirt, feeling soreness on her cheek.

Doherty ran to her.

'I'm all right,' she kept saying in a squeaky voice that sounded nothing like her own. 'I'm all right.'

'She's all right,' he called out to the other figures moving in the gloom.

Reinforcements had arrived.

'Is he dead?' Even to her ears, her voice hadn't quite gone back to normal.

Doherty glanced towards the dark bundle lying still on the floor.

'With the side of his head missing? I should think so.'

Honey rejected his offer to help her to her feet. 'I'm OK.' She looked down at her favourite suit and groaned. 'Why did I choose white?'

'Because you're contrary and won't be told anything.'

# Chapter Thirty-seven

A guy wearing a lop-sided toupée and a carnation in his buttonhole smiled in her direction. For a split second his shiny shoes pointed her way. His course altered the moment John Rees appeared.

'Have you had a good day?' he asked, once the drinks were on the bar.

She nodded. 'Good enough. My daughter hasn't told me she's pregnant, the chef hasn't sliced off a customer's ears, and no one's caught the curtains alight with a double Sambucca.'

He nodded affably. Being affable as well as good-looking was definitely one of John's things. She told herself he was exactly what she needed; nothing too macho, too cocksure and too much of a lad with the ladies. She knew a policeman who fitted the latter category.

'You seem good, you know, kind of relaxed.'

She licked a dewdrop of wine from her bottom lip.

'I'm wearing my relaxation hat.'

'Do you have many? Hats that is.'

She counted them off on her fingers. 'There's my Father Confessor hat – people tell you all sorts of details about their private lives over the bar. Then there's my 'the customer is always right hat'. That's the one I reserve for the loudmouth who insists on his consumer rights when a greenfly lands on his salad. Then there's …'

'Whoa! And what about your amateur detective hat?'

The sound of her sigh seemed to echo through her

body.

'Not tonight. Case solved and the butler DID do it – well sometimes butler. Most times mechanic.'

'So how do you intend to celebrate?'

Honey pursed her lips, eyed the ceiling and thought about it.

'I could buy something really old, silky and outdated at Bonhams' next collectibles auction, but I've got a long wait. They held one yesterday and there were some good items going under the hammer. But never mind. I'll catch the next one.'

John smiled. 'It was a good auction.'

'You went?'

He nodded. 'Indeed I did.'

'Lucky dog!'

'I was. I bought you a present.'

He reached down to the gap between their bar stools.

'Here,' he said. 'I saw this and thought of you.'

She started to undo the black plastic bin bag he'd handed her.

'Stylish wrapper,' she mused.

He shrugged. 'It was practical.'

Her fingertips touched something familiar.

She smiled at him. 'Whalebone running through crisp lace and soft silk feels like nothing else in the world.'

She peered in and saw red satin trimmed with black lace. Probably French, just like the one she'd missed on the morning when Casper had summoned her to his office.

John's hand covered hers. 'Best if you didn't get it out in here. People might get jealous.'

She grinned and looking up at him felt all warm inside.

'A corset. Should look nice encased behind glass with the rest of my collection.'

The look he gave her was almost serious, certainly unsmiling.

'In my opinion it's the corset that should do the

encasing. What do you think?'

A slow smile spread across her face. 'You must have read my mind.'

The hollow sound of a phone ringing in the deep recesses of her favourite Gucci handbag cut the conversation short, though the inclination remained.

'Mother!'

Her smile was stiff and barely patient.

'Hannah, I've arranged for Mr Paget to meet you in the bar of the Francis Hotel at nine o'clock. Are you far from there?'

'Mr Paget?'

'My dentist.'

'I'm sorry, Mother, I'm not. I'm in Bradford on Avon,' she lied. 'I'll have to take a rain check I'm afraid. Can you tell him that?'

The response was grumbled.

An echo of another phone trilled from the other end of the bar. The guy with the toupée answered the call, shoved the phone away and ordered a double whisky.

Honey eyed him feeling like a rabbit that's just outwitted the fox.

'Do you know him?' asked John.

'I think he's a dentist.'

'Well we certainly don't need him, do we?' said John. 'A bottle of champagne is very well deserved.'

She leaned closer to him. 'A bottle of champagne, a four-poster bed and a red satin corset.'

Her phone rang again. This time it was Doherty.

'Hi! We're partying, having a right humdinger of a celebration. Fancy joining us?' He hesitated before saying the words she wanted to hear. 'After all, you put so much into this. I need to show my appreciation.'

'I'm sorry, Sergeant. Not tonight.' She smiled at John. 'I'm inspecting the facilities at a prominent Bath Hotel.'

'Never mind. Another time? Just the two of us?'

'Always willing to oblige the police.'

She snapped the phone shut. Blue eyes and stubble. Why was that so attractive? She also liked the way his hair flopped over his forehead, and that lop-sided smile. He also looked pretty good in jeans. Some guys just didn't fill them as they should be filled. She hadn't realised she was so deep in thought until John's voice broke through.

'Shall we take a rain check too?'

She jerked her head up. 'What?'

He smiled at her. 'Look. I wouldn't want to rush anything …'

She bent her head over her bag, unwilling to let John see the sudden confusion she knew would show in her eyes. That was the trouble with having an open face – anybody could read it.

She fiddled with her phone as she thought things through. Suddenly the four poster and all the trimmings didn't seem quite as attractive as they had done.

'I'm sorry.'

'Don't be. As I said, I wouldn't want to rush things.'

But Doherty would, she thought as she left the bar. Damn him for phoning, for being lustful, masculine and annoyingly attractive. Damn her feet for heading towards Manvers Street and a party that she just had to be a part of.

Her phone rang again. 'Are you coming?' It was Doherty.

And damn him for being so sure that she'd come.

A Honey Driver Mystery

A Taste to Die for

Jean G Goodhind

**Next in the Honey Driver series**

Chefs can be arrogant, competitive and downright murderous at times, so when Bath International Taste Extravaganza (BITE for short) organizes a best chef competition, Honey Driver, the Hotels' Association police liaison officer, senses trouble. Her instinct proves correct when the winning chef is found dead in his own kitchen. Then a second, and a third ... On top of this Honey's mother has fallen for the charms – and the white Rolls Royce – of a wealthy butcher, supplier to the catering trade. Is he really after her mother's body – well preserved as it is – or is he after the hotel's meat account? Honey's own relationship with dishy DS Doherty is on hold. He's pooped – too tired even to fall for Honey's ample charms. As for the murderer, is this a case of past grievances? And once it's solved, will Honey finally get her man?

**ISBN    9781909520196**

www.accentpress.co.uk

15232875R00173

Printed in Great Britain
by Amazon.co.uk, Ltd.,
Marston Gate.